What the critics are saying about:

No Escape

"Incredible...ingenious. Ms. Black only gets better and better, improving upon a talent that was superior to begin with." - *Pandora's Box*

"NO ESCAPE is packed with action and intrigue. Ms. Black has an incredible talent for taking the unbelievable and unimaginable and making it engrossing." - *Romance Reviews Today*

"In NO ESCAPE, Black's intricate balancing of characters becomes evident as the Trek Mi Q'an universe grows. Fans of the series have no doubt waited for this volume since finishing book 1. (I know I did!)" - *Ann Leveille for Sensual Romance*

No Fear

"This exciting sequel is not to missed." – *All About Murder*

"... follows in the path of its predecessors with blazing sexuality, charming characters and an ample dose of humor. Ms. Black teases the reader with tiny bits of knowledge that are guaranteed to make the wait for the next installment of this fascinating tale too long. For a fun and erotically sinful read, don't miss NO FEAR" - *Terrie Figueroa, Romance Reviews Today*

"Book five in the Trek Mi Q'an series is another delightfully unique tale. I don't know about anyone else, but I think I'm going to be lost when Ms. Black completes this series!" - *Amy Turpin, Timeless Tales*

Trek Mi Q'an Series

ROMANTICA PUBLISHING

Discover for yourself why readers can't get enough of the multiple award-winning publisher Ellora's Cave. Whether you prefer e-books or paperbacks, be sure to visit EC on the web at www.ellorascave.com for an erotic reading experience that will leave you breathless.

www.ellorascave.com

Ellora's Cave Publishing, Inc.
1337 Commerce Dr. #13
Stow, OH 44224

ISBN # 0-9724377-8-9

Edited by Cris Brashear.
Cover art by Bryan Keller.

CONQEST

2 Trek Mi Q'an Tales

Jaid Black

WARNING:

No Escape and *No Fear* are part of a series and not meant to stand alone. We suggest reading *Enslaved* by Jaid Black before attempting to read *Conquest*.

NO ESCAPE

"Immigration is the sincerest form of flattery."
– Jack Paar

Prologue I

Airspace within the Kyyto Sectors, Planet Tryston
Trek Mi Q'an Galaxy, Seventh Dimension
6044 Y.Y. (Yessat Years)

She had nigh unto given up hope of ever escaping him.

Already four years had gone by — four incredibly long years since the moon-rising of her eighteenth *Yessat* year when her ownership had been transferred from her sire to Cam K'al Ra.

She had been given several opportunities to escape him since she'd turned eighteen, yet nothing had come of any of them. Leastways, she had made a pact with her cousins. They had made vows unto the others that it would be all of them who would flee together or all of them who would stay behind and remain prisoners to the fates. The closer she had gotten to the moon-rising of the claiming, the more Kara had sometimes wished she'd made no such vow. But a vow was a vow and she had given hers freely.

It had turned out to be the right decision. She had kept her oath and now the three of them would be free the soonest, together for all time.

From the moon-rising her cousin Dari had been forcibly carted off to Arak and onward, Kara Q'ana Tal had made certain to always give the appearance of being all things demure and submissive. She had given Cam K'al Ra no reason to doubt her acceptance of their impending joining and because of that fact he had been lenient toward her over the *Yessat* years, allowing her to remain in her family home with minimal guarding. He had come visiting upon occasion, kissing and licking at her body as though he'd never get enough of her, but for the most part he had left her alone, confident in her obedience.

'Twas paying off.

Kara had no desire to hurt Cam—truly she didn't. And truth be told, she felt more than a little guilty turning her back on him that she might be free.

But freedom. She shivered under the rouge-colored *vesha* hide wrapped about her. 'Twas a heady thing, a state of being Trystonni females took for granted they would get to experience after their twenty-fifth *Yessat* year. And yet that very thing, the rite of passage into Trystonni womanhood so many thought nothing of for 'twas considered a given, she and her cousin Dari had been systematically denied.

Nay, Kara hadn't the desire to hurt Cam, yet she hadn't the desire to succumb to his wishes either. What's more, she had matured enough through the years to realize that if she were to flee from him, she could never again return to him. Like as not, his pride would be sorely wounded and he would seek to punish her in ways she couldn't begin to imagine—terrifying, whispered-about-under-one's-breath ways that she had overheard her sire tell her *mani* about.

Kara sighed. Had she thought Cam might give her no more than a small punishment she might have considered returning to Tryston and to him after a time. But nay, he had changed too much over the passage of time, had become grimmer and more formidable with the advent of each new moon-rising. 'Twas for a certainty she'd be doled out the most horrific and final of punishments were she to return to him after fleeing.

The older Cam grew, the fiercer he had become. Kara had watched with much trepidation as the young, carefree hunter she had known since her youth had grown into an unbending, ruthless warlord. From untitled hunter to high lordship, from high lordship to lesser king, from lesser king to king of planet Zideon, each rise he had taken up the political ladder had come at a price. And the price he had paid in battling and bloodshed had created a formidable, domineering warrior she had no desire to be bound to. He frightened her.

Kara hated admitting as much for over the *Yessat* years she too had come into her own, had grown into a strong woman unafraid of most things. And yet there it was. Fear. Fear the likes of which she'd never before known.

"We will be free and clear of Kyyto airspace the soonest." Princess Jana Q'ana Tal whispered the words to Kara as she navigated the stolen high-speed conveyance through the shimmering gold twilight.

Kara closed her eyes briefly and sighed. "Praise the goddess. If Uncle were to catch us within his own sectors, 'twould be spankings for the deuce of us, twenty-two *Yessat* years apiece or no." She kept her voice lowered, as did Jana. It was as if both of them feared he'd hear them, regardless of the fact that they had almost breached the Trystonni atmosphere altogether.

Jana thought of their uncle Kil and swallowed a bit roughly. "Yet further proof that we have made the correct decision." Her nostrils flared. "Leastways, we shan't be spanked on Galis."

Kara smiled at that. "I shall still miss him," she said softly.

"Aye." Jana's eyes gentled, though she didn't turn her head from her navigating duty. "So shall I."

Kara's eyes flicked over her cousin. "'Tis fortunate indeed your sire permitted you to learn how to navigate a conveyance." She looked away, glancing out the wide front porthole as they breached outerspace. "My sire would permit me nowhere near one."

"Mayhap he expects you to flee. Mine believes I've no reason to do so." Jana's lips curved downward into a grim smile. "In truth he would have permitted me to learn even if I'd had a reason to flee."

Kara patted her knee sympathetically. "Uncle Dak has not been the same these four *Yessat* years Dari has been removed to Arak."

Jana's spine went rigid. "Neither has my *mani*," she gritted out. She was silent a long moment, then said, "Leastways, I feel that by removing Dari from her prison, I am evening the score on my parents behalf a wee bit."

Kara nodded. Her eyes narrowed in thought. "I dislike the notion of bringing you bad thoughts, cousin, yet am I worried for Dari. The holo-call she sent out was nigh unto chilling..." Her voice trailed off. "My apologies," she murmured. "'Twas not necessary to say—"

"Nay." Jana's jaw went rigid. "But mark my words as truth, Kara. If Gio has beaten her, 'twill be the last action he ever makes without consequence."

Kara agreed. She couldn't begin to imagine what else could have possibly upset Dari enough to be frightened to the point of tears. It wasn't like Dari to have tears in her eyes at all, for she tended toward the stoic for a certainty. The best Kara and Jana could figure was that she was being maltreated—yet further proof 'twas past the time to flee.

Quiet fell between the cousins, giving Kara time to think. 'Twas something she didn't desire to do much of these days for when she did it inevitably meant that her thoughts would turn to her betrothed, or her former betrothed as it were.

Cam was going to be furious when he found out, more angered than she felt comfortable thinking on. He'd be furious at her for fleeing, at himself for being fooled by her displays of obedience, and at her *mani* and sire for not keeping a close enough vigil regarding her whereabouts. Aye — he'd be angered with them all.

Kara could live with knowing of his fury, however. 'Twas not his fury she'd be thinking about for she would be forever removed from him and any punishments he might think to inflict upon her.

She sighed. 'Twas not Cam's inevitable anger that made her flinch when she thought on him — 'twas the possible hurt and embarrassment she might cause him by fleeing. She would that it could be otherwise, yet the course had been set and there was no turning back. But then, neither did she wish to turn back.

Freedom. Her sire and betrothed had tried to deny her, but she would not be denied. Daughter of the Emperor or no, she would be no warrior's battle prize.

"We've reached the shield," Jana murmured.

Kara's head shot up. Her hearts rate began to accelerate, knowing as she did that all of their planning came down to this one moment in time. If the codes she had stolen from the warring chamber were accurate, their ship would be permitted to breach the invisible energy field her sire had ordered commissioned only three *Yessat* years past to guard the planet. But if the codes were wrong...

"Let us pray to Aparna that our ship is not instantly disintegrated." Kara took a deep breath then looked at her cousin. "Are you ready for the codes?"

Jana did a little deep breathing of her own. Moisture gathered between her breasts and on her brow as an acute sense of fear settled into the pit of her stomach. "Aye," she whispered hoarsely. "Read them to me."

Kara closed her eyes briefly and sent up one last prayer to the goddess. Clutching the *trelli* parchment firmly in both hands, she opened her eyes and began reading off the hieroglyphic-like symbols that corresponded to Trystonni numbers. "*Sii, Sii, Fala, Sii...*" She continued to read off the numbers in a slow, measured tone until the last one had been keyed in by Jana.

"'Tis done," Jana said quietly.

Kara nodded, her breath coming out in a rush. "'Twill take but mere seconds." She sucked in a lungful of air and unconsciously held it. Her eyes wide, she grabbed her cousin's hand and squeezed it as the deuce of them awaited their shared fate together. 'Twould be death or freedom.

As their ship thrust through the Trystonni energy field, they both released a pent-up breath, grinning as they hugged each other. "We did it!" Kara beamed. "We well and truly did it!"

Jana smiled fully as she switched on the dimmer control. The dimmer allowed the high-speed conveyance to become invisible to detection scanners, but it also made her job as navigator more difficult. Leastways, passing-by conveyances and other assorted ships wouldn't be able to see their craft to know to steer clear of it. 'Twould take much concentration to navigate the conveyance to Arak.

"Aye." Jana chuckled. "'Tis nigh unto impossible to believe, but we are free and clear of Trystonni airspace."

"How many *Nuba* hours to Arak?"

"Approximately five."

Kara nodded. "I shall remain quiet so as not to distract you."

The next few hours proved to be the longest of Kara's life. Nearing Arak also meant nearing the chance that the three of them would be caught and punished accordingly. She couldn't begin to imagine how horrific their punishments would be, but she knew they'd be harsh for a certainty.

There were approximately six hours left of the moon-rising, six hours until the dominant sun broached the Tryston sky and declared it morn. Her absence would be noticed mayhap an hour or two after that. That gave them seven *Nuba* hours at worst and eight *Nuba* hours at best to snatch Dari away and hightail it to Galis. There was no time for mistakes.

A horn-like sound blared just then, breaking both escaped princesses out of their quiet reverie. Kara's gaze shot toward the communicator. Her eyes rounded. "'Tis another holo-call from Dari," she muttered.

Jana's forehead wrinkled. Why would her sister be calling an hour before they were scheduled to dock? "A recorded message or a living dimensional representation?"

Kara's fingers flicked over the complex keyboard. She punched in directives until the requisite information appeared on screen. "'Twas recorded two *Nuba* minutes past and 'tis labeled as urgent." She keyed in another sequence, commanding the communicator to play the recorded memory. "'Twill take a few seconds for it to rewind and play—ahh here we go."

A moment later, Princess Dari's three-dimensional image appeared on a display screen that emerged from the front ceiling of the conveyance. She looked frightened, Kara thought nervously. Something had spooked her for a certainty.

"*Greetings unto you, sister and cousin. I fear I haven't much time to speak, so this message will be brief...*"

Dari looked over her shoulder, apparently ascertaining that she hadn't been followed. She turned back around to face the recorder, throwing three long micro-braids over her shoulder as she did so. Her almond-shaped eyes were wildly rounded, the fear in their glowing blue depths obvious.

"*Head for Galis with all speed,*" she choked out. "*Do not come here to aid me for I cannot leave. Not yet.*"

Horrified, Kara glanced at Jana with her mouth agape. She couldn't begin to imagine why Dari would want them to leave her behind. Leastways, it made no sense. Dari hated —

"*An evil dwells here,*" Dari murmured. "*An evil that must be destroyed.*" She swallowed shakily, closing her eyes briefly. "*I mayhap have not the power to destroy it myself, yet I will not leave Arak until I've enough information to —*"

The sound of approaching footsteps caused Dari to stop speaking and turn on her heel to gage who it was that was about to come upon her. She turned back to the recorder and spoke quickly.

"*I must go. Vow it to me that the deuce of you will not return to Tryston. Forge onward to Galis and create your new destinies. I will join you the soonest. 'Tis a vow amongst cousins,*" she adamantly swore.

Dari hesitated, mayhap deciding how much time she had left to speak. In the end she decided to risk another few *Nuba* seconds worth of speech.

"*Worry not o'er me, for I will be passing fair. The Evil One knows not that I am aware of its existence. Please,*" she begged, "*do not return to your impending matrimonial prisons. I will join you the soonest,* she whispered fervently. "*I have figured out how to escape —*"

The holo-call abruptly ended, leaving Kara and Jana more than a little frightened for Dari's safety. They turned to look at each other, both of their expressions horrified. It wasn't necessary to speak, for both of them implicitly understood what the other one was thinking.

What evil one had Dari spoken of? Why had the recording ended so abruptly—had Dari been caught or had she merely switched off the holo-recorder device herself? Should they risk returning to Tryston and mayhap get caught in the doing to inform their sires of Dari's predicament, or should they continue onward as Dari had directed them to do? Would she truly be able to escape without aid?

"What do we do?" Jana whispered. She sounded lost. Frightened and lost.

Kara nibbled on her lower lip as her fingers danced once again over the main communicator's keyboard. "First things first, cousin. I must ascertain whether 'twas Dari who ended that holo-call or if 'twas an unexpected interloper who ended it for her."

Jana nodded as she steered the conveyance away from Arak and toward Galis. "If the genetic map of any but Dari shows up on the fingerprint scan, we must turn ourselves in for a certainty that we might inform our sires of what we know."

"Agreed." Kara pulled up the recorded memory and punched in a sequence of keystrokes. She waited what felt like forever for the communicator to analyze the fingerprint scan. When it was done, she turned to Jana.

"Dari ended it," she murmured. "'Twas her genetic map and no other's."

Jana blew out a breath of relief. "Thank the goddess."

"Aye."

They sat in silence for a suspended moment, both of them realizing they had little time to make a decision. Their sires would send out hunting calls the soonest. If they chose to continue onward to Galis as Dari had instructed them to do, it was now or never to see it through.

Now or never, Kara thought anxiously. They had to breach Galis airspace before every hunter in Trek Mi Q'an was alerted to their escape.

Jana swallowed a bit roughly before she spoke. Her voice came out in a shaky whisper. "I vote we carry onward."

Kara's eyes widened. "But what of D—"

"In my hearts," Jana said adamantly, "I know my sister will make good on her word. I know this for a certainty."

Kara said nothing to that. It was true blood siblings shared a mental bond that others could not feel or understand the why of. Yet still…

"I, more so than you, have my reasons for desiring to continue on to Galis. But I will not go unless 'tis certain you are that—"

"I am," Jana said simply. "I know Dari will come to us."

Kara blew out a breath. She turned away from Jana and stared out of the front porthole of the conveyance.

"What is your final decision?" Jana asked anxiously. She was clearly too emotionally charged up to trust her own judgment on so critical a matter.

Kara pondered that question over for a torturous moment. For a certainty neither Jana nor herself would know happiness again if anything happened to Dari. And yet her cousin had seemed so certain of herself, so convinced that she could escape Arak and join them on Galis…

"We will continue onward," Kara said quietly. Her glowing blue gaze tracked the movement of a passing meteorite that Jana's navigating had expertly dodged. "And we will pray to the goddess 'tis the right decision."

Prologue II

Palace of the Dunes, Sand City on planet Tryston
Fourteen Nuba hours later

Cam K'al Ra, the King of planet Zideon, strode through the great hall in haste. His harsh features grew all the grimmer when he took notice of the weeping *manis* seated at the raised table offering each other solace. The High King Jor was seated between them, his large palms stroking both his mother and auntie's backs.

This, Cam conceded, did not bode well. He hadn't the faintest notion why he had been summoned before the Emperor, yet he was now certain that it somehow involved his betrothed. The Empress would not be weeping otherwise. He would not have been summoned otherwise.

"Ari predicted something bad would happen," Kyra choked out. She leaned against her son as though she couldn't hold herself upright without aid. "But I never thought..."

"I don't believe it," Geris said shakily, her normally authoritative voice subdued, her eyes unblinking, "my firstborn baby is gone."

Cam's entire body stilled. The breath went out of him at the Queen's words. He stopped in his tracks and slowly turned on his boot heel to face the family that would one day soon be his own.

Jana was gone? he thought warily. That could only mean that—

"We'll find them," sixteen-year-old Jor murmured. "Already the finest hunters of Tryston are scouting for the conveyance."

Them, Cam thought as his hearts rate sped up. His future brother-within-the-law had used the word *them*.

Wasting no more time, Cam made an abrupt about-face and strode briskly toward the warring chamber. Something had happened to Kara, he told himself as his mind raced with the possibilities. Something bad. Mayhap she had even been kidnapped. His nostrils flared as he considered what would happen to his betrothed if she had been captured by insurrectionists, what would become of her if they —

Nay. He could not allow himself to think on it. It was sorely apparent he would need his wits about him to find her.

When he entered the warring chamber, Cam knew for a certainty that his assumption had been correct. Every of the Q'an Tal warriors was present, the four ruling brothers gathered around the planning table with their commanding captains at their sides.

Kara was gone.

Cam could see it in their expressions as they noticed his entrance and looked up at him from their seats. He could see it in the bloodshot eyes of the Emperor and King Dak as they stared at him with troubled expressions. They had both lost daughters today.

But, he thought with a sudden flash of premonition, there was something more to this...

As Cam's eyes flicked about the warring chamber, he noticed for the first time that some of the warriors within it were throwing him pitying glances. Kil's gaze shifted from Cam's eyes and looked away as if he felt...embarrassed.

But that made no sense. Why would the King of Morak be embarrassed for him? And then Cam noticed yet the same shifting of eyes from King Rem. Rem's face flushed slightly before he too looked away from him.

Something was wrong—something was very wrong.

"Just tell me," Cam said hoarsely, the muscles in his heavy body cording. He felt the eyes of every warrior in the chamber turn to him as he spoke. "What has become of Kara?"

Throats cleared. Eyes darted away. Warriors shifted uncomfortably upon their seats.

Cam's nostrils flared. In that moment he knew for a certainty that his betrothed had not been kidnapped. But nay, he thought angrily, if she had not been kidnapped then that could only mean that she had—

"'Tis sorry I am," Zor muttered as he met Cam's gaze.

His hands fisted at his sides, inducing the veins on his forearms to bulge. "Just tell me," Cam gritted out. He cared not that his tone of voice bordered on impudence. "Tell me what has happened."

But he already knew, of course. He just wanted to hear the words aloud, needed his worst fears confirmed.

"She is gone," Zor said softly. "Kara and Jana have fled Tryston together."

Cam stood there rooted to the ground for what felt to be an hour. His breathing was labored—labored in the way all warriors' breathing becomes when they are in a temper with their wenches yet trying to control it. His nostrils continued to flare with each heaving of angered breath he took. His hands fisted and unfisted at his sides as he allowed the impact of the Emperor's words to sink in.

She was gone. Kara had run away from him.

Cam's head shot up. He narrowed his glowing blue-green eyes at the warriors looking upon him with pity. "I will find her," he growled. His heated gaze found Zor. "And when I do 'tis my right to remove her from her birth home since 'tis obvious she has not been watched o'er properly here."

Zor's nostrils flared at the words that had been hissed at him like venom. "I watched o'er her well," he ground out. "'Tis not I that my hatchling fled from."

Zor's face flushed guiltily when he heard his brothers suck in their breath on Cam's behalf. He took a deep breath and expelled it. "I offer you my apologies, Cam." He stood up, looking as weary as Cam felt. "You are correct for a certainty," he rasped out. "Had I guarded her more vigilantly then—"

"Nay." Cam held up a palm, then ran it over his chin as his thoughts turned back to his betrothed. He sighed. "I offer you my apologies as well. We are both—we are...we are not ourselves just now."

Kil stood up and walked towards the deuce of them, his fingers intertwined with those of his three-year-old son, Kilian. "We will find her. We will find both of them." When he was upon them, he drew his face closer that none but Zor and Cam might hear him. "I ask but one boon, Cam."

One of Cam's golden eyebrows arched in inquiry, but he said nothing. He was beyond words really. He was so angered that—

"Do not cause my niece a harm when you find her," Kil said under his breath to keep their conversation private. "'Tis for a certainty you feel shamed, yet I still ask that you show Kara a bit of mercy. She is but young and confused."

23

Cam's nostrils flared. He felt the need to attack something, to punch at someone until his fists bled. But he would never—could never—hurt Kara. "She will be spanked as is my right," he gritted out, "but nay, I shan't harm her."

Kil nodded his understanding. Had he been Cam he would have done the same.

"'Tis time to talk strategy," Dak announced from across the chamber as he motioned toward them to take their seats. "We best get on with it."

Cam was about to join him at the planning table when the sound of loud footfalls jogging towards the warring chamber snagged his attention. A *Nuba*-second later, High King Jor strode in briskly, his pathway veering straight towards Zor and Cam.

"What is it?" Zor bellowed to his heir. "Has word come back from any of the hunting parties?"

"Aye," Jor confirmed as he panted for air. He jogged the remaining space that separated him from his sire, coming to a halt before him and Cam. His glowing blue gaze flicked back and forth between the two warriors. "'Tis bad news," he rasped out.

Cam's entire body went deathly still. He awaited Jor's words much like one would await a sentence to the gulch pits—quiet dignity on the outside, dread on the inside. "What has happened?" he asked hoarsely. "What has become of wee Kara?"

Jor closed his eyes briefly and inhaled a calming lungful of air. His chest rose and fell with each labored breath that he took. "Kara and Jana attempted to land on Galis," he murmured as his eyes opened and bore into Cam's. "Leastways, they did not make it."

"What do you mean, son?" Zor asked softly.

"Their ship was disintegrated." Jor's gaze flicked from Cam to his sire, then back to Cam. "Kara and Jana are dead."

The warring chamber fell into silence. Not a word, not a sound, not even a breath could be heard.

Cam tried to control himself, tried with all of his *Yessat* years worth of brutal training to remain stoic—but he could not.

"Nay!" he bellowed, his arm flinging wildly through the air. "They are not dead. Those hunters know nothing!"

Cam felt Kil's hand upon his shoulder, attempting to comfort him, but he shrugged it off. "Nay," he ground out. "I am not mad! Think you I would not know it in my hearts if Kara had passed through the Rah?" He backed away from Kil, from Jor, from the distraught Emperor. "They," he said distinctly, his teeth gritting, "are wrong."

But as Cam's eyes flicked over the chamber, as he took in the solemn expressions of those around him, his breathing grew more and more labored for he knew he was grasping at nothingness in a futile attempt to hold on to the only woman in existence who could complete him.

Tears came to his eyes. "Nay," Cam said softly. He continued to back away from the other warlords until a crystal wall stopped him from going further. "Nay," he rasped out.

The sound of Zor's footsteps leaving the chamber broke the quiet. Cam's eyes tracked the movement and he noticed that the Emperor was on the verge of losing any tentative control he might still have left over his emotions. Not wanting to shame himself in front of so many, Zor made his exit before he did.

Cam wished he had the energy to do the same. But nay. All he could do was stand there. All he could think of was—

"Kara," Cam said softly, his eyes unblinking, "why did you run from me, *pani*?"

His love for her and need of her had been an all-consuming one. So strong were his emotions where she was concerned that he had purposely stayed away these past four *Yessat* years, afraid as he was that he wouldn't be able to keep himself from claiming her if he didn't. Mayhap, he thought as a renegade tear slipped unchecked down his cheek, mayhap if he had spent more time in her company she would not have feared him enough to flee.

Yet now it mattered not, for she was gone. Kara was gone and she wasn't coming back.

King Cam K'al Ra fell to his knees and wept.

Chapter 1
The Trefa Jungle
Approximately one Nuba-hour outside of Valor City
Planet Galis, 6049 Y.Y. (Yessat Years)

With the silent and agile cunning of a *heeka-beast* stalking its prey, Kara Gy'at Li, nee Kara Q'ana Tal, slithered on all fours atop the dense tropical forest floor of the Trefa jungle. Like the other pack-hunters accompanying her today, she wore a pair of thigh-high leather maroon combat boots, but was otherwise completely naked. Her body had been smeared all over with maroon *tishi* paint by male servants, allowing her and the other female warriors she hunted with to blend in with the maroon jungle that surrounded them.

"Jana," Kara murmured into the communication device fastened into one ear, "I have a visual confirmation of the prey. Proceed with Operation Bag and Tag."

Ten *Yessat* yards away, Jana raised one fist — the Galian equivalent to the thumbs-up symbol — to the bride-to-be situated to her left. "Ready your hunters, Tora." She whispered the words under her breath whilst simultaneously clicking on her *maltoosa* to stunner mode. "Proceed on three." Her eyes narrowed in concentration as she stealthily crept under a *tu-tu* bush. "One," she murmured into the communication device shared by every pack-hunter on the mission. "Two…"

Kara felt her muscles clench in anticipation, awaiting the final signal from Jana to ambush. When Jana said "three", all the hellfire in *Nukala* would break loose. A quick glance to the right confirmed that the other Gy'at Li sisters were ready to strike as well. Kari and Klykka held their *maltoosas* firmly in hand, whilst Dorra prepared her laser scan.

All was prepared.

The prey had been surrounded on all four sides.

It was ridiculous in the extreme to hunt humanoid males, she thought grimly.

"…Three!"

"Banzai!"

In unison, the pack-hunters roared out the battle cry that had been taught to them by Kari Gy'at Li as they exploded from the jungle on all sides and encircled the frightened Galian males. The males screamed out their terror, two of them fainting dead away at the sight of so many women warriors preparing to subdue them as marriage chattel.

The remaining two males began to slowly back away, their eyes wide with upset and their lips threatening to break into sobbing quivers.

Crying males, fainting males—Kara half sighed and half harrumphed. Her lips pinched together disapprovingly. Five *Yessat* years past, she had sought freedom from a certain Trystonni warrior for this? *Ahh, 'tis ironic for a certainty…*

"Kara!" Dorra bellowed as she sprinted away from the enclosure of males. "The big one is getting away. Aid me, sister!"

Kara's head shot up. Her glowing blue eyes narrowed at the form of the retreating male. By the sands, she silently grumbled, it was the six-and-a-half-footer hightailing it into the thick of the jungle. Males of that height and brawn were highly coveted hunting booty because they garnered such large sums from the brides who desired a marriage union with them. Leastways, that particular six-and-a-half-footer would garner them no sum at all for Dorra coveted him as a mate for herself.

"I'm right behind you." Kara wasted no time in aiding Dorra. She had spent the last five *Yessat* years on Galis learning to become a proficient warrior and pack-hunter. It was what she excelled at. It was why all hunting parties desired to count her amongst their numbers. She was fast, she was agile, and she was wicked-good at bagging and tagging.

Bagging and tagging, the Galian equivalent to courtship, was a sport Kara had never dreamed existed back when she'd been a little girl on Tryston. Wenches hunting down males for mates? It was unheard of on a planet where it was the males who did the hunting and the females who got captured.

But Galis was a different culture altogether, a fact that reared its head in just about every facet of daily life. Bagging and tagging pack-hunting parties, for instance, operated every moon-rising during the hunting season. Sometimes Kara was a part of the pack, sometimes she was not. Leastways, if the price offered by the potential bride desirous of having a particular male bagged and tagged was exorbitant enough to lure her, Jana, and the other Gy'at Li sisters into hunting, she usually was a part of it.

This particular hunt would reap Kara, Jana, and their adoptive sisters a large sum of credits. Having decided to kill five *haja* birds with one *trelli* stone, the Gy'at Lis had set out last moon-rising to capture four prime male specimens at the same time. One of those males, the six-and-a-half-footer, would be Dorra's mate and therefore garner them no wage, but the other three they had been contracted to hunt down by their brides-to-be would reap them nigh unto fifty thousand credits in total.

Hunting season was over in a fortnight, so it was necessary to earn as many credits as possible. With the close of hunting season, the Gy'at Lis would holiday for a month, then recommence their tutelage in the erotic arts. Leastways, now that the five of them garnered such high pack-hunting wages, it was no longer necessary to perform serving wench jobs at dives to earn a living. Instead, their family unit devoted itself to pack-hunting, which reaped a living that was large enough to pay for all five of them to be schooled in the erotic arts.

For a Galian female, there was no greater honor than being named a High Mystik of Valor City — a title none but the most schooled in the erotic and warring arts could claim. Kara was proud of the fact that one member of her adoptive family — Klykka — was already a High Mystik. It was Klykka who ruled over the sector of Gy'at Li. And then there was Kari — it would take her mayhap one more season of apprenticing before her mistress granted her with a sector of her own to rule over.

Kara clicked on her *zorgs* and took flight. She concentrated on recapturing the retreating male, ignoring Jana's cry-out to Kari that a six-footer was escaping. Kari could handle the six-footer without aid. It was nigh unto child's play for a wench so close to becoming a High Mystik.

Flying at high speed directly toward the six-and-a-half-footer, Kara waited until the precise moment she was upon him before aiming her *maltoosa* down and firing it. The male bellowed, making a sound of pain before stumbling to the ground and landing on his backside. Unable to move, he could do naught but watch as Kara landed before him, wearing her thigh-high maroon combat boots, and the maroon warpaint spread all over her naked body.

"Shh," Kara soothed as she squatted down beside him. "'Twill do you no good to get yourself all worked up." She could see his chest heaving up and down from his labored breathing, which she'd come to realize over the years meant that the male was both tired from the stunning and frightened of his impending fate.

The entire ritual was too close to Trystonni mating for her to have a care for. Only in this situation the roles had been reversed and it was the male who had been rendered nigh unto unconscious that he might not flee from his future mate. When Kara searched the male's terrified gaze, she couldn't help but to think of her own situation—or the situation that would have been hers had she remained on Tryston.

Kara knew that although the bagged male was frightened just now, he would be happy for his fate after he joined his body with Dorra's. On the next moon-rising when Dorra claimed him for a mate, his hearts would belong to her as well as his body. It was ever the way of things on Galis.

Nay—she cared not for the similarities between the Galians and the Trystonnis for it made her wonder whether or not her hearts would have swooned with love if—

Nay. There was no sense in dwelling upon it. She was dead to Cam now.

Kara sighed, not having a care for the direction her thoughts were straying in. She shook her head as if willing them away, then absently wondered to herself how long it would take Dorra to catch up with them. The six-and-a-half-footer wasn't the only tired one. This pack-hunt had lasted two straight moon-risings, the four males having escaped once before. Dorra had chosen her mate well, she conceded. The male was cunning and agile and would gift her with many strong daughters.

The captured male's breathing grew more labored, which induced Kara to break out of her contemplative thoughts. "There now," she cooed as she removed the loincloth he wore, "'tis naught to fear of your mistress Dorra." She came down on her knees beside him and leaned over him, that her breasts dangled before him. "She is the bravest of warriors and skilled in all things erotic. No male could be happier with a bride such as Dorra Gy'at Li."

The male's breathing began to calm, which caused Kara to smile. She grabbed his thick cock by the root and began to slowly masturbate it up and down with one hand whilst she soothingly stroked his chest with the other. It was the least she could do to keep him bagged and calm until Dorra caught up with them and tagged him.

The male's eyes closed on a shaky expelling of breath. Kara could tell from his innocent, unschooled reaction to her touching that he was still a virgin — a fact that would please the future mother of his children immensely.

"Please," the male whimpered, realizing he could do naught to stop her from stroking his manpart for the stunner had zapped his energy, "I — ohh," he breathed out. His teeth gritted. "Please do not make me do bad things, Mistress."

He sounded as if he were about to cry. Kara sighed. Sure enough, she espied tears welling up in his lavender eyes. His bottom lip began to tremble. "I'm not that kind of boy," he sobbed.

Kara resisted the urge to roll her eyes. Leastways, she had learned over the *Yessat* years that all Galian males were given to extreme emotion. So instead she smiled down at him, but did not cease the stroking of his cock. "What is your name?" she asked gently.

His bottom lip continued to quiver as his eyelashes batted away his tears. "Vrek," he said shakily.

"'Tis a nice name, Vrek." She smiled as her voice gentled yet further. "I think it best do you allow yourself to be a naughty boy, Vrek. 'Tis for a certainty your mistress will expect much more from you on the next moon-rising when she takes you to the *vesha* hides."

She immediately realized it was the wrong thing to say. The six-and-a-half-footer's eyes widened on a gasp, then ten seconds later he broke down into a fit of uncontrollable crying.

Kara winced. By the sands, what had she been thinking, scaring him as she had in regards to his wedding night? She sighed. Her only excuse was that her mind was distracted as of late. Distracted with thoughts of a warrior she had no business musing over. She had given him up all of those *Yessat* years past, and now it was for a certainty he would never again welcome her home with open arms.

As her adoptive sister Kari would say, hindsight is 20-20. The past could not be changed.

But she didn't care, she firmly reminded herself. She would one day be named a High Mystik of Valor City and would rule over a sector all her own. It was what she wanted. It was what she had aspired to when first she'd arrived on Galis with Jana. So why then must she keep reminding herself of her own happiness?

Because, she thought forlornly—because naught had turned out the way she had envisioned it would when she'd been a young and immature twenty-two *Yessat* years and determined to carve out her own destiny. She hadn't truly considered the fact that she'd never again be able to go home to Tryston. Aye, she had known it in her head, but not in her hearts. She missed her family. And she hated the fact that they all thought her long dead. Her beloved sire, her equally beloved *mani*...

An image of her favored sibling Jor popped into her mind, causing her to smile sadly. Jor would be twenty-one *Yessat* years now — nigh close to the age when Cam Ka'l Ra had first made his claim to Kara's future known.

Cam, she thought with a nostalgic smile. When she had been a girl-child still clinging to her *mani's* skirt, she had loved him with all of her hearts. His tall, muscled form and golden good looks had made him seem larger than life to her. The way he'd always had a care for her, the way his glowing *matpow*-colored eyes had always promised to cherish her. Mayhap it was possible he had coveted her as more than a marriage prize. Mayhap he had actually loved —

Cease your mental babbling, Kara! You are free. Independent and free. 'Twas what you wanted, remember?

Kara's nostrils flared as she began masturbating Vrek in fast, firm strokes. Bah! It was ridiculous, this bagging business. The males of Galis were far too weak and unschooled to have a care for.

The male began to moan loudly at the frenzied milking of his cock, replacing the weeping he had been doing but *Nuba*-moments prior. "Mistress," he said hoarsely as his chest heaved up and down and sweat broke out on his forehead, "please do n—*ooooh*."

Vrek closed his eyes as his entire body shuddered, then convulsed on a groan of completion. Warm liquid shot up from his cock, spewing from the hole at the thick tip and saturating his belly.

Kara grinned at the look of bliss on his face. It was much the way she had felt the first time her favored *Kefa* had brought her to peak.

"Now that wasn't so bad, was it?" she asked in an exaggeratedly patient tone. It was said with more patience than she felt for a certainty. "'Twill feel even better when your mistress impales her channel upon your cock and rides you into spurting within her."

Vrek's eyes rounded. "'Twill feel better?" he whispered.

"Aye." Kara smiled, making the pep talk up as she went along. In truth, she had no notion what being mounted felt like for she was still a virgin herself. Try as she might, she hadn't been able to bring herself to couple with the male servants as other Galian wenches were wont to do. "'Twill feel like bliss."

Her adoptive sister Kari had told her that the inability to couple with the servants was an affliction brought on by having dabbled with a warrior. Leastways, it was the very affliction Kari had suffered from ever since she'd been mounted by a warrior nine *Yessat* years past. Kari had coupled with no one since she'd fled from the warrior — the same as Kara had been unable to couple at all.

Vrek's breathing calmed as he considered that. "For a certainty?" he squeaked.

Kara nodded her head. "Aye."

Just then Dorra burst through the maroon jungle trees, the severe look of the huntress making her features appear grim. It was a sight that sent Vrek's eyes back into tearing fits.

Kara grunted, her lips puckering into a frown as she rose to greet her sister. "I had him calmed, dunce. Look what you've gone and done."

Dorra grunted back, her severe look softening when she laid eyes upon her hunting booty. Naked but for her thigh-high maroon boots and the warpaint she was sporting, her breasts bobbed up and down as she strode briskly toward the six-and-a-half-footer and prepared to tag him. Her nipples hardened into tight points as she came down beside him and ran a hand along the sleek contours of his body. For a male who was not a warrior, Kara had to admit he was impressive of face and form. She knew for a certainty why Dorra coveted him so.

"Calm thyself," Dorra murmured as she gently swiped away his tears with a thumb. "'Tis naught to fear of me, handsome one."

She placed the laser scan across the length of his cock and detonated it. The highly advanced chemical branding device made a whirring sound, then a moment later Vrek was officially tagged.

It was done. The six-and-a-half-footer could never couple with any wench but Dorra or his cock would explode.

When Vrek whimpered, Dorra soothed the stinging sensation the laser scan had left behind by running her tongue across the length of the brand. "'Twill be all healed in time for me to claim you next moon-rising," she murmured between licks. "From the morrow onward, thy body will know naught but sweet bliss from mine."

As she watched the Galian claiming scene unfold, Kara idly considered the fact that a warrior would never submit to being tagged. A warrior would have done his own brand of tagging via a bridal necklace. When the noise of hysterically sobbing Galian males reached her ears through the dense Trefa jungle, she wondered if that would have been such a bad thing.

Kara grimaced at the inferior sound. Trystonni females might grow frightened when they are claimed by warriors, but the wenches are never so weak-willed as to succumb to tearing fits. She sighed, realizing as she did that she had better grow accustomed to Galian males and their inferior temperaments the soonest.

She had no choice. It was either that or never be mated.

Kara gritted her teeth. It was ironic for a certainty.

Chapter 2

Holo-Port 3, Trader City, Planet Arak
Trek Mi Q'an Galaxy

Dari Q'ana Tal released a pent-up breath of air when she felt the *gastrolight* cruiser lurch upwards and broach the Arakian atmosphere. From her hiding place within Pod Nine, she quickly calmed herself, carefully ensuring that she made not even the smallest of sounds. She would do naught to give herself away. Even her eyes were kept closed that her glowing blue orbs might not give so much as a hint that a stowaway was aboard ship.

Dari tightly clutched the hand of the boy-child she had rescued, letting him know without words that all would be well. She could feel Bazi shaking beside her, not a surprising reaction for a child who had seen but nine *Yessat* years.

In truth, she was a bit wary of their predicament. She knew that if their hiding place was discovered they would be sent back to Arak in all haste.

Dari shivered. Neither she nor Bazi could ever go back, for the Evil One now knew that they were aware of its existence. It would have killed her and Bazi had she not fled the palace in all haste. Mayhap it would even have killed Gio when he discovered how and why she had died…

Gio, she thought on a pang of emotion. She had tried to remain steadfast, had attempted to thwart him at every turn over the past nine *Yessat* years, yet he had managed to do the unthinkable: he had gotten under her skin and into her hearts.

Yet she could not return to him. There were reasons. Reasons he would never forgive her for.

Leastways, that was a separate story.

Chapter 3

Kopa'Ty Palace, Planet Zideon
Trek Mi Q'an Galaxy

Panting for air, King Cam K'al Ra emerged naked from the lulling silver waters of Loch Lia-Rah. His darkly bronzed skin glistened of dew droplets, his hair dark gold with wetness. This moon-rising, as he'd done every moon-rising for more *Yessat* years than he could remember, Cam had circumnavigated the loch four times, which kept his heavily muscled body fitter than that of most warriors. He had an endurance few could match let alone surpass.

When he had been naught but the lowly son of a credits-poor *trelli* miner, he had swum the polluted, dirty loch of his sector every moon-rising. The waters had been so dirty it was nigh unto impossible to see where one was swimming, yet he had done it without complaint.

He had been raised amongst the ruins left behind by greedy sector lords—insurrectionists who thought naught of burning an entire village to the ground did it help them make their point and scare the people they ruled over into submission. Cam supposed that because he hadn't known any other way of life, he had accepted his surroundings unthinkingly, never realizing there was a better way.

One morn Cam had gone off to labor within the *trelli* mines—slave labor he now realized himself to have been—and when he returned home for the eve, it was only to find that his own village had been burned to the ground. Everyone that he loved—his *mani*, his ailing papa, even his wee siblings — all of them had died in the *gastro-gel* fire set ablaze by the sector's own High Lord.

Cam had gone crazed — as crazed as the starved gulch beasts that sometimes deserted their pits in Koror in order to hunt humanoid flesh if their food supply grew too low. Like a hungered gulch beast, Cam had spent the next few *Yessat* months hunting down the humanoid flesh of the rebel leader who murdered his family. He had tracked him, stalked him, waited for the right moment to make his move, and then he had killed him. He had experienced no guilt for the High Lord had deserved his fate for a certainty. Cam had played the part of the executioner and had thought no more on it.

Once his family had been avenged he decided it was time to move on and find work in another *trelli* mine. The mines were, after all, the most he had ever expected from life. But then he hadn't realized at the time that the High Lord he'd executed was wanted by the Emperor for treason. Or that a warlord named Kil Q'an Tal had witnessed the death sentence Cam had handed down to the rebel.

Two months later, Cam had been working the mines in a sector twenty days walk from his birth village when three finely dressed warriors had entered the squabble of a place where he had found employment. They had demanded to speak to him directly.

The warriors had been donned in blue leathers — the emblem of High Lords — so Cam had absently wondered if they had been sent to kill him for murdering one of their own. Leastways, he would have welcomed death at the time, for it was all he really had to look forward to in those days. With his family on the other side of the Rah, there had been naught in life to recommend living — and worse yet he had barely been earning enough credits at the mines to rent a cheap chamber to sleep in.

But nay, the warriors had not come to murder him. They had come instead to inform him that he had been handpicked as one of the few select to study the warring arts under the Emperor's tutelage.

Cam could still recall the way his good friend Jek had grinned at him when Cam had hoarsely told him there must have been a mistake. Of course, Jek hadn't been his friend at the time—it was the first time they'd ever laid eyes on the other. Cam had argued that he was but the son of a *trelli* miner—that he knew naught of the warring arts, but Jek had insisted that no mistake had been made, that the Emperor's brother and heir apparent had witnessed Cam's hunting prowess with his own eyes and wanted him trained to be on the right side of the battling.

The first time Cam had laid eyes on the Palace of the Dunes he had nigh unto swallowed his own tongue. The wealth of the stronghold had been beyond his ken. Finely dressed and highly skilled warriors were everywhere. Beautiful, topless serving wenches abounded, their lush breasts bobbing up and down as they saw to their duties. Gorgeous, enchanted *Kefa* slaves created in every hue imaginable stood passively about, doing naught else but await the attention of the master.

All of those women—enchanted and real—had belonged to one man, to the Emperor. Their channels existed to milk him, their mouths to suckle him—and Cam had admired the arrogance of the warrior able to bring so many under his dominion.

The first time he had swum the loch contained within the grounds of the Palace of the Dunes, Cam had felt a boyish giddiness move through him. He, Cam K'al Ra, son of a *trelli* miner, was living in Sand City training under the most powerful male in existence and was permitted to make use of the most elaborate and clean loch his eyes had ever beheld. That water had been as sweetly silver as the waters of the loch he now swam in—his very own.

But where the mirror-clear waters of the loch within the lands of the Palace of the Dunes had inspired him, Loch Lia-Rah's waters haunted him. Every moon-rising back in Sand City, Cam had stared at the reflection cast back at him from the waters before he'd jumped in and did his nightly exercise. The reflection had been one filled with promise, with hope for a new life and a better future. For the first time ever, he had felt as though he were at last on the right track, that there was naught to look forward to but bliss.

But now in the present, Cam had not a care for his reflection, for it held none of the promise that his man-child reflection had. He deliberately never gazed upon himself before jumping into Loch Lia-Rah, for he knew there was naught there to see but grim lines and harsh features.

In Sand City, there had been hope. On Planet Zideon, there was naught. When Kara had died, his hearts had died with her. There was naught left on the inside of him now, just an empty space.

Why Kara, he asked himself as he strode from the loch. Every day he went through this same ritual. Every day he went over the past in his mind, wondering where it was he had gone wrong. *Why did you run from me?*

Cam sighed, realizing no answers would be forthcoming. They never were. Pulling on his leathers, he strode back toward the palace, and to his harem.

* * * * *

"What?"

Cam's head came up as if in slow motion. He summoned a bottle of vintage *matpow* and settled into his *vesha*-bench. Gio sat at the raised table directly across from him.

"I think it best do you start from the beginning before you tell me the whole of it."

"Dari ran from me a fortnight past," he said harshly.

Gio's jaw clenched. He refused to let anyone see how broken he felt without her nearness, how anguished he felt by her betrayal, and concentrated instead on his ire. He had thought she had come to have a care for him. Now he realized he had been played for the fool.

"I thought her sleeping when in reality she'd fled, so she had a good ten *Nuba*-hours head start on me."

A distant, yet still painful memory flickered through Cam's mind. It was much the same method Kara and Jana had used prior to their ill-fated sojourn away from Tryston. Kara too had feigned sleep, giving her a head start that, sadly, was never recovered.

"She's gone off to Galis for a certainty? How can you know this?" Cam murmured.

Gio's harsh features grew grimmer. "When I followed after her, my path crossed with that of an escaped bound servant—a *male* bound servant from Galis." He shook his head as if he couldn't believe he'd lived long enough to bear witness to such things as male sex slaves. "Leastways, the escaped servant sought me out at Galis' main holo-port and offered me information of Dari in exchange for his safe passage off the matriarchal planet."

"You agreed, I take it."

"Aye. Aye, of course." Gio's jaw clenched impossibly tighter. "The escaped servant swore a vow that he witnessed Dari within the presence of a male humanoid," he gritted out. "A male humanoid who stands approximately a *Yeti*-foot shorter than most warriors."

Cam grunted in sympathy. He realized it was the last thing in the galaxies Gio would have wished to heard tell of. Dari with another male — possibly being mounted by him — it was definitely not the sort of situation a warrior could stomach. If Dari coupled with that male, it would drive Gio to death or devolution. Leastways, every time he claimed her body for his use, the scent of the lesser male's would always be there, slowly driving him mad. Once a warrior had a lock on his wench's scent, there could be no other male for her.

Cam waved a hand toward Gio as his thoughts turned in a new direction. "Why did you seek me out afore venturing onward to find Dari?"

"I didn't," Gio admitted. "I immediately set off to track her to the sector the runaway servant claimed to have seen her in." He ran a hand through his black hair and sighed. "Yet she was gone before I got here. The Galian wenches, tightlipped and secretive as they are, would not tell me in which direction she had headed."

"And their men are too bedamned weak and timid to do aught but their wenches' bidding." Cam's gaze narrowed speculatively. "But I still do not understand why you've come to Zideon, my friend."

"'Twas closer to refuel and rearm myself here than to return to Arak. And," he murmured, "I have not yet told you the whole of it."

Cam felt his stomach muscles clench, though he hadn't any notion as to why. The tiny hairs at the back of his neck stood up, as if portently. "Aye?" he said in low tones. "Tell me then."

Gio sighed. "The male servant espied Dari in the company of someone other than the lesser male's."

"Who?" Cam asked softly.

Gio's gaze clashed with his. "With a golden wench Dari hugged and kissed as though she hadn't laid eyes upon her in nigh unto five *Yessat* years." His nostrils flared. "With a golden wench she joyfully embraced whilst calling her names such as 'sister' and 'Jana'."

Cam's eyes widened. His hearts rate picked up. If Jana was alive that meant also that—

Nay. Such was not possible.

"What are you saying, my friend." It was a question that had been issued as a statement, for Cam knew exactly what it was that Gio was telling him.

Gio's nostrils flared. "I'm saying 'tis possible that your betrothed is alive, Cam. And I'm saying 'tis possible that my betrothed accompanies her."

Chapter 4

Kara was having a wicked-good time watching Dari's jaw hang agape all throughout the evening meal. She knew how her sorely missed cousin felt, for it was the same way she'd felt when first she and Jana had arrived on Galis five *Yessat* years past.

Everything on Galis was different. It was as if the planet was the mirror reflection of Tryston, yet in reverse. In many ways Galis reminded her of a saga her *mani* had once told her about a little girl named Alice and her adventures in a place called Wonderland. Like Alice, they had fallen into a world where everything was the opposite of the world they had once dwelled in.

Dari sighed as she finished the last bit of her stew. She turned to Kara. "Remember the wetted *vesha*-towels the bound servants would hand to us after we partook of a sticky repast?" Her brow furrowed as she studied her sticky hands. "Have they *vesha*-towels here?" she asked almost absently.

Kara grinned. She could scarcely wait to witness Dari's reaction to her answer. "Aye. The male servant attending to you holds yours."

Dari glanced over towards him, her lips puckered into a frown much reminiscent of her *mani's*. "I don't see—"

Kara bit down onto her lip to keep from laughing aloud, but the shocked look on Dari's face was nigh unto hilarious. She cleared her throat, grinning from ear to ear. "Do you see it now?"

"Aye," Dari squeaked. She cleared her throat. "I mean aye, I see it." Reaching up, she snatched the wet *vesha*-towel that dangled from the male servant's erect manpart and briskly washed her hands with it. Her nostrils flared. "I don't understand the way of things here, Kara," she grumbled. "And it makes me look the fool."

"Nay." Kara chuckled, a dimple popping out on either cheek. "You look much less the fool than Jana and I did when first we arrived. 'Tis a vow amongst cousins that my jaw hung open for at least a solid fortnight."

Dari found her first grin. A rarity for her, so Kara knew she was well-humored.

"Aye, I believe it. 'Tis a passing fair place, yet different for a certainty." Dari glanced at the male servant attending to her, then turned back to Kara. "How is it possible that..." She waved a hand about. "How do their manparts stay forever erect as they do?"

Kara tossed a *migi*-candy into her mouth, savoring the sweetness of her favored dessert. "They've spells placed o'er their cocks by High Mystiks." She shrugged, having had five *Yessat* years to grow accompanied to the sight. "'Tis so they are able to perform sexually at any time a wench desires to sample of their charms."

Dari's eyes widened. "Have you ever sampled of their charms?" she murmured.

"Nay." Kara sighed as her teeth sank into another *migi*-candy. "Leastways, I have been tempted a time or two by the sight of so many erect cocks, yet I've never felt as though 'twas the right man or the right time..." Her voice trailed off. "Mostly I've felt it was never the right man," she admitted in a whisper of a breath.

Dari looked away. She didn't wish to think on Gio any more than Kara wished to think on Cam. There was naught but hearts-ache down that *trelli*-paved road.

"I've decided to attend the final hunt of the season," Kara said, turning the topic. "'Tis on the moon-rising of the morrow. Would you like to accompany me?"

"Aye," Dari said, nodding. "I should very much like to — ahh I forgot." She sighed.

Kara's forehead wrinkled. "What? What is wrong?"

"Kari and I are trekking into Valor City on the morrow. There is...information there I might find useful."

When Dari's features schooled themselves into a grim mask, Kara realized she would say naught else on the subject. She frowned. She wished she knew what it was that her cousin had endured before finding passage to Galis. She wished too that she understood how the six-foot man-child named Bazi who had accompanied Dari to Galis factored into it. Yet it was sorely apparent on both accounts that her cousin cared not to divulge any information as of yet.

Thirty *Nuba*-minutes later, as Dari rose from the bench to see Bazi off to his rooms, Kara vowed to herself that she would find a way to get her cousin to confide in her. She sensed it was important that she did.

* * * * *

Jana's gaze meandered over the male servant's body, hovering at the erect manpart holding her *vesha*-towel. It was the biggest, fiercest specimen of manhood she'd ever laid eyes on. She felt her mouth watering as she gingerly plucked the small towel from his large cock and patted at her lips with it.

It would be bliss, the pummeling that cock would give her in her chamber this moon-rising. She'd never taken a male servant to the *vesha* hides, or any other male for that matter, but for a certainty she would be impaling herself upon the cock of this formidable male within the hour.

She'd never experienced a compulsion so strong, so basic and primal. It was as if her body was being summoned by the goddess to couple with the servant.

"Take yourself off to my rooms," Jana said arrogantly, not so much as deigning to glance upwards at his face. She feared if she did he would see her bizarre need reflected in her glazed-over eyes. "Await me in my bedchamber. I shall be up shortly."

When the male made no move to see to her bidding, she was startled enough to glance up. Leastways, males did not disobey females on Galis — not ever.

Her glowing blue eyes clashed with his piercing silver one. He possessed the eyes of a predator, she thought somewhat warily. The irises of his eyes were the most formidably honed silver she'd ever gazed upon.

And, what's worse, the anger radiating from the servant was a tangible thing. She could see the rage in the clenching of his jaw, feel it in the way his eyes bore into hers, sense it as his heavily muscled body corded and tensed. He stood as tall and as big as any warrior, yet she knew from the silver of his eyes that he was no warrior. He was sired of a different species altogether. What species he could have possibly been sired of she hadn't any notion.

Jana forced herself to remember that it was her right to avail herself of the servant's charms at any time she so desired. He was but a gift from Klykka and therefore hers for the taking. She narrowed her eyes as she spoke to him.

"No matter your species, humanoid, you belong to me for five *Yessat* years. Klykka captured you fairly in battle and 'tis mine you now are." She kept her words soft, but forceful. "Obey me in all things, handsome one, or 'tis my punishment instead of my pussy that you shall receive."

The servant's nostrils flared. His silver eyes promised retribution. "I beg to differ with you, *Mistress*," — he spat the word out, "but I would not call capturing a drugged and otherwise unawares male in any way fair battling."

Jana waved that away. She didn't know how Klykka had captured him, nor did she care. Her body fair screamed for release just gazing upon him. He elicited primordial reactions from her she'd never heard tell of.

The desire to mate with him was so paramount as to be painful. Perspiration dotted her forehead as the most intense wave of heat suffused her.

She whimpered as her nipples painfully hardened, a reaction that induced one side of the male servant's mouth to curl upwards in an arrogant half-smile. He knew something that she didn't, she thought warily. What in the name of the holy sands was happening to her?

Jana had heard tell of *heeka-beasts* and *gazi-kors* going into heat when the need to reproduce was upon them. Leastways, she had never heard tell of such a thing happening to a Trystonni wench. She was overcome with the need to milk the male's rod with her channel, to allow him to plant a hatchling within her womb…

She gasped at her distressing thoughts, then schooled her features into a formidable mask as her teeth ground together. She would entertain her bizarre thoughts no longer. She needed to mate. It was all that was of importance.

"Fair. Unfair. It matters naught for you are mine." Her eyes devoured the length of his swollen cock — a cock Klykka's potent magic had commanded to remain hard at all times — then licked her lips. "Take yourself off to my bed anon, slave." Her eyes found his. "Or I'll have you tied to it."

A tick began to work in his jaw. "If you tie me up, *zya*," he said too softly, "you will know my punishment."

Jana was startled enough to frown. A moment passed in silence, their proverbial horns locking. Her eyes narrowed determinedly as her jaw did some clenching of its own.

"Never threaten your Mistress, slave." Her nostrils flared. "Guards!"

* * * * *

Cam strode toward Gio, his stride brisk and efficient.

"Well?" Gio asked, his glowing violet eyes scanning Cam's clenched jaw, his flaring nostrils. "Did you learn anything useful?"

"Aye," he bit out. "I did."

Gio sighed. "Kara is alive I take it?"

"Alive and well," Cam growled. "And going by the family name Gy'at Li."

Their gazes clashed as a moment of silence passed between them. Finally, Gio murmured, "Did you get the sector coordinates?"

Cam fisted and unfisted his hand, causing veins to bulge on his forearm. "Aye," he ground out. "I did."

Chapter 5

Kara slithered atop the Trefa jungle floor, naked except for her thigh-high maroon combat boots and the maroon *tishi* paint smeared all over her body. She was the only of the Gy'at Li sisters who had decided to partake of the last hunt of the season. The others had made different plans.

Kari, Klykka, and Dari had all three ventured into Valor City in the hopes of gaining an audience with Talia, the Chief High Mystik of Galis. Talia, known amongst the women warriors as Flash for her quick reflexes and unsurpassed skills in pack-hunting, held court but twice a *Yessat* year, this moon-rising being one of them. Jana had decided to remain behind to bring her wayward and newly acquired male servant to heel, whilst Dorra was still busily enjoying the benefits of teaching Vrek all there was to know in the *vesha* hides.

Thus, the only of the Gy'at Li sisters pack-hunting on this the last official moon-rising of the hunting season was Kara. Leastways, she now wished she hadn't given her vow to do so, for she very much would have preferred trekking into Valor City with her cousin and adoptive sisters over gaining more credits to add to their already impressive hoard of them.

Crawling on all fours over the dense jungle's maroon terrain, it occurred to Kara that she had somehow managed to separate herself from the rest of the pack. She sighed, wondering when she'd become such a careless huntress. It wasn't like her to become distracted for a certainty, yet on this moon-rising she had obviously managed to become distracted enough to wander too far off from the others whilst she tracked the Galian male she'd been hired to bag.

Cam. *He* was the reason, she thought with a harrumph.

Kara had thought back on her former betrothed often over the years, hoping against hope that when they met again on the other side of the Rah, he would forgive her of all her transgressions against him. She doubted that he would ever forgive her, even in the next life, yet she had still hoped.

Aye, she had thought back on Cam K'al Ra more times than she could count over the years, wondering how he was, hurting herself with jealous thoughts concerning which highborn mistress he might be dallying with, yet during the past fortnight she had been plagued with haunted memories of him stronger than ever before. It was as if her connection to him had been rebirthed. And it was driving her mad.

Sometimes she felt overcome with the need to return to him, knew even that she should, yet she also knew he would always hate her. She didn't think she could bear to see the turquoise eyes that had once glowed with love of the hearts for her glow with naught but revulsion and hatred instead.

Kara took a deep breath and expelled it, deciding there was no use in thinking on Cam. What was done was done. She had chosen her own path and she had willingly traveled down it. Like as naught, she would spend the rest of her days regretting that course for she missed her family—and Cam—sorely, yet the past could not be changed.

It was all her own doing. She had made choices in her youth and they were choices she must now pay the price for as a wench full grown.

The sound of a crackling frond caused Kara's ears to perk up. She slithered closer to the next bush then came down on her elbows when she neared it, planning to take a look on the other side of it through the gaping hole that always appeared near the bottom of a *tu-tu* bush. Still crawling upon all fours, her naked buttocks were high into the air as she pressed her face closer to the ground that she might glance through the bottom of the *tu-tu* bush and ascertain where the sound had come from.

"Well what have we here," a chillingly cold voice said.

Kara's entire body stilled. She sucked in her breath, knowing precisely who that voice belonged to. She had heard it whisper to her in her every waking fantasy and sleeping dream these past five *Yessat* years. And right now, it was fiercely angry with her.

She felt the anger penetrate her body, sweeping through her in a current of emotion much like a *gastrolight* discharge. The feeling was frightening, and somewhat physically painful. She made a small whimpering noise, then immediately chastised herself for making a sound that could be interpreted as naught but fear and submission.

"Oh aye, you should be afraid," the voice growled as it drew closer.

Kara closed her eyes on a wince, her hearts rate beating rapidly as she quickly tried to think of what she should do. She was frightened—powerfully frightened— and because of that fact she refused to look back at him.

Cam K'al Ra had been terrifying to her before she'd disobeyed him. Her fear was a thousand times worse now, knowing he would punish her for a certainty.

In that moment, the past five *Yessat* years melted away, the rationality of a matured wench along with it. She felt two and twenty again—young and driven by desperation. No matter that she'd missed Cam. No matter that a part of her hearts had secretly hoped this day would come. Now that it was here and she felt the tentative control he had on his emotions threatening to snap, her only thought was to once again flee. Without thinking, her eyes flew open and every muscle in her body corded and tensed as she made a move to lunge to her feet and sprint away.

And yet—nothing happened. Her body remained unmoving. She began to sweat.

"Oh goddess," Kara quietly cried out, feeling somewhat hysterical. Cam's gaze was commanding her body to his bidding. She couldn't move, couldn't flee, could do naught but remain upon the jungle floor on all fours, her face submissively lowered to the ground whilst her buttocks were thrust up high, showcasing her naked pussy for him. Her hearts rate was so high she feared she might do something embarrassingly weak like swoon.

"Now now Kara," the voice said mockingly, "'tis just now that I've found you." Cam drew closer still until Kara was certain he had come down upon his knees behind her. When his large palms settled upon her buttocks, she knew that she had been right. "Don't tell me you think to flee me again so soon," he murmured.

Kara's nostrils flared at his superior tone. "If you are so certain of yourself and your abilities, why not release me from your hold that we might decide my fate as equals," she ground out.

When he said nothing for long moments, Kara began to nibble at her lower lip. When she tried to swivel her head that she might look upon him, she found that she couldn't. Even the simple movement of her neck had been summoned, disallowing any part of her body save her voice to move.

"Will you not speak?" she asked warily.

Just then she heard a sound, not of Cam's voice, but of his labored breathing. His large hands began to knead her buttocks and she could tell without needing to look upon him that his eyes were feasting on the ripe flesh between her thighs. Perversely, when but a *Nuba*-second ago she had felt naught but terror at the sheer worrying over what he might do to her, she instead felt her nipples harden and her belly clench in anticipation of what he might do next.

"Your channel still drips for me," he murmured as his hands kneaded and massaged the soft globes of her buttocks. He pressed his face against her swollen channel and inhaled the scent of her. "You've been with no male of any species," he rasped out, his happiness apparent in the carnality of his tone. His breathing grew heavier, more labored. "I shall never allow you from my sight again, *pani*." His jaw clenched. "Never."

Kara closed her eyes against what his usage of the word *pani* did to her hearts. How could he respond to her this way? she thought guiltily. How could he call her by the very endearment he'd used for her whilst she'd been growing up on Tryston? After all that she had done to shame him, why would he—

With a groan, Cam buried his face between Kara's thighs and began to lap frenziedly at her channel. "Mmmm," he growled as his tongue streaked wet paths all over her flesh. "All mine."

Down on all fours and unable to move, her buttocks submissively raised into the air for him to do to her what he would, she could do naught but shudder and gasp, every fear she'd harbored of him moments past forsaken for pleasure. "Oh aye," she shakily breathed out.

His tongue flicked at her clit in hard, rapid, mind-numbing thrusts and continued to flick at her until she thought she'd go mad. Beads of sweat broke out all over her body at the frustration. She wanted him to suck on her, to take her clit into his mouth and suckle hard, yet he continued to toy with her instead, working her up into a delirium whilst knowing she was unable to move to do anything about it.

"*Please*," she gasped, her nipples stabbing out. "Please do not—" She moaned long and loud. "—do not punish me this way."

Cam raised his face from between her legs. His fingers replaced his tongue, rubbing her clit in that maddening way that was firm enough to arouse her, yet too weak to allow for completion.

"Make no mistake, *ty'ka*. You will be punished at my hands for a certainty," he said in a low, dark rumble. "Yet no punishments shall be given to you on this the moon-rising of our joining."

Kara's nostrils flared at his arrogant words. She was accustomed to being an independent wench—long accustomed. How dare he inform with such calm stoicism that he meant to punish her *after* they had mated? She would never submit, she thought as her teeth gritted. She would never—

"*Oh goddess.*"

Kara moaned out the platitude when Cam's face dove once more for her flesh, his tongue this time curling around her clit and drawing it into the heat of his mouth. "Suck it," she groaned. "Oh aye—*suck it.*"

With a low growl, he gave her what she wanted, his lips and tongue coiling around the erect little piece of woman-flesh, then frenziedly suckling.

"Aye," she gasped. "Harder."

He suckled her harder, wringing gasps and groans from her. Being unable to move, being unable to do naught but accept the pleasure, made her orgasm come all the sooner. And all the harder.

"*Cam.*"

She came on a loud groan that started low in her throat and worked its way up to her hair and down to her toes. Blood rushed to her face, to her nipples, then he thrust his tongue deeply into her channel whilst she contracted around it.

"*Aye,*" she cried out. "*Oh Cam — aye.*"

Kara closed her eyes and breathed in deeply. The orgasm had been so harsh that she felt shaky and yet the summoning of her body prevented her from shaking. The effect drove her mad. She felt in a frenzy. She needed to move. She needed — something.

"Please," she panted out, her entire body tingling almost painfully, "release my body from your summons. I — *ooooh.*"

A bridal necklace was summoned around her neck at the precise moment a long, thick cock slid into her from behind in one fluid motion. She gasped at the sensation of being so full, then moaned when she felt her body being released that she might move about. Immediately, instinctively, she arched up onto her elbows, raised her head, and prepared to look back at him. Unable to refrain from looking upon him any longer, Kara slowly, cautiously, turned her head and raised her eyes to meet his.

She sucked in her breath. She had nigh unto forgotten how powerfully handsome he was. Large and fiercely muscled, golden and perfect, with eyes that glowed a turquoise the likes of which not even vintage *matpow* could compete. Such handsomeness had always been Cam K'al Ra. That visage had caused her to feel lucky as a girl-child, knowing he belonged to her as he did. And yet somehow throughout the years, that feeling of luckiness had been replaced with a fear of him, fear that odd though it was, she no longer felt now that she'd looked upon him as a wench grown.

She had hurt him. It was so apparent in his eyes that the knowledge of it caused yet another stab of guilt to lance through her hearts. Feeling defensive, her nostrils flared as she looked away from him. There was too much pain between them. How could they ever carry on as Sacred Mates?

He began to move his cock in and out of her in long, deep strokes. All her worries were temporarily forgotten on a moan.

"'Tis mine you are, *pani*," Cam said thickly, his voice a rasp. His fingers dug into the flesh of her hips as he rotated his own hips and plunged into her in a series of slow, mind-numbing strokes. His jaw clenched. "You will never leave me again."

Kara closed her eyes and moaned as she threw her hips back at him. She wanted more. She wanted it faster. Where non-Trystonni females sometimes felt pain upon the loss of their virginity, a Trystonni wench experienced naught but bliss. Why, none could say.

"Aye," she breathed out, the sound of their flesh slapping together as much a turn-on as the pummeling itself. *"Harder."* Her breasts jiggled and her nipples stiffened with each hard thrust.

Cam's fingers burrowed deeper into her hips. "Like this?" he asked arrogantly, his thrusts coming harder, deeper, more rapid. "You want this?" he gritted out.

"*Oh aye.*" Kara moaned as she threw her hips relentlessly at him, the need to be pounded into harder and deeper inducing her breath to come out in a hiss. "Fuck me," she ground out in Trystonni. "Fuck me harder."

With a growl he mounted her hard, taking her like an animal as he thrust into her from behind. "My pussy," she heard him rumble out in their tongue. "*My pussy.*"

Kara moaned loudly. Their flesh made suctioning sounds as it slapped together. Their breathing was heavy and labored. The sound of him moaning and groaning as he pummeled obliviously into her depths made her belly clench and knot. Being down on all fours made her breasts bounce around wantonly, which sensitized her nipples to the point of pleasure-pain. She knew she was about to come — harder than she'd ever come in her life.

"*Caaaam.*"

His name was torn from her lips on a loud moan that echoed throughout the dense Trefa jungle. She threw her hips back at him in a state of near-delirium, greedily wanting fucked as hard and as much as he could give it to her whilst her belly burst and orgasm tore through her insides.

"Oh goddess," she groaned, her hips rocking back and forth. "Aye — *oh Cam.*"

His nostrils flared as he pounded into her mercilessly, holding back nothing. He took her hard, ruthlessly, his teeth gritting as he staved off his orgasm for long minutes, thrusting in and out of the channel he'd been denied for five torturously long *Yessat* years. "Mine," he ground out over and over again as he took her. "*My pussy.*"

He could endure no more. Her moans. Her gasps. The way her flesh sucked him back in every time he withdrew to thrust into her again...

"*Kara.*"

Every muscle in Cam's body corded and tensed as he animalistically pounded into her channel three times more. On a groan that was loud enough to make up for five years outside of twenty *Nuba*-minutes, he closed his eyes and spurted hot seed deep within her.

It took but three seconds for Kara to understand why a Sacred Mate could pleasure a wench as no other. As her bridal necklace began to pulse, as her belly began to contract with spasms that were nigh unto painful, she threw her head back and moaned whilst they burst together in a maddening peak of euphoria.

She felt faint, dizzy. Kara felt Cam gather her into his heavily muscled arms a sheer moment before the blackness came and began to overtake her. She had to wonder at her fate. It was for a certainty that when she woke up she would be long removed from Galis.

As she surrendered to the blackness, Kara could only speculate as to how harsh a punishment she would receive when she woke up. Thankfully, mercifully, and before she could grow too hysterical, she fell into a deep sleep.

Chapter 6
Meanwhile, back on Galis…

Jana's nipples hardened as she gazed down upon the chained male servant. The women warriors of her command had laid his eight foot long and heavily muscled body out in spread-eagle fashion, then chained him to the red crystal floor with *boggi*, a set of four shackles that protruded up from the crystal ground. Galians used *boggi* rarely, needing them only on the sparse occasions such as this one when it became necessary to break a recalcitrant male to their bidding.

She took a deep breath as she lowered her gaze to the slave's erect cock. The need to mate with the male, to impregnate her body with his hatchling, tore at her insides until she felt as though she might be crazed. Her breasts heaved up and down as she stood over him, her breathing labored.

"Feeling warm, *zya*?" he asked with an infuriating arrogance no slave should feel let alone display.

Jana's nostrils flared. Standing over him, she threw a golden tress over her shoulder whilst her breasts continued to heave up and down. For a certainty she would not answer a question put to her by a slave so bold as this one. And what, she thought idly, did *zya* mean? Twice now he had called her thusly.

One night-black eyebrow rose up fractionally as his silver eyes insolently drank in the sight of her naked breasts. "You have delicious nipples," he murmured. "Made for suckling."

Galian wenches always left their breasts unbound, so she was accustomed to her nipples being looked upon, yet the effect this male's possessive gaze had upon her nipples was nigh unto unnerving. They poked out as stiff as she didn't know what, and she wanted them suckled on more than she wanted to breathe. She began to pant—from need and fear.

"What manner of species are you?" she whispered. "What magic have you ensorcelled my body with?"

His heavy-lidded eyes were narrowed with lust, with need as powerful as her own. "'Tis no potion or magic trick," he said in a low rumble that brought to mind the growl of a male predator. "'Tis something far more powerful than that, *zya*." His acute silver eyes raked over her covered mons, inducing his nostrils to flare. "A *vorah* should never be clothed," he said with irritation. "Remove your *zoka* anon and let me gaze upon you as is my right."

Automatically, Jana's hands rose up to her hips, and her fingers prepared to remove the flimsy, see-through g-string she wore, which on Galis was referred to as a *zoka*. She had to obey him, she thought unblinkingly. It was necessary to obey him in all things. He owned her. He was her Master. Her body was his to command. He—

Eh? Yeeck!

Jana shook her head to clear it. She groaned as her hand flew up and clamped to her forehead. She was crazed for a certainty.

Her body, she thought uneasily, felt compelled to obey him. Not merely desirous, but literally compelled. It was as if her brain had been hypnotized and her womb wanted naught but to do the male's bidding.

When she realized that he had been purposely compelling her to think the thoughts he'd desired her to, her lips pinched together in a severe frown as she regarded him from her superior position standing over him. "What species are you?" she gritted out. "I would know why it is you are able to mesmerize my mind."

He didn't answer her, and she knew that he wouldn't. At least not yet.

"My birth name is Yorin," he murmured, his predator's eyes raking over her. "'Tis all you need know for mating me, *vorah*."

Jana's breathing was so labored she thought it was possible she might faint. Her need was so great, the desire to mate so powerful, that she felt as though she might die if she didn't impale herself upon his jutting cock the soonest—this moment.

She tried with every fiber of her being to resist the mental push he was giving her, but in the end his will was too strong to be overpowered. Her hands trembled with the effort of resisting him and a silky sheen of perspiration covered her body as her fingers threaded through the strings of the flimsy blue *zoka* and slowly pushed the g-string down her hips, then lower to her ankles. Her breasts heaving up and down, she stepped out of the *zoka* and stood over him naked.

Yorin's sharp silver gaze honed in on her pussy, then flicked back and forth between her nipples and the thatch of golden curls between her thighs. "You are mine," he purred, his eyes finding hers, "all mine, *zya*."

Jana closed her eyes briefly, just long enough to drag in a calming breath of air and regain her sanity for a spell. Her eyes flicked open as she warily looked down upon him. "I've changed my mind," she rasped out.

Her breathing grew more and more labored as sexual need turned into acute fear. This male meant to keep her. That he was chained to the floor did naught to quell her anxiety. She needed to remove herself from his presence before she mated him. Somehow, and she knew not how, she was fundamentally aware of the fact that mating him would bind her to him for all times.

"I will send the guards to release you," she whispered as she turned on her heel and began to drag herself away. Every step felt heavy, as though crystal weights were tied upon her ankles. "I—oooh."

Jana gasped when a pair of large hands seized her from behind. As he whirled her around to face him, she had little time to digest the knowledge that the chained male had managed to escape his bonds before she found herself being lifted into his arms. It was unfathomable how he had accomplished his escape. Unfathomable and terrifying.

Her eyes widened as she gazed up into his face. Shoulder-length black hair. Piercing silver eyes. A strong jaw.

Silver eyes, she mentally murmured as her gaze narrowed in thought. Silver—

Oh goddess.

"Nay," Jana whispered. She swallowed roughly as her rounded eyes flew wildly up to meet his. "Your species is naught but a legend..." Her voice trailed off disbelievingly.

The look he gave her was arrogant, male. "I am very real, *zya*." Yorin palmed her buttocks whilst he held her and kneaded them as though he had the right of it. "And you are my mate."

Definitive. Unwavering.

Jana's breasts heaved up and down as her breathing grew heavier. "Let me go," she said shakily.

Frightened. Terrified.

Yorin closed his eyes and breathed deeply. His nostrils flared as he inhaled her scent. "Nay," he murmured as his silver eyes slowly opened and clashed with her glowing blue ones. His jaw tightened. "Never."

Jana gasped as an intense wave of heat surged through her, hardening her nipples and inducing her face to flush. She could feel her clit pulsing. Her body screamed for surcease. She knew without a doubt he had done this to her. Or that his nearness had done this to her. She knew naught which.

"Release me, Barbarian." It was a plea issued as a command.

He raised her up by the buttocks and slowly, achingly, rubbed her soaking wet labia over the hardness of his cock. "Nay," he rumbled out. His callused palms continued to knead her buttocks as he stared down into her face with a dark, brooding intensity. "Impale yourself upon me, *vorah*," he murmured.

Jana moaned as another, stronger, wave of heat suffused her. She knew then and there that he had won. She had to feel him rutting in her—needed his seed implanted in her womb with a compulsion the likes of which terrified her. She could endure no more.

In a series of swift movements, Jana reared up her hips, guided the entrance of her sopping wet flesh to the head of his cock, and bore down hard upon him. She cried out in pleasure as his flesh impaled hers, as his large fingers dug into the padding of her buttocks. Panting, she wrapped her arms around his neck.

"Yorin," she breathed out. She felt as though she was in a semi-trance, as though her body was but a vessel doing his bidding. "What do you to me?"

She didn't need to open her eyes to know that his hard silver gaze was drinking in the sight of her parted lips, of her flushed cheeks. She didn't need to see him to be aware of his nostrils inhaling the scent of her as though she smelled of the sweetest Galian perfume.

"I make you mine," he said thickly.

Fill your womb – fill your womb – fill your womb...

The words pounded through her mind, pierced through her hearts, vibrated through every cell of her being, until she felt like an animal—like an all powerful she-beast who would not and could not be stopped. With a ferocious growl she never would have made whilst mating with any other male, Jana bore down upon his cock once more, and frenziedly began fucking him. Up and down she rode him whilst he held her, moaning and groaning more wantonly than a harem of bound servants.

"Harder," Yorin murmured before nipping at her ear. "Suckle me with your flesh, *zya*."

"Aye," she gasped. Jana's breasts jiggled with every rapid movement, her hips slamming downward in fevered strokes.

Seed. She craved his seed. She needed his seed like she needed air to breathe and food to eat.

"*Aye*," she moaned, the sound of her wet flesh enveloping his. Her hips slammed down harder, faster, more, more, more—

"Harder," he growled, his teeth gritting as her pussy clenched tighter around his cock. "Milk me of seed, Jana."

"*Yorin.*"

Jana screamed out his name as she slammed her hips down hard and threw her head back, mercilessly impaling herself. Half groaning and half growling, she was too delirious with the desire to milk his cock to question why it was that she felt a compulsion to bite him. Purely on instinct, her teeth bared and with a she-beast's growl, she bit down hard onto his jugular vein.

"*Zya,*" he groaned loudly, his cock growing impossibly harder within her.

She could feel him tense with pleasure and knowing she had made him feel thusly emboldened her. Jana clamped down as hard as was possible on his jugular vein, her flesh making sucking sounds as it enveloped him within her. Slamming down hard upon his erection, her teeth held him tightly whilst she groaned against his neck. Within moments she was bursting, and her channel was frenziedly contracting around him.

"*Zya,*" he rasped, his voice drunk on arousal.

He carried her to the raised bed, their bodies never disjoining as he came down on top of her and pounded ruthlessly into her depths. Jana's teeth held tight to the jugular, pinching the vein together in a way that she somehow knew would drive him to a state as delirious as her own. Yorin moaned and groaned as he pounded into her, his eyes closed in bliss as he mounted her hard.

He rode her long and animalistically, his eyes closed tightly as though he was trying to stave off his orgasm and allow the pleasure to go on and on and on. But finally, when he could endure no more, the primordial instinct of his species took over, and on a groan loud enough to wake the dead, Yorin burst and he spurted his warm liquid deep inside of her.

Only then, only once her womb had been gushed with potent seed, did Jana release his jugular. Exhausted, and still half delirious, she could only find enough energy to gasp when she felt fangs tear through the flesh of her neck. "*Yorin.*"

She came immediately. Loudly. Violently.

Her last conscious thought before the blackness overtook her was that he had bound her to him for life.

And that her womb had been impregnated with a species not her own.

* * * * *

Kari Gy'at Li nibbled on her lower lip as she ended the holo-communication with Klykka. She took a deep breath, sucking in the pure nighttime air of Valor City. Wide-eyed, she turned to Dari. "Kara and Jana are missing."

Dari's eyes rounded to the shape of full moons. *"What?"*

"Kara disappeared from the Trefa jungle a few hours past and Jana seemingly disappeared from her own bedchamber."

"Good goddess," Dari breathed out. Unblinking, she shook her head. "Is there any guess as to what became of them?"

Kari sighed. "Yes." She bit on her lip for a moment as she studied Dari's face. "Klykka thinks they've fled for safety."

"Fled? But why?"

"Because it gets worse," Kari muttered.

When Dari looked at her quizzically, she took a deep breath and expelled it loudly. "The Emperor and his men—your betrothed included—are demanding that Galis raise its shield and allow them passage inside." Her voice quieted. "They've come looking for Kara and Jana. And," she said pointedly, "you know what else it is that they want as well."

"Me," Dari murmured.

As loathe as she was to admit it, the temptation of surrendering herself to Gio was a bewitching one, yet for a certainty she could not. Her eyes flicked to a few feet behind them where Bazi stood. If she was found before she had time to prove who the Evil One was, and what it really was, the young man-child would be brought back to Arak with her and murdered for a certainty. Mayhap she would be murdered too.

"What do you want to do?" Kari whispered. She reached for Dari's hand and squeezed it in a soothing manner. "Whatever you choose to do, I'll stand by you."

Dari took a deep breath whilst she studied the visage of the six-foot Bazi, the man-child who was at peace for the first time in weeks. There was but one choice, she knew. Leastways, she could never live with herself if death were to come to him.

Turning back to face Kari, she nodded her head, her mind made up. "We flee. Name the place and let us be gone."

Chapter 7

Airspace approximately five Nuba-hours outside Planet Zideon
The next day

Kara sat across from Cam at the raised table aboard the *gastrolight* cruiser and partook of the evening repast. Or tried to partake of it was mayhap more to the point. She found it was hard to enjoy a meal when her only company to share it with stared blankly into space, not so much as deigning to glance in her direction whilst he ate.

She looked away from him and sighed. "Will you not talk to me?" she asked tiredly as she rubbed at her temples with her hands. "'Twill be a long trip if we sit in silence throughout—"

"What is there to say?" he cut in, his voice a low murmur. She could feel his turquoise eyes boring holes into the side of her face. "'Tis sorely apparent you've no wish to be my *nee'ka*."

She didn't need to look up and see him to know that his jaw was clenched unforgivingly.

"'Tis also sorely apparent to any warrior with half a mind that you will attempt to flee me again when given the chance." His nostrils flared. "And so when we arrive on Zideon you will be granted few, if any, rights. I cannot trust you," he gritted out. "You sentenced me and your birth family to five *Yessat* years of hellfire with your childishness."

Kara's eyes closed at his words. She felt sick in the pit of her stomach realizing as she did that his words were true. She and Jana had caused much pain for many. This was fact. And yet...

"Why will I be granted no rights?" she asked bitterly, her eyes opening once again then flying up to meet his gaze. She felt a little girl-child again, but refused to show him her weakness. "Think you I have not suffered as w —"

"Silence."

Kara grimaced at the ice in his voice as well as at the strong hurt in his tone. She had shamed him — shamed and embarrassed him. And, she thought with a stab of guilt, she had also betrayed him and hurt him in the doing. Another fiercer stab of guilt lanced through her.

"Cam," she said softly, "'tis sorry I am. I never meant to —"

"You never meant to do what?" His jaw clenched impossibly tighter as he slowly rose to his feet. "Hurt me?" he ground out. He began to walk towards her, the look in his eyes frightening in its intensity.

She would not, she reminded herself, show him her fear. Her nostrils flared instead. "What are you doing?" she asked with more staunch than she felt. Her eyes watched him warily. "Mayhap 'tis best do you seat yourself — oh."

Kara swallowed a bit nervously as she studied him through rounded eyes. She gasped when one of his hands clamped about her wrist, then gasped again when he picked her up and carried her over to his *vesha* bench.

"What do you?" she whispered, her voice slightly shaking.

"I do unto you what is my right. Guards!" he called out loudly. "You may enter this chamber anon."

She sucked in her breath. His voice was like ice and it frightened her for a certainty. When he stretched her out over his lap that her head dangled over one side of his thighs and her feet over the other, her fright escalated into panic.

"Nay!" she gasped, unable to believe he was going to punish her this way. "Cam I beseech you—"

"'Tis best," he ground out, "that you accept your token punishment with the grace befitting a Queen." He waited until ten warrior guardsmen had filed into the chamber before he hiked up the back of her *qi'ka* skirt and exposed her bare buttocks to the men of his command. "You knew the price you would pay when you disobeyed me," he gritted. "Verily, I have twice bore witness to the Empress being punished thusly o'er the years. 'Tis the way of it when a wench disobeys her Master and well you know it."

Kara closed her eyes, blushing at the impending humiliation. Cam believed her to be aware of her *mani's* public spankings at her sire's hands when in fact she had been kept in the dark. She had heard the rumors. She hadn't believed them—until now.

"Please," Kara said quietly. "I do not wish to be spanked before your men." She bit down onto her lower lip, heat suffusing her face at the mere thought.

"You would have me look the fool after all that you have done?" he asked softly. Too softly, she thought warily.

"Nay but—ouch!"

Kara grimaced at the impact of the first sharp spank he awarded her backside. She steeled herself for the next one, her buttocks clenching together, intuitively figuring as she did that there were four more to come—one for each *Yessat* year she had spent in hiding.

And, inevitably, she was right. Four more sharp spanks crashed down upon the flesh of her buttocks, each one harder and more painful than the previous one.

Throughout the whole of it she managed to retain her quiet dignity in front of Cam and his men, but by the time the last of the five stinging spanks had been awarded to her, her buttocks were fierce sore and she was unable to avoid the release of a small whimper.

His large hand stilled upon the cheek of one red buttock. "Will you disobey me again, wench?" he asked loudly, making certain all in the chamber could hear his words.

Kara felt her teeth grind together at the cool command of his tone. It was no wonder wenches rarely disobeyed their Sacred Mates, she thought acidly, for to be splayed out like this and publicly spanked was embarrassing in the extreme. She wanted to curse Cam, to tell him exactly what was on her mind, but she knew that to do so in front of his warriors would only further shame him, which in turn would garner her naught but a fiercer spanking.

"Nay," she hissed.

He gave her a small, stinging whack to her backside, letting her know that naught but a properly chastised tone of voice was acceptable. "I did not hear you, *nee'ka*. Answer me again."

Her nostrils flared, but she gave him the bedamned word he sought and spoke it this time in a neutral tone of voice. "Nay," she repeated. It was her guilt and naught else that induced her to say it, she decided. And then she added for clarity, "I shan't shame you again."

He ran a soothing hand over her buttocks, inducing her to whimper. She gritted her teeth at the submissive sound, chastising herself.

"'Tis a good wench," Cam murmured whilst he stroked her buttocks. "Now show these warriors proper respect unto me."

Kara's nostrils flared to wicked proportions. If the rumors concerning public spankings were true, then so too were the rumors concerning how a wench might show proper respect to her Sacred Mate following a punishment. She closed her eyes briefly, realizing as she now did that the spanking was naught in terms of embarrassment compared to what was to come.

For a suspended moment she didn't move, just continued to dangle there across his lap. She flirted with the idea of disobeying him again, but in the end decided against it. Cam needed to save face. And such, whether she had a care for it or not, was apparently how a Trystonni male when shamed by his *nee'ka* restored his pride.

After taking a deep breath, Kara raised herself up off of Cam's lap and stood before him, waiting whilst he summoned off her *qi'ka*. When he had done so, she came down to her knees before him and began to remove the boots that covered his feet.

Cam's eyes raked over her body as he watched her perform the ancient ceremony that bespoke of complete and total submission to one's mate. He felt his cock stiffen merely watching her and wanted more than anything to fill her up with it.

In front of him, Kara's cheeks showed crimson. Mayhap if her mating Mistress had informed her of this custom years ago whilst she had been of the schooling age, she never would have been so bold as to flee Tryston in the first.

"Show them," Cam murmured. "Show these warriors your submission to me."

Her eyes widened at the challenge she heard in his voice. This was his way of saying that if she was truly sorrowful over the pain and shame she had caused him in the past, then she would cause no more by shaming him yet again in front of his men.

On a sigh, she relented.

Naked on her knees before him, Kara spread out her thighs as far apart as they would go, then lowered her face to his bared feet. She was careful to keep her channel on full display for the warriors gathered behind her to watch, her buttocks raised high as she began kissing his feet.

She knew it was up to Cam how long this phase of her punishment was to go on and, indeed, he allowed it to go on for quite some time. Perversely, it was only then that Kara realized just how sorely she had injured him.

Cam was not the type to inflict revenge upon her, yet the fact that he was allowing the kissing of his feet whilst her channel was on display for others to go on for so long was proof positive of all that he had endured at her hands. She grimaced at the thought, wondering if even after all this had transpired he would forgive her.

"Enough," Cam murmured. "Rise up, *nee'ka.*"

She closed her eyes at the gentleness of his tone. It was then that she knew for a certainty he harbored no desire to see her splayed out the way that she had been. He had merely done it because it was what was expected of him. To do aught else would have made him appear weak—a death sentence for a warlord who forged his way in life by commanding the respect of so many.

Mayhap it was guilt, mayhap it was the desire to show him she well and truly wished for peace between them, but when Kara raised herself up before him, she lifted only her face and remained upon her knees. Her thighs still spread submissively wide, her channel still on display for all and sundry to gaze upon, she removed his thick cock from his leathers and wrapped her lips about it.

Cam shuddered, his breath escaping in a hiss. He cupped her face with his palms, watching through eyes narrowed in bliss as she sucked him off for all to see. She took her time with it, allowing him to feel the pleasure of her warm mouth for long minutes before she began working him frenziedly, suckling his stiff erection in rapid sucks.

"Kara," he murmured, his breath catching. He came hard, spurting into her mouth on a groan. "Kara," he hoarsely repeated.

His breathing labored, Cam flicked his hand toward his men, indicating it was time for them to take their leave. They filed out one by one, until only the deuce of them remained in the chamber.

Kara's head slowly rose from his lap and their gazes clashed together. Cam's nostrils flared as he studied her face, wanting as he did for all to be healed between them, yet simultaneously afraid to trust her.

Kara took a deep breath as she studied his face in return. Everything Cam had punished her for—and more—was true. She had hurt and betrayed both him and her family. She had fled from her husband without giving him the chance to calm her fears of him. She had schemed and lied, connived and even stolen to achieve her means. There was much she had done that was wrong. And yet, there was one thing her Sacred Mate was wrong about himself.

"I won't try to run from you again," she said gently. "I say that now not that you might save face before your warriors for they have departed, but that you might know in your hearts 'tis true." Her eyes softened as she looked at him. "'Tis a vow amongst Sacred Mates."

He looked away from her, afraid to believe. "As if a vow from you means aught," he defensively ground out.

Wounded, Kara sucked in her breath. She quickly stood up and backed away from the raised table a few steps.

"There is much I have done that is wrong," she rasped out, her naked breasts heaving before him. "Leastways, I have never uttered a lie unto you."

The hurt in her voice caused Cam to look up. He studied her face but said nothing.

"Even once in the five years you thought me dead," she asked angrily, "did you ever wonder why 'twas that I ran from you?" She didn't wait for an answer. "I wanted a taste of freedom, aye, but I've come to realize o'er the passing of time that freedom wouldn't have been enough of a lure to make me flee."

His nostrils flared. "Oh aye, *nee'ka*, I know why 'twas you fled from me. Leastways, it's all I've been able to think upon every moon-rising for the last five *Yessat* years."

Kara squinted her eyes and cocked her head. She could tell he was serious in his thinking, yet something told her they were not thinking along the same lines. His voice was too bitter. "What mean you?" she whispered.

"Because I was not a warrior born," he ground out. Cam's eyes bore into hers. "I spent year upon year upon year proving myself to be a better hunter, a better fighter, than any highborn warrior in existence." His eyes flicked longingly over her form. "I did so that you might be proud to call me your own, that you would feel pride of the hearts instead of embarrassment for being Kara K'ala Ra." He looked away. "Yet all that I did 'twas never enough. You never felt pride. And you never came to love me," he murmured.

A numbing chill worked its way down Kara's spine. She couldn't have been more shocked by his confession had he sprouted metallic skin and turned into a *gazi-kor* right there at the raised table. Her eyes haunted, she took a deep breath. "'Tis ironic for a certainty," she whispered as she stared at him.

"I don't follow." Cam shook his head, then looked up to meet her gaze once more. "Of what do you speak?"

"'Tis my sire that wanted you to be a great warlord, but 'twas never what I myself wanted."

His brow furrowed uncomprehendingly.

"I ran from you because I feared I was naught but a battle prize to you," she said sadly. "It had naught to do with your titles or lack thereof."

Cam's entire body stilled. Every muscle in his body corded and tensed. He wanted so much to believe her for he loved her as he could love no other, and yet so much hurt had passed between them that he was afraid to cling to the small hope she'd just thrown his way.

"Do you speak the truth to me?" he rasped out.

Her smile was poignant, sad. "Aye, 'tis true."

She took a deep breath, too overcome with emotion to remain in the chamber with him. She needed to go to her apartments aboard the ship and think for a spell.

She loved Cam K'al Ra. She had always loved him. She had tried to forget it for a time, yet she could suppress the truth of it no more. And now, ironic though it was when at last she had admitted her buried feelings to herself, it appeared as though all was lost. He didn't trust her. He didn't believe her. And mayhap he never would again.

Kara turned around to walk away. She could feel his eyes upon her. Swiveling her head, she took a calming breath and then looked at him from over her shoulder.

"You became a great warlord that I might love you," she said quietly. "Yet 'twas the son of a lowly *trelli* miner that I fell in love with."

Cam felt tears sting the backs of his eyes. He blinked them away as he watched her take a deep breath and walk away from him.

It hadn't escaped his notice that her eyes had been glowing a dimmed blue. She believed that all was lost between them.

Chapter 8
Meanwhile, back on Galis…

Zor's lips tightened into a grim line as he glanced around at the bevy of bound male servants attending to the evening repast. It was nigh unto disgusting, the sight of so many erect manparts standing about. He sighed, telling himself he had now lived to see it all. And to think that his wee Kara had lived amongst the Galians for five *Yessat* years…

As his beloved *nee'ka* would say, good grief.

Zor rubbed his temples as he listened to his brother Dak put questions to the High Mystik of the Gy'at Li sector. It was going to be a long moon-rising, he decided on a martyr's sigh. He was anxious to leave, anxious to take his *nee'ka* to Zideon that they might be reunited with their hatchling. Yet he was also of a mind to know that wee Jana and Dari were passing fair.

"I want," Dak ground out, "to have my hatchlings back anon." His nostrils flared. "I do not believe for even a *Nuba*-second that you've no idea where they've gone off to."

Klykka's eyebrows rose at his imperious tone, but she said nothing of it. "Mayhap if you warriors had shown a care for their feelings whilst growing up they never would have fled to begin with."

"I was given no choice," Dak gritted, pausing in his speech long enough to throw a sour look Zor's way. "I had to remove Dari to Arak. Leastways, this talk is all for naught. Your Emperor has issued you a direct order and 'tis for a certainty you *will* obey it."

"You are lucky, wench," Kil hissed, his eyes narrowing at the High Mystik from where he was seated next to Lord Death across the raised table, "that my brother did not sentence you to the gulch pits for your treason." He flung an arm wildly about. "You aided and abetted the escape of three royal hatchlings!" he shouted. "Our family has grieved Kara and Jana's 'passing' for o'er five years." He slashed his hand through the air. "For a certainty you would be gulch beast food if I were Emperor."

Klykka rolled her eyes, not at all intimated. "I shall praise the holy sands that you are not then," she said dryly.

Kil merely grunted.

Klykka schooled her features into a fashionably bored mask. In truth, she was more than a wee bit frightened. Not for her own fate, for she knew she had been within the rights of the Holy Law to aid wenches she believed to be political prisoners on their home planet, but more so she was worried for Dari, Jana, and Kari.

She hadn't been telling untruths when she'd declared to the warriors that she had no clue as to their whereabouts. A *gastrolight* storm the moon-rising prior had sizzled out the main holo-communicator within her stronghold and the last she'd heard from the women warriors of her command the wretched thing was still not functioning properly. And so, sad though it was, it was also the truth that she had no notion as to their position.

Leastways, the High Mystik told herself, she could do naught but try to distract the warlords, and hope against hope that her stalling would provide enough time for the lot of them to flee Galis. She prayed to the goddess that they had not yet been caught, sending up a quick plea to Aparna to humbly ask for her omnipotent intervention. These warriors, she thought acidly, considered naught but how the absence of the wenches affected *them*. If she was forced to endure one more diatribe on the rights of a Sacred Mate or the rights of a sire, she would like as naught gag.

Klykka sat up straighter on her *vesha* bench, her dark eyes narrowing seductively as she ran a tongue across her lips. When the nipples of her unbound breasts began to harden and elongate of seemingly their own volition, Zor narrowed his eyes.

"Stop it," he grunted.

She batted her eyelashes as if innocent. "Stop what, Excellent One? I am but your humble servant thinking to entertain you in the proper, traditional Galian manner."

He harrumphed at that. "You think to distract us more like."

Klykka pretended to be shocked. "Whatever do you mean?" she asked in a tone of voice sweeter than *migi-candy*.

Kil grunted, his eyes narrowing. "Thrice you have been issued a direct command to tell us where the Q'ana Tal hatchlings are hidden, and thrice now you have answered us by bringing us to peak." His jaw clenched hotly. "I do not wish to be brought to peak!" he bellowed.

When it occurred to him what he had just said, he felt his cheeks redden. As the warriors gathered about began to uncomfortably clear their throats, said cheeks flamed from red to scarlet. "Leastways," he sniffed, "my leathers are fair soaked from the last two times. 'Tis hard to find replacements for them so far removed from Morak," he finished dumbly.

Zor rolled his eyes.

Klykka paid neither warrior any heed whatsoever. She threw a long black tress over her shoulder, then stood up and removed the bottom to her *zoka*. The warriors moaned when they felt her telekinetically send out sexual pulses, then groaned when she began to massage her nipples as she slowly walked towards Jek Q'an Ri, Kil's commander.

"Oh nay," Dak said hoarsely as he closed his eyes tightly, "the wench thinks to impale herself upon our cousin's rod this time."

Zor whimpered. "'Twas a hard enough spurt the last time. And that with naught but a mental push."

Kil's head fell back on a groan. "'Tis for a certainty we shall sleep for hours rather than minutes this time." He clamped a hand to his forehead. "I pray to the goddess Mari packed me a fresh pair of leathers."

"Geris will know," Dak said grimly. "Leastways, she knows everything." He moaned as another wave of sexual titillation was sent his way. "'Twill be the war of wars when I remove myself to Ti Q'won."

Zor's eyes began to roll back in his head. "If the erotic arts performers who ventured into Sand City had been so talented, I would have expired before ever I'd set out to capture my *nee'ka*." He moaned grimly. "Where is Kyra when I need the wench? She and Rem have been removed to Valor City o'er long."

Their chatter turned into fierce groans as they watched the naked High Mystik run her fingers through Jek's mane of hair. Their cousin tried to remain strong, tried to fight off the desire to couple with Klykka, but being unmated…it was looking as though it was mission impossible.

Jek's gaze ran over the length of the High Mystik. "Stop it, wench," he hissed. "You will tell the Emperor anon where the hatchlings are."

Klykka ignored him, deciding instead to remove his cock from his leathers. "Oh," she breathed out. "'Tis exceedingly large." She licked her lips, meaning the compliment. No males within her harem were possessed of such huge manparts.

Jek gritted his teeth when she cupped his balls and began massaging them. His cousins had long teased him that he was the wiliest warrior amongst them for it was common to find his cock buried within a hot channel at any given time. Whenever none within the Palace of Mirrors could find him, they knew to check within the harem chamber. If he was not training or warring, it was where he could always be found. Yet now his strong need was working against him. He needed to resist her. If only he could distract—

Jek sucked in his breath when the wench wrapped her lips around the head of his cock. Her hands continued to massage his man sac whilst her tongue suctioned his shaft into the heat of her mouth, taking him all the way in until he could feel the back of her throat. His nostrils flared.

"Cease this," he hoarsely commanded her.

"Mmm nay."

Klykka closed her eyes and enjoyed the feel of him, speaking on the subject no more. She loved cocks. She loved sucking them and fucking them. It was why she was forever battling, finding more to add to her collection of bound servants. But warriors...

Galian wenches went out of their way to avoid them, so it was a rare treat indeed to suckle a cock so large and thick. She intended to savor the moment.

Jek groaned as he watched his shaft disappear into the High Mystik's mouth, over and over, again and again. Down on her knees before him, her head bobbing up and down upon his lap, he couldn't resist the urge to watch her work upon him. And so before he could think better on it, his hand moved to grasp her dark hair, and he brushed it out of her face that he might watch her suckle of him. "Good goddess," he ground out.

She was like an animal. Klykka sucked harder and harder, faster and faster, her eyes closed in bliss, her throat issuing primitive moans whilst she feverishly worked up and down the length of him. The sucking sounds her lips made coupled with her extreme talent at doing so, made his jaw clench. As if on instinct, his hands reached down for her breasts, and he cupped them whilst he massaged her nipples and watched her mouth devour him.

"Oh aye." Klykka's head bobbed up into his line of vision when the nipple massage became too arousing to continue suckling him. Naked, she climbed up onto his lap, gasping at the sensual jolts going through her. "Tug at them," she whispered, arching her back that her chest was thrust closer to him. "Please."

Beads of sweat broke out upon Jek's forehead. He wanted to stop, wanted to keep her from causing the room to pass out in a fit of peak, yet the arousal she was experiencing was being transferred to him, making him feel the same way, making him crave more and more, making him want—nay need—to bury his cock deep inside of her body. He could hear the moans of the warriors around him and knew that he had to remain strong.

The High Mystik smiled slowly, knowing as she did that his trying was all for naught. "'Tis no use, handsome one," she whispered as she cupped one of her breasts and ran her elongated nipple over his lips. "Open up for me. 'Tis impossible to resist and well you know it."

Jek's nostrils flared at the taunt. He removed his lips from her nipple. "Cease your witchery," he said thickly.

The nipple looked so ripe, so suckable, so hard and delicious. He gritted his teeth. "Cease this anon." Each word became quieter, less forceful.

She grinned. "I have studied the art of peaking for more *Yessat* years than you've been alive, feisty one." Her dark eyes narrowed, glazing over in passion as they found his glowing blue ones. "Suckle me," she murmured as she ran the tip of her nipple over his lips again. "You are not mated. I can give you pleasure as no other ever has," she breathed out.

Jek felt as though he was going mad. He was a warrior. Nature had declared that his sexual need would always be great. He was torn between instinct and duty. It was torture, this.

His breathing grew labored as he felt his large hands clutch her fleshy buttocks and dig into them. Before he could stop himself, his mouth opened and his tongue darted out to curl around the High Mystik's nipple.

"Mmm aye," she said on a breathy moan. She began to rock her hips atop his lap, the entrance of her wet pussy running over the head of his engorged manhood.

Jek's nostrils flared, his jaw clenched, and yet he could no sooner stop breathing than stop sucking on her nipple. He drew the piece of elongated flesh between his lips and firmly sucked it from root to tip, over and over again. Her moans made his stomach muscles clench. Her soaking wet cunt continued to tease the head of his manhood, until he felt as though he'd die on the spot if she didn't impale herself upon him.

The torture of fighting her combined with the torture of wanting her was making him delirious. Teasing him — she kept teasing him. The engorged flesh of her channel kept stroking over his cock, promising to envelop him within but never doing so. He had to fight her, he thought desperately. He had to—

"Just do it," he heard Kil groan from across the chamber. "Take her and get it o'er with."

It was all the justification he needed. Tearing his mouth away from her nipple, he growled low in his throat, surprising the High Mystik. She sucked in her breath as he clutched her hips, then groaned long and loud whilst he sheathed himself fully within her flesh.

"Aye," Klykka moaned, her eyes closing as he used his large hands to force her hips down upon him in deep, rapid strokes. Her breasts jiggled with each thrust, sensitizing them all the more. Against his large frame she knew she looked like naught but a doll, riding up and down the length of his huge shaft. The thought turned her on all the more, so she threw back her head and bounced away upon him, gluttonously loving every moment of the impaling. "Harder," she panted. "More."

Jek gave up the fight entirely, the nature of his species taking over to revel in the feel of her tight, milking flesh wrapped around him, preparing to contract about him. "Aye," he murmured, his teeth gritting. "Reach your pleasure upon me."

Klykka gasped as she rode him, her moans coming harder and louder as she bounced up and down. Her clit was stimulated with each down stroke, which in turn hardened her nipples further and induced need to knot in her belly. She could hear their flesh slapping together, could smell the heady scent of their combined arousal. When his tongue curled once more around her nipple and drew it back into his mouth for a suckling, she could take no more.

"*Aye*," she cried out, her hips rocking deliriously against him. Another fiercer contraction tore through her. She screamed as her entire body clenched and then convulsed atop him.

Jek gritted his teeth, the sexual flickers her peaking sent out catapulting him into a near maddened state. He groaned low in his throat as his fingers dug into the flesh of her hips, then spurted his warm liquid within her on a growl.

All throughout the chamber, warriors convulsed and moaned. On Klykka's third, final, and harshest peak, moans turned into tortured groans as the entire room orgasmed, then passed out.

Breathing roughly, Klykka smiled down at Jek. Unable to resist touching him before climbing off his big body, she bent her head and sipped softly at his lips. Telling herself there was no time to lose, she removed his cock from her pussy with a suctioning sound, and then scrambled to her feet.

Her eyes flicked toward the crystal staircase above. She glanced back at the chamber of passed out warriors once more to make certain all were in deep slumber before she darted toward the twisting stairs, taking them two at a time as she ran up.

She had to find her sisters via the holo-communicator. She could only pray the wenches of her command had fixed it whilst she'd been busily stalling.

* * * * *

Kyra's lips pinched together in a frown as she gazed down at her snoring husband. Her eyes narrowed in confusion when she took note of the large wet stain permeating the pair of leathers he wore. Crouching down to touch them, her nostrils flared when she realized it was semen.

"What the hell is going on?" she bit out to Rem without looking up at him. "Why are all of these warriors passed out?" She huffed as she glanced around. "And why are all of them wet from their own orgasms?"

Rem sighed. "It looks as though the High Mystik sought to stall their questions."

Kyra harrumphed, her arms crossing under her breasts. "It looks like she did better than stall them. It looks as though they've been knocked completely out of commission for a while now."

"Aye."

She harrumphed again, then began gently slapping at Zor's face in the hopes of rousing him. "Wake up," she chided him. "Please Zor—wake up!"

When five *Nuba*-minutes had passed by and her husband continued snoring as loudly as ever, she gave up with a groan. "Now what do we do?" She looked up at Rem. "Where is the High Mystik anyway?"

Rem's gaze was narrowed thoughtfully. "I know not for a certainty," he murmured. "But I think I've a lock on her. We had best go find her."

Kyra studied his face for a suspended moment. She knew he still hadn't totally recovered from his brush with devolution. Almost, but not quite. The result being, she reminded herself, that he sensed things a lot clearer than the average warrior did. Like an animal, his hearing was keener, his sense of smell more acute. If he thought he'd located her, then he probably had.

"Okay," she said as she made to stand up. "I'm right behind—oomph."

Kyra sighed as she lost her balance and landed flat on her rump. "These damn boobs," she muttered as she came up onto her knees and held a hand out to Rem for aid. "How many more years of not bearing children do I have left until they go away already?"

Rem chuckled. "Mayhap just a few more, sister." He took her hand and pulled her up to her feet. "Gis is the exact opposite of you. She nigh unto worships her *moosoos*."

Kyra shook her head and grinned. "How many children do the two of you have now? Twenty? Thirty?"

"Eight," Rem said proudly. He guided her toward the staircase. "All sons save Zari."

Kyra looked up the long, twisting flight of stairs and sighed.

Rem wiggled his eyebrows. "Too much effort with the *moosoos*?"   .

"Yes," she said forlornly.

He was preparing to sweep her up into his arms and carry her, when the sound of the warriors coming-to caught up with them. They both turned around and watched them.

Kyra's lips puckered into a tight-lipped frown as she studied Zor. His hair was a mess, his big body stretching and yawning, as he roused himself from what looked like a ten-year slumber. When at last their gazes clashed, she saw his cheeks go up in flames.

"'Tis about time you arrived, *nee'ka*," Zor said defensively as he took to his feet. "Leastways," he sniffed, "'twas wicked-bad torture that the High Mystik put us all through."

Kyra rolled her eyes. "Gimme a break."

Zor blushed profusely but said nothing. "Stay down below whilst we search for the nefarious Klykka," he mumbled. His gaze shot back to the raised table where the male servants were starting to regain consciousness. "And stay away from those bedamned males whilst I'm searching," he grumbled.

* * * * *

"Hurry!" Klykka ordered the woman warrior who was fiddling with the holo-communicator. "We've no time left. Those bedamned warlords will wake up the soonest and they will like as naught be feeling surly." Her nostrils flared as she paced back and forth within the war-planning chamber. "This is taking far too long!"

"'Tis sorry I am, Your Worthiness," the warrior woman demurred. "I am working as fast as I—ahh here we go."

Klykka took a deep breath and released it. "Send out a distress call to Kari's communicator anon."

The High Mystik resumed her pacing whilst she awaited a signal to come back from Kari. She realized it was a race to the finish line for if those warlords woke up before she spoke to her sister she would never get another chance to warn her. Finally, after a gut-wrenching two *Nuba*-minutes had slowly ticked by, the holo-screen on the far wall lit up and Kari and Dari's faces shown through.

"Thank the goddess," Klykka breathed out. "Are the deuce of you passing fair?"

Kari tucked a tress of fire-berry hair behind her ear. "Yes. I was worried when I couldn't get through. Is everything all right there? Was Jana found? Are you and Dorra—"

Klykka interrupted her questions with a wave of her hands. "We've no time for this. In a few words," she said hurriedly, "Dorra and I are passing fair, yet Jana has not yet been located. Kara was captured by her betrothed—"

She ignored their gasps and continued on, knowing time was of the essence. "And I've a great hall full of passed out warlords, all of whom want to find Jana and Dari." She tugged in a breath of air. "Are the deuce of you safely removed from Galis with the man-child?"

"Aye." Dari nodded, answering the question for Kari. "Bazi sleeps the sleep of the innocent whilst Kari steadily navigates us from Trek Mi Q'an."

"Where do you go?" she asked quickly. "Tell me that I might send aid."

Just then the doors to the warring chamber exploded open and angry warlords materialized seemingly out of nowhere. Klykka whirled around and gasped, startled. Thinking quickly, she closed her eyes, preparing to send out the strongest wave of sexual titillation in existence.

"Nay!" she bellowed when Jek's strong hands clasped her arms and forced her to cease her mental incantations. "Release me!"

"'Tis best if you remain silent, wench," Jek murmured into her ear. "You've already made me look the fool. I shan't hesitate to return the favor."

Klykka gulped a bit nervously, but said nothing.

Her body in fight-or-flight mode, Kari was preparing to end the holo-communication so their position couldn't be traced when a sight she had not at all been expecting to see appeared before her. Her eyes wide, her face draining of all color, she gasped as her silver-blue gaze raked over a very familiar and very imposing eight-foot tall frame.

"You," she breathed out as her eyes found his face.

Death's entire body stilled as his golden gaze drank in the sight of Kari Gy'at Li for the first time in nine agonizingly long *Yessat* years. He felt as though he'd been punched in the stomach so powerful was the effect on him. He had scoured Galis and searched the dimensions for her these past years, yet until this moment had never heard tell of her.

"You disobeyed me, wench," Death rumbled out, his nostrils flaring. He ignored the feelings she evoked in him and concentrated on the tangible. "Come back here anon and bring the princess with you."

Kari said nothing. She was so stunned that she could scarcely think let alone speak. Her eyes drank in the sight of him. He looked so powerful, so masculine and handsome. His huge, massively muscular body looked to be riddled with even more battle scars than he'd sported since the last time she'd seen him.

She sighed. She'd fantasized about him for nine *Yessat* years. And now here he was.

Taking another deep breath, Kari briefly closed her eyes and snapped herself back into the proper frame of mind. She wanted to see him, wanted to touch him so incredibly much, but...

"I can't," she whispered, looking away from him. "I can't come back."

Death's eyes narrowed at her words. "Do not flee from me again, little one, or when I catch you 'twill be hellfire to pay," he finished grimly.

Her eyes flew open. "Why?" she asked hoarsely. "Why do you want me? For a toy to add to your collection?"

Death's golden gaze never wavered from Kari's. "You are mine," he said firmly to Kari. "You are my mate."

Klykka gasped. Stunned, and uncertain what to say, she joined in the conversation for the first time. "This matters naught, Kari, and well you know it." Her nostrils flared. "Dari has a mission at hand and naught, not even emotions, can interfere with it," she reminded her.

Kari nodded, but didn't open her eyes.

Kil's gaze widened as it flew to Dari. "What does she mean, Dari? What has happened? Of what mission does she speak?"

Dari nibbled at her lower lip and looked away.

"You can tell me, Dari," Rem chimed in. "You and I were ever close whilst you were growing up. Come, *pani*, tell us—"

His words were interrupted by the crashing sound of Dak making his way into the Gy'at Li warring chamber. Dari cried out when she saw him, her usual formidable resolve cracking under the emotion of seeing her sire once again.

Dak came to a halt in front of his daughter's holo-image and took a deep breath. His eyes raked over her, ascertaining that she was passing fair. "*Mani* and I are worried," he rasped out. His eyes were troubled. "Please remove yourself to Arak, *ty'ka*."

"I can't," Dari said quietly, her glowing blue eyes in mourning. "I can't chance it until I have...more information." She swore under her breath, immediately chastising herself for giving away even that much of a hint as to her activities. She could take no chances.

Dak's brow furrowed in confusion. "Information?" he murmured. "What sort of information do you seek, *pani*?"

When she did naught but remain rigid in her silence, chills raced up and down Dak's spine. He knew—*knew*—something horrid had happened and mayhap was still happening. "Please, wee one," he said pleadingly, "I can't help you if you don't—"

Her sire's words were brought to a halt a moment later when Gio stormed into the warring chamber and made a direct path toward Dari's holo-image. To her credit she held his gaze, even though he looked as though he wanted to murder her. He was angry, she realized. Fiercely possessive and angry.

"Remove yourself back to Arak," Gio ground out. His eyes grazed over her, the longing he felt to simply touch her overwhelming to him. His nostrils flared. "Do not make me hunt you down, *ty'ka*."

Dari's nostrils did some flaring of their own. She ignored the sunken feeling she had inside, and her reaction to the way her hearts thumped in her chest when he called her *ty'ka*. She tried to ignore the chance she'd been given to gaze upon him once more, but the memories pounded through her mind, forcibly reminding her of the wondrous way he'd been intimately touching her hearts and body ever since her seventeenth *Yessat* year had passed.

She reminded herself of how she'd loathed him when first she'd been taken to Arak so many *Yessat* years ago. It was more than necessary to call upon those emotions now.

"You shan't find me until I am ready to be found, Gio Z'an Tar." Dari took a deep breath. "If ever I want found."

A tick began to work in his cheek. "You would cause this much grief to experience naught more than a time of freedom? Have you not learned by Kara's example?" he murmured.

Dari sat up regally straight, her chin going up a notch. He *would* attempt to remind her that even though Kara had fled, in the end she had been recaptured by Cam.

Well, it didn't matter, she firmly reminded herself. Her sire and uncles had nigh unto choked a confession out of her, but now that she'd regained her wits, it was necessary to remember she had to keep Gio in the dark. Let him think she desired naught but freedom. Let him think what he would if it kept him from the Rah.

Just then Bazi awoke and the masculine sound of his voice calling to Dari captured the attention of every warlord in the chamber. Dari gulped a bit roughly, uncertain what to do. She wanted no one, not even her sire, let alone an entire chamber of warriors, to know that Bazi was aboard ship.

Gio's entire body stilled, for he knew not whom the voice belonged to, only that it was male. His breathing stilled as he narrowed his gaze at his betrothed. "Who is that?" he rasped out. "And why does the male beckon to you?"

Dari took a deep breath, but remained silent.

"Answer me wench!" Gio bellowed, his arm flailing wildly about. A low growling sound erupted from his throat a split second before he hurled himself toward the holo-image as if trying to jump through it. "I'll kill him!" he shouted. "Do you hear me, Dari? You have issued your lover a death sentence!"

Dari's eyes widened and then closed. Good goddess, what should she do? What should she—

Dak and Kil surged toward Gio in an effort to restrain him. Dari's hand flew over to grasp Kari's wrist and her fingers dug into the flesh there whilst she watched the fight unfold. Gio had gone wild. Primal. She knew how strong her uncle and sire were, yet it was not until Lord Death and her Uncle Rem added their strength into the mayhem that Gio was successfully restrained.

Dari released a pent-up breath, then let go of Kari's wrist a moment later. She knew it was impossible for Gio to jump through a virtual image, yet she didn't want him to do himself a harm trying either.

"Cease this!" Dari said fervently. "Please, Gio, do not do this," she said in a tone of voice that coming from any other wench would have sounded a plea.

His breathing was heavy, his chest constricting up and down with the movement. Restrained by two warlords at either side, he could do naught but stare into her eyes.

"How could you hurt me this way?" he rasped out. His eyes were wild, panicked, as though he had to recapture her anon lest he go mad. "I thought you had come to...to love me." His voice was hurt. Choked and hurt.

Dari closed her eyes briefly and took a deep breath. She wanted to scream at the fates that had made it necessary to tear out his hearts this way. She yearned to shout out to him that it was not true, that she had coupled with no male, yet an inner voice kept telling her to remain silent until Bazi was safely removed from Trek Mi Q'an.

Gio's jaw clenched. "Have you naught to say?" he ground out.

Dari held his gaze for a suspended moment. Dead silence enveloped the warring chamber. But finally, realizing there was naught that could be said whilst she needed to protect Bazi, she gently shook her head and looked away.

"I see," he murmured.

For the first time in she didn't know how long, Dari felt her eyes filling up with tears and her bottom lip trembling. Before she could disgrace herself, before she began weeping right there in front of all and sundry, she stood up and left the chamber she had been seated within, leaving Kari to deal with the situation alone.

"Dari! Dari!"

Dari could hear Gio yelling for her as she walked away. She could feel his panic, wondering as he must where she was walking off to...or *whom* she was walking off to. She could feel his anger, his hurt, his possessiveness, his sense of betrayal. Weeping, she fled as fast as her feet would carry her.

Back at the holo-communicator, Kari sighed. This was the most confusing and gut-wrenching day she'd lived through since that day so many years ago when forces she still didn't comprehend had snatched her from earth and placed her on Galis. Her mind said that they were doing the right thing, yet her body and heart wanted to return to Galis...and to *him*. It was obvious that Dari was experiencing the same emotions. She took comfort in that, realizing she was not alone.

Kari gazed into Death's golden eyes once more. The intense way that he stared at her told her he would never let this decision go unchallenged. He would hunt her down, she realized. He would never stop, never relent, until he had her firmly under his power once more.

Heat rushed through her as the renewed memories of the week they had spent together in Crystal City took over. The way he had touched her, commanded her, and perhaps...loved her? She sighed, knowing that week could never again be relived.

Closing her eyes and taking a fortifying breath, she switched off the holo-communicator.

Chapter 9
Planet Zideon, Kopa'Ty Palace
A sennight later

Cam laid abed, moaning as he watched his cock disappear into the mouth of his ever-voracious *Kefa* Muta. He wanted Kara, would give anything to have her lips wrapped about his manhood thusly, yet knew also that he would have to content himself with his favored slave. Kara had made that plain when she'd sent Muta to his rooms to see to his comforts this eve. For a sennight now she had done the same every moon-rising, not deigning to see to his needs herself.

He gasped as he spurted, his eyes closing tightly as he pretended it was the mouth of his *nee'ka* he was spurting into. He needed to see her, needed to touch her, yet was afraid it was too soon to approach her. Already they had been removed to Zideon for over a sennight, yet not once in that time had they coupled or shared a bed. This was unnatural, he conceded on a mental sigh. And what's more, it was like as naught destined to drive him mad.

He wanted her powerfully, Cam admitted as he opened his eyes, watching as Muta's blue lips took to suckling his man sac. He needed to be inside of Kara's flesh like he needed to breathe. Yet he knew not what could be done to correct the bad feelings that lay between them, feelings that were keeping them divided better than any crystal walls could ever do.

Twice he had attempted to reassure her of his emotions, to gently let her know that she had never been a mere battle prize to him, yet he knew not if his words had been believed. She had quietly thanked him, smiled softly up to him even, but then she had removed herself from the chamber without another word, lost in her own thoughts.

Cam gritted his teeth. He would give anything — everything — to be able to read his *neek'a's* mind.

The only thing that had kept him going this past sennight was the certain knowledge that her emotions were in turmoil. She might avoid him, she might even go so far as to purposely hide from him, but he knew her emotions had rarely strayed from him.

He figured that was a promising sign for over the passage of time Kara K'ala Ra had learned well to school her emotions that they might not spill over to alert him of their existence whilst she'd been in hiding. The fact that they were now spilling over powerfully enough to make him aware not only of their existence but also of the fact that they were focused upon him and no other was telling unto itself.

Cam turned his head, latching his mouth around the plump nipple of a green slave who pillowed him. He sucked on the nipple, closing his eyes whilst his manhood hardened for the insatiable Muta, her lips working up and down the length of his rod once again.

He slowly fell asleep that way, much the same as he had in his youth, feeling empty inside yet knowing it was necessary to have his needs seen to.

His emotions were in turmoil. He could understand Kara's reasoning, goddess help him, and that meant he could understand both why she had fled in the first and why she kept herself hidden away from him even now. And yet he also knew for a certainty that he could not continue on like this.

Cam sighed. He needed his *nee'ka* in a way he'd never needed anyone or anything before.

* * * * *

Kara swam through the waters of Loch Lia-Rah with sunken hearts. Returning from the dead was overwhelming to her. Every day, every hour, every moment, she was learning of new things that only served to further remind her of all the pain she had caused to her Sacred Mate by fleeing from him.

Cam's haunted eyes bespoke of torment, of pain. Even the possessions of his dominion told the same story, reflecting the fact that he had lived out five *Yessat* years as a man tortured. Before she had "died", Cam had christened the stronghold of planet Zideon the Palace of Dreams. When she had passed on, he had renamed it Kopa'Ty.

A Warrior's Sorrow. Or, more simply, *My Sorrow.*

She wanted naught more than to make amends to him, to let bygones be bygones and carry on as they should have from the first. Yet she feared his rejection more powerfully than ever, feared too that it would take a miracle from the goddess before Cam forgave her of the transgressions she'd committed against so many.

Kara closed her eyes in grief, knowing as she did that her husband must think she hated him. She could see in his eyes how much he longed for her despite everything, yet she had sent *Kefas* to his bedchamber each moon-rising rather than joining him there as she wanted to, as she should have.

She knew not why she continued to do so, except for the fact that she was afraid that after their passion had been spent together she would see naught but revulsion for her in his beautiful, haunting eyes. But she was stronger than this, she reminded herself staunchly. Leastways, if she wanted a happy life with Cam she had to at least let him know she was desirous of one.

No more bedamned pride, she vowed, as she emerged naked from the waters. She would go to him this very eve and make her charms available to him. But from there, she told herself resolutely, whatever happened betwixt them was in Cam's hands.

* * * * *

Cam slowly awoke in the thick of the night, his mind groggy yet nevertheless registering the fact that he was being suckled off. He sighed, not at all in the mood to spurt for the *Kefas* yet again.

"No more," he said gruffly, his hand reaching down to thread through Muta's hair. "'Tis time for me to sleep..." His voice trailed off disbelievingly.

Cam's eyes widened. His breathing stilled when it dawned on him that the hair in his hand was not the blue hue he'd been expecting, but the black hair he'd forever dreamed of. "Kara," he rasped out, "what do you here?"

She met his eyes whilst she sucked up and down the length of him, but never stopped in her ministrations long enough to answer his question. His large palm settled at the back of her head, cradling her there.

"Aye," he said thickly, his breathing growing labored, "do not stop, wee one."

She didn't. Kara closed her eyes and took him in clear to the back of her throat, working up and down the length of his cock just as her mating Mistress had instructed her to do in her youth whilst she'd been made to practice on lesser males the way of pleasing her future mate. Apparently, she thought with a secret smile, the instructions had at last paid off, for Cam was moaning and groaning, his chest heaving up and down with the effort to stop himself from spurting.

"*Nee'ka*," he rasped. "*Aye*."

When he could endure no more torture, he gently prodded her face up from his lap. She removed her lips from his cock, a suctioning sound as it popped out echoing through the bedchamber.

"Ride me," he murmured, his gaze clashing with hers. "I've long dreamed of it," he thickly admitted.

Kara crawled up the long length of him, naked and as aroused as was he. She didn't make him wait, neglected even to tease him in the ways the mating Mistress had suggested, for her need was as fierce as his own.

"Aye," she whispered as she guided the thick head of his erection to her channel. "As have I."

On a groan, Kara sheathed his manhood within her flesh, her nipples hardening when she heard him suck in his breath. The two *Kefas* that lie abed with Cam made mewling sounds, their enchanted senses attuned to any flesh that hardened before them. Kara was more than happy to provide each one with a plump nipple to suckle, her eyes closing in bliss as the slaves further aroused her whilst she slammed her hips down upon a hungry Cam.

"I love watching slaves suckle you," he said hoarsely. "Before you fled, I looked forward to visiting with you just to see the look upon your face whilst the slaves brought you to peak after peak."

Kara's eyes narrowed in desire as she rode him harder. "I enjoyed the peaks you gave me even more," she said breathlessly.

His fingers dug into the flesh of her hips. His jaw clenched in pleasure. "As did I, *pani*."

And then they spoke no more, for they were busy with the pleasure of mating each other hard. Kara moaned and groaned as her hips slammed down upon him, the feel of his stiff cock buried within her causing her to peak. The *Kefas* continued to suck on her nipples, their throats emitting mewling sounds each time her nipples grew harder and more elongated within their mouths.

"Come for me again," Cam ground out, his thumb massaging her clit whilst she rode him. "Let me feel that sweet pussy—oh aye," he praised her thickly, "just like that, wee one."

"*Cam.*"

Kara moaned long and loud as she bounced atop him, her flesh contracting around his whilst she burst. "*Aye,*" she groaned, her hips slamming down to impale him within her channel again and again. "*Cam.*"

Cam's teeth gritted whilst she burst, his hands digging into the flesh of her hips to hold her steady that he might spurt his hot liquid deep within her. He groaned whilst he spewed, his muscles clenching hotly, the veins in his arms cording as he came. "Kara," he groaned. "I love you."

Kara's body stilled atop his, her eyes wide as she panted for air. "Do you say this in passion?" she asked, her voice a rasp. "Or do you say this in truth?"

He was given no time to answer, for her bridal necklace began to pulse and in the blink of an eye both were moaning and groaning as they rode out endless waves of sexual euphoria. Kara gasped at the sensation, knowing why it was that Sacred Mates would never even consider separating once they'd been joined.

It was more than the peak, she knew. It was also the emotions that assaulted them whilst they rode out the waves together.

After long minutes had passed and she was lying securely stretched out atop Cam's chest, Kara heard his voice whisper down to her. "In truth do I love you. In truth, I have always loved you."

She closed her eyes whilst she steadied herself, having been raised to believe as all Trystonni were that tears were inferior to stoicism. "Can you forgive me?" she asked quietly, hopefully.

Cam stroked her hair behind her ear. "Of course, *nee'ka*."

Kara raised her head, unable to suppress the single tear that misted in her eye. "I love you too, Cam. I've always loved you. The reasons I gave you for running were true. Misguided I see now, yet still true."

"I know—I believe you." He took a deep breath. "We've lost a lot of time due to misconceptions on both our parts. I don't wish to lose even another moment."

"Nor do I."

He smiled, his eyes finding hers. "I think," he said softly, "'tis time to change the name of this palace once more."

Kara smiled back. "Aye," she agreed, her head coming down to rest over his hearts. She hugged him tightly. "Naught shall come between us again."

Five years had been stolen. Five years where they could have been loving and caring for the other. It was mayhap wrong to call the years wasted for she'd learned much about herself during her time on Galis, learned too how much she longed for Cam's embrace. Nay, she could not call those years wasted. Nevertheless, she never wished to stray from his side again.

Kara smiled into the night, a blue moonbeam shining through the bedchamber window. She held onto her husband tightly as they both fell into a happy, contented slumber.

Chapter 10
Planet Khan-Gor, "Planet of the Predators"
Zyrus Galaxy, Seventh Dimension

Jana gritted her teeth as the last of her *zoka* was ripped from her body and thrown to the ground. "What are you doing?" she sputtered, whirling around to face Yorin. Her nostrils flared. "Why did—oh goddess."

Jana gasped as she watched the pupils of Yorin's eyes light up a frightening red. She took two steps away from him, instinctively backing up as she watched lasers of sorts shoot out from his eyes and singe the material of the flimsy *zoka* until naught remained of it. Her eyes wide with terror, she continued backing up, her mind desperately racing through different scenarios of escape.

Yorin's nostrils flared. "Do not back away from me, *zya*, or 'twill be another spanking for you."

Her lips curled into a snarl at the reminder of the child's punishment she'd received two moon-risings ago, the very punishment that had been doled out to her a mere *Nuba*-hour after she had awoken from her sennight long state of unconsciousness. Back on Galis he had vowed to punish her if she ordered him bound and tied down. He had stayed true to his word, turning her over his knee and spanking her bared bottom at first opportunity.

Afterwards, he had carried her to the bed of furs aboard his ship and had taken his pleasure within her flesh more times than she could count. For a certainty she was with child. Leastways, no wench of his species could be mounted so many times without conceiving, she knew. And she indeed *was* of his species...now.

She knew not what had happened to her during the sennight she had been in a coma-like state, yet for a certainty a metamorphosis of sorts had occurred within her body. Her senses were keener than once they had been, her reflexes faster, her movements more agile, and her passions more pronounced. The need to couple overcame her every other hour, and the automatic compulsion to obey him in all things forever drove her to do his bidding. It was driving her mad—all of it.

Jana ignored his not so subtle threat and concentrated instead on the injustice that had been done to her. "I want to return to Galis anon," she hissed. Her eyes narrowed. "And I want the *zoka* you ruined replaced with your own credits. 'Twas an expensive material possession you just charred as naught but waste."

Yorin raised a dark brow. "You will not speak to me in such a tone, *vorah*." He gentled his voice a tad so as not to frighten her further. "And what's more, there is no such thing as credits on Khan-Gor."

She harrumphed. "Why does this knowledge not surprise me?" she asked bitterly. "You are naught but Barbarians, the lot of you." She crossed her arms under her breasts and rubbed briskly at her lower arms. This primitive planet of silver ice was cold indeed.

"What know you of my species to make such a judgment?" he murmured.

Her nostrils flared. "I know that you have kidnapped me against my will. I know that you have denied me the use of clothing though 'tis cold enough out here to kill me. And you just admitted you've no bartering system here which can only mean you have naught worthy of bartering for!"

His sharp silver eyes raked over her naked body. "I never said we've no bartering system," he replied absently, his mind focused on his arousal. "I only said that we do not barter with credits."

She was intrigued despite herself. She didn't want to express any interest over his planet in the slightest, yet her curious nature won out. "What do you barter with then?" she mumbled.

Yorin walked a step closer to her, separating the distance between them that quickly. "We barter with *yenni*."

Her eyes narrowed uncomprehendingly. "*Yenni*?" she asked incredulously. "What in the sands are those?"

His eyes flicked toward the entrance of the silver, ice-coated cave that was his lair. "Let us go inside and I will show you. 'Tis past time to feed them anyway."

Jana's eyes darted from the cave back to Yorin. "Your species barter with living creatures?"

"Aye."

She sighed, thinking that was the strangest custom she'd ever heard tell of. Waving away the enigma of *yenni* for the moment, she returned to her earlier demand. She had no desire to enter that cave with him, but she also realized that she had no choice—for now. Eventually she would escape him and all this nonsense would be naught but a dream, but for the interim she could only bide her time.

"If you want me to accompany you of my own free will, then 'tis for a certainty," she said staunchly, "that you will clothe me." Her hand swept about in a manner meant to broach no argument. "'Tis nigh unto chilling out here. 'Twill be a thousand times colder within a dark cave."

Yorin's lips curled into a half-smile. "'Tis not exceedingly cold within our lair, *vorah*. Nor is it dark. 'Tis lit of gel-fire."

By this point in the conversation, Jana's teeth were chattering from the frigid temperature of Khan-Gor. Her bared feet were freezing, standing upon the silver icy ground as she was. Every second they remained without grew worse. "Why d-do you not c-clothe me?" she asked again, for some perverse reason wanting to hear the real answer.

His gaze devoured her naked body as the thumb and index finger of one of his hands reached toward a nipple and rolled it around between them. She sucked in her breath, immediately aroused.

"Because," he murmured, his predator eyes narrowing in possessiveness, "males of my species do not take chances with their mates."

Jana's breathing stilled as she considered the significance of his words. She feared she already understood his meaning, but asked the question anyway. "What d-do y-you mean?" she chattered out.

Yorin plucked her up off of the icy ground, no longer willing to abide her foolishness. She would catch her death if she continued to stand out here in the cold. Cradling her close to his body, he swaddled her within the warmth of the animal pelt he was wearing, then made for his lair.

"I mean," he explained in an implacable tone of voice as he strode toward the entrance to the cave, "that males of my species allow their mates no clothing because 'tis impossible to flee from us whilst naked."

Jana bit down on her lip to keep from whimpering aloud. He was telling the truth and she knew it. In an icy climate such as this one, a wench on the run from the male who'd claimed her would last mayhap a *Nuba*-hour before expiring without clothing to warm her.

If she was considering ways she might thieve animal pelts from Yorin, she kept her thoughts to herself.

* * * * *

Piloting through the black depths of deep space, Kari Gy'at Li glanced over to where Dari sat beside her. The princess was silent, her eyes narrowed in thought as she stared out of the *gastrolight* cruiser's wide porthole.

It had been a long day, an even longer week, Kari thought wearily. They had followed the trail dictated to them by Talia, the Chief High Mystik of Galis, yet so far they had learned very little in the way of useful information.

They still didn't know where the Evil One had originated from, nor did they even know who or what it really was. All that they knew was that the information was out there — somewhere — and that they needed to find it before the Evil One found them.

"Where should we go now?" Kari asked softly, turning back to face the vastness of space.

Dari sighed as she tiredly smoothed back a few strands of micro-braids. "I think you should pilot us to the far reaches of this galaxy, just to see if what we learned on the last planet has any truth to it at all."

Kari snorted at that. "I doubt it. As exploratory a people as the citizens of Trek Mi Q'an are, surely somebody would have discovered this ice planet if indeed it truly exists." She shook her head. "Those males on planet Brekkon didn't look to be the most reputable or reliable of sources."

Dari tried to smile at her words, but found the movement too taxing. "Have you a better idea then?" she challenged.

"No." Kari sighed. "Unfortunately I don't."

"Then what harm will it do us to at least go see for ourselves?"

"Point taken."

Neither woman said anything more on the subject as Kari Gy'at Li steered the *gastrolight* cruiser toward an encroaching wormhole. But then there wasn't much that could be said. They could either check out every possibility no matter how small, or they could surrender themselves in defeat and be killed off in the process.

By now the Evil One surely knew that Dari and Bazi had escaped. It was only a matter of time until it came looking for them…and possibly found them.

* * * * *

"This," Jana squeaked, "are *yenni*?"

She stared unblinking down at the creatures, unable to believe what it was she was seeing. They hadn't even reached the lair proper yet, she thought apprehensively, and already, only three feet inside the cave's entrance, they'd come upon these…pets. What in the sands else would she find here?

"Aye," Yorin absently answered her as he removed the animal pelt that had covered his upper body, exposing his massively muscled arms and chest. His lips curved into a frown. "It looks as though they haven't been fed in days," he said angrily. "My brothers know better than to go off without one of them remaining behind to feed them."

When Yorin began removing the animal skin kilt-like covering that he wore, Jana's jaw dropped open. "How do you plan to feed them?" she sputtered.

His eyebrows rose fractionally at her reaction, but he said naught to chastise her. This was all new to her, he realized. Given time she would accept the ways of Khan-Gor as her own. "With seed, of course."

Jana thought it was possible her jaw was hanging open wide enough for it to touch the ground. "Life-force?" she squeaked. "The staple of their diet is life-force?"

"Aye." Naked, he strode toward the pen, stopping only briefly to apologize. He combed his fingers gently through her hair. "'Twas not my intention to take the time to feed them on the very moon-rising I brought you home, yet 'tis apparent from the fact that these creatures of the night are sleeping whilst 'tis dark that they are lethargic from lack of food."

Jana's teeth clicked shut. She could only stare at him dumbly.

"Go on and explore your new home, *vorah*," he said on a nod. "'Twill like as naught take me a couple of hours before they've had their fill."

She returned his nod, yet never moved from her position. Too curious to leave just yet if at all, she watched in fascination as Yorin entered the pen and walked towards a bed of soft animal pelts.

Tethered by golden choke collars that were secured to the wall of the cave by long leashes, were a pack of creatures that looked much like humanoid wenches save for their luminescent white skins and sharp, icy looking tails. And, of course, the fact that they preferred moving about on all fours to standing upright.

Otherwise, however, the *yenni* looked remarkably like humanoid wenches. They sported large, full breasts, puffy labias that looked ripe and ready for a male's thrusting, as well as beautiful faces. If the staple of their diet was Khan-Gor male life-force, it was obvious now to Jana why these creatures were used for bartering. Much like *Kefas*, they were insatiable pleasure-givers. And just as the *Kefas* had no thought processes, the *yenni* too looked to harbor none either. Leastways, if they were possessed of thought processes, it was the simplistic reasoning of lower animals, their main goal in life to stay well fed.

If Jana had thought the creatures were too similar to humanoid wenches for her to have a care for, such doubt was laid to rest when she saw the first *yenni* take notice of Yorin's presence and bound over to him. She leapt on all fours in a lightning-fast movement, her tail whipping about excitedly at the realization that she was nigh close to being fed. A scarce second later the rest of the pack took notice of the Master and in the blink of an eye, they had tackled him in their excitement, causing him to land upon the bedding with a thump.

Yorin laughed as he landed on his backside. He groaned when the dominant female of the group popped her suctioning lips around his cock.

Yet another difference from humanoid wenches, Jana noted with interest. The lips of the *yenni* were exceedingly puffy when wrapped around a cock, as if they had been made to suckle males dry.

She sighed. By the holy sands of Tryston, why had she ever left Ti Q'won? Had she not fled, she tiredly conceded, then she never would have went to Galis. And had she never ventured into Galis, then she never would have been kidnapped by Yorin only to end up here watching this bizarre event unfold.

Jana took a deep breath as she absently smoothed a tendril of golden hair back from her brow line. She was tired. Cold and tired. The temperature was not so cold as it had been outside of the cave, but it was still chilly enough to keep her nipples hard and goosebumps dotting her skin.

She was confused. For two moon-risings now she had been awake and at Yorin's side, yet she still didn't understand why she had been stolen by him in the first. Nor did she understand what he had been doing on Galis, or how he had ended up within Klykka's harem. When she had put her bevy of questions to the giant predator, he had but smiled in that aggravating way of his, then murmured that all would be revealed to her when at last they'd reached his lair on Khan-Gor.

Well, she thought tiredly, they were on Khan-Gor and strictly speaking within his lair, yet still she had no answers. And, she thought on a sigh, judging by the ferocious cock-suckling Yorin was receiving just now, she doubted anything in the way of enlightenment would be hers anytime soon.

Jana's eyes flicked down the rocky path that led to the lair proper. She bit her lip, wondering if she should go inside without Yorin that she might rest for a spell. She was exhausted. So bedamned bone-weary and—

"Mmm, aye."

Yorin's dreamily uttered words induced her head to pivot back around to watch him as he fed the *yenni*. His eyes were closed in bliss, his cock poking straight upwards as it disappeared within the dominant female's mouth. Since Jana had already heard him spurt twice, she knew this was a third feeding for the dominant female. She could only speculate how many spurts it would take before she was filled.

Having been raised on a planet where males kept harems until they were mated, and indeed kept *Kefas* even after they'd been mated, Jana felt no pangs of jealousy whilst watching the feeding take place. Instead she felt mere curiosity, for she'd never heard tell of natural creatures that needed seed to exist. And, if she were honest with herself, she also felt arousal coalescing and cording within her, for the sound of so much purring whilst the females of the pack licked all over Yorin's body was unexpectedly provocative.

The *yenni* licked him everywhere, the saltiness of his skin apparently a treat of sorts to them as well. Whilst the dominant female continued to feed, her suctioning lips working up and down his thick cock in a frenzied manner that induced Yorin to moan and groan, the beta females lapped at every other part of his body, their tongues sucking salt from his neck, his nipples, his man sac, even his knees and toes.

The look on Yorin's face was one of carnal bliss mixed with pain. He kept moaning and groaning, then, his eyes shut tightly, eventually began crying out in sounds that were nigh unto tortured.

Jana winced, wondering to herself if the females were harming him, then walked closer to the pen to see what they were about. Her eyes widened.

Yorin was definitely not being tortured. In fact, just the opposite. The reason the giant Barbarian was crying out so loudly was because the dominant female was allowing him no surcease. She suckled upon his cock frenziedly, wildly, in a manner that would cause any male to spurt hard and long, yet she kept him from bursting by gripping his man sac in her hands and gently tugging it away from his body.

The dominant female knew how to feed, Jana thought as her arousal grew more pronounced. The lead *yenni* was forcing Yorin's man sac to jam up with seed that when she released it and allowed the tight sac to hit his body, his spurt would be violently hard.

Jana watched in fascination as the *yenni* continued to suckle him, one of her hands still firmly latched around his man sac, her suctioning lips working up and down his shaft with incredible speed. Yorin moaned and groaned, his head flailing about wildly, his man sac turning from a bronzed color to a bluish one.

"Feed from me," Yorin commanded the female in the Khan-Gori tongue. His nostrils flared as his chest heaved up and down. "Drink of me anon!" he bellowed.

On a mewling sound that further reminded Jana of *Kefa* slaves, the dominant female obeyed, releasing his man sac and allowing it to flick back at his body. Yorin growled as he burst, fangs exploding into his mouth, his eyes lighting a primitive red, as he spurted a ferociously hard load of seed into the female's awaiting mouth.

His chest continued to heave up and down as he patted the *yenni* atop the head. "Good girl," he murmured as she lapped up all the seed there was to be had from his spurt. "Now go lie down and let the others feed." When a mew of protest issued from her throat, Yorin gave up on a sigh. "You must be nigh unto starving." He laid back and allowed her to continue, his eyes closing once more as the process began anew, repeating itself for the fourth time.

Minutes later, after four wicked helpings, the dominant female moved away from Yorin and strolled lazily on all fours to the other side of the pen that she might sleep. Jana could tell she was well sated, for a contented purring sound rumbled low in her chest as she licked at herself before falling into a deep sleep.

Now it was the turn of the others and each of the *yenni* saw to it that they got their fill of Khan-Gori seed. Jana knew not how much time had gone by when at last the final female moved away from him, contentedly purring as she crept to where she would sleep, but she knew it had been hours. By the time the feeding was done, Jana had been worked up into a state of need that could rival any *yenni's* hunger.

Yorin's eyes raked over her, the need within them apparent. "Come here, *zya*," he said thickly. "I've the need of your flesh...and blood."

Jana's breathing grew labored, sporadic. Ever since she had awoken from her metamorphosis, the need to couple came upon her urgently and regularly. She had been denied the impaling she needed whilst Yorin had fed the *yenni*, and now her body wanted that fact remedied. She closed her eyes, wondering for the hundredth time what had become of her.

"Come," he murmured. "I'm stiff for need of you."

"How can you be stiff," she gasped, arousal hitting her hard, "when you have spurted no fewer than twenty times to feed your pets?" Her eyes opened slowly, and she saw the proof of his words for herself. He looked so wicked, she thought, so powerful and masculine as he laid there amongst the animal pelts, his cock poking upward, drunk on his own arousal. "'Tis unfathomable," she muttered.

One black eyebrow rose. "Is it?" he asked softly. His silver eyes narrowed in lust as they ran over her. "Do you not remember," he said thickly, "what it feels like when we mate...what it feels like when we drink of each other whilst we are both spurting?"

Jana's breasts heaved up and down as she tried in vain to stifle her body's reaction to him and his words. Oh aye, she remembered. She remembered too well.

"Twenty spurts into the mouths of starving *yenni*," he rasped out, "cannot hope to compare to even a single spurt within your milking cunt, *zya*."

Sweat broke out onto her brow. Her breasts heaved violently. Her clit swelled and pulsed with the need to couple.

"Come to me, *vorah*." *Come to me, wife.*

Fangs exploded into her mouth. A growl erupted from her throat. In an animalistic instinct that seemed almost second nature, Jana flung herself over the wall of the pen in one far-reaching leap. She came down upon him and impaled her flesh with his cock in one fluid motion.

She fucked him hard and primally, inducing him to bellow and growl. Her breasts jiggled up and down as she milked moan after moan out of him. His hands reached out to cup them that he might massage her nipples in the way she liked.

Jana's hips slammed down upon him as she frenziedly fucked him, her flesh wanting his seed. The sound of blood pulsing through his jugular vein unleashed a knot of arousal in her belly, and on a growl, she burst and exploded around him.

Yorin groaned as her fangs tore through his neck and suckled of his warm, fresh essence. He was so delirious with pleasure that his eyes rolled back into his head. As she fed of him, as she continued suckling at his ripest vein, his fingers dug into the flesh of her hips and aided her body in slamming down upon his, his cock ramming and cramming further and further into her suctioning pussy with each thrust.

She never once released his jugular whilst she rode him, and Yorin thought it would drive him mad with arousal. Her wee six-foot frame stretched out upon his like a doll's, her face buried against his neck, her hips frantically slamming downwards, all of it instinctually done in the need of finding surcease.

"Aye," he gritted out, his orgasm fast approaching, "you've the juiciest cunt in all the galaxies, wee *vorah.*"

And then he was spurting within her, a growl of completion torn from his throat as his man sac burst of seed. In a matter of seconds, his fangs were tearing into the flesh of her neck and he frenziedly sipped of her whilst she screamed in maddening pleasure atop him.

Yorin rolled her to her back and fucked her flesh long and primitively. He mated her hard, rode her body to peak countless times, pounded in and out of her until she'd milked his cock twice more.

When it was done, when he'd mated her to satiation, he rolled over once more and bade her to sleep upon his belly. She purred contentedly atop him, her much smaller stature intimately snuggled against him.

From where she lay atop him, her fangs at last retreating into her gums, Jana fell asleep feeling loved and secure in a way so powerful it was for a certainty she had never before experienced it. And yet as she stretched and yawned, she couldn't help but to wonder what other Khan-Gori surprises lay in wait for her, what other astonishing things would be thrust upon her.

Instinctually, and unable to resist, Jana's tongue darted out and curled around Yorin's flat male nipple, suckling the salt from his skin. She was no better than a *yenni*, she thought with a pang of fright, for there was naught in this world or any other that could keep her from milking him of seed, or from lapping away the salt upon his sweat-soaked skin.

She fell asleep thinking about Yorin's lair, apprehensively wondering what she would find within it.

Chapter 11

Meanwhile, back on Zideon…

Kara's eyes filled with tears as her sire swung her up into his arms and hugged her as though he never wanted to let go. She wept openly, allowing her hot tears to track down her cheeks unchecked, wetting them both.

She had expected to feel overwhelmed with joy upon seeing her *mani* and sire again, yet nothing could have prepared her for the surge of emotion she had felt when first she had embraced her *mani*, and now as she was held by her papa. After all that she had done to hurt them, after allowing them to believe her dead for five *Yessat* years, they were both accepting her back into their lives with open arms — and without recrimination.

In truth, Kara wished that they would yell at her, that they would accuse her of all that she was guilty of, for it would do much to ease her plaguing guilt. Instead, she was being showered with naught but love of the hearts and genuine gratitude of the fact that their beloved daughter had at last returned home. Their unconditional love was wondrous indeed, yet it was for a certainty that she felt she didn't deserve it.

"Ah goddess, my hearts," Zor whispered into her hair. "You have been sorely missed, wee one."

Kara smiled through her tears, hugging her sire tightly. "As have you," she choked out. "There were many moon-risings throughout the years that I longed to come home, yet I feared 'twould be no welcome for me there."

"How could you think that?" he rasped out. "'Tis naught I wouldn't have given to have you safely back."

Kara held onto his neck tightly, having missed him so much. She could feel Cam's eyes upon her, so she raised her face from her sire's shoulder and gazed at him through teary lashes. He winked, a silent communication reminding her that he had been right and that her parents had wanted her back regardless to everything. She smiled at him softly, telling him without words how much she loved him, how much she would always love him.

"I'm telling you sweetheart," Kyra said shakily as Zor set their daughter back down on her feet that his *nee'ka* might embrace their hatchling again, "if you ever pull any dumb stunts like that again I'll…"

"Oh goddess, *mani*," Kara said on a groan. "Think you I could ever bear to be separated from Cam, papa, and you again?"

"The answer had better be no," she sniffed, reaching out to run her fingers through her daughter's hair. "My heart couldn't handle it."

"Nor could mine," Cam murmured as he walked up to join the hugging, teary-eyed trio. He put his arm around his *nee'ka* and squeezed her gently. "Mayhap now you understand why 'tis important you tell us all that you know in regards to Dari and Jana's whereabouts." He bent down and kissed her atop the head. "Just as your parents grieved o'er you, so too do Queen Geris and King Dak grieve the loss of their hatchlings."

Kara shook her head. "'Twas truth I told you, husband. Verily, I know not where they have gone." She sighed, her expression growing troubled. "Though in truth I fear the worst. Jana and I have always been best friends. If 'twas possible for her to contact me…"

"Then she would have done so," Kyra murmured. She took a deep breath and gazed up at her husband. "I hope Dak finds them—both of them. I have a bad feeling about...something I can't quite put my finger on," she muttered.

"As do I." Zor's look was thoughtful as he gazed down at his daughter. "In truth, my hearts, I am fair bursting with questions to put to you about the years you spent removed from us. And yet—" He waved toward the raised table within the palace's great hall. "—'tis mayhap best if I save those questions for later that we might discuss Jana and Dari anon."

Cam nodded. "Gio and Death have sent word of their imminent arrival. They wish to put questions to my *nee'ka* as well."

Kara sighed, but nodded. "I will be what help I can be, Cam, yet I truly do not—"

"I know," he said softly, his turquoise eyes glowing lovingly. "I believe you when you say you've no notion where they've gone."

Kara smiled, secure in the knowledge that the deuce of them would never again lack for faith and trust in the other. "I'll see what I can do," she murmured.

* * * * *

The desperateness Gio felt to reach Dari was so tangible as to make Kara feel a pity for him. She briefly closed her eyes, reminded anew of the grief Cam must have felt whilst she'd been removed to Galis.

"I must," Gio rasped out from his bench at the raised table, "have Dari back anon." His mind raced with memories of the male that had called to her aboard the *gastrolight* cruiser. It was enough to make his stomach knot up and feel sickened. "For a certainty," he continued on, "you must know something—anything—I could find useful."

"And I must find the fiery-headed wench who accompanies her," Death rumbled out. He ran a strong hand over his jaw. "'Tis of dire consequence that I find her."

The Empress's forehead wrinkled. "Fiery-headed?" she asked. Her eyes narrowed thoughtfully. On earth, the color of her hair had been considered rare. In Trek Mi Q'an, it was a downright anomaly.

Kara nodded. "'Twas much the same as yours, *mani*," she confirmed. "In fact, she looked so much like you I found it eerie at times." She smiled, remembering the woman who had cared for her, who had helped her grow into a strong wench. "Leastways, Kari Gy'at Li never spoke much of her past, though I know she heralded from a place outside the seventh dimension."

Kyra's heart began to race. She felt chills racing up and down her spine. It couldn't be...could it? "How strongly did she resemble me? Was her accent similar to mine?"

"Aye." Kara frowned. "'Twas one in the same now that I think on it." Her eyes narrowed thoughtfully. "I wish I could tell you more, truly I do, but Kari Gy'at Li never spoke of her former life. 'Twas as if..."

"What?" Kyra asked quietly. She leaned in closer to her daughter. "It was as if what?"

Kara sighed, not quite able to eloquently express the gut feeling she'd long harbored in respect to Kari. "'Twas as if she felt too haunted by memories to think back on her past," she murmured. "I think she mayhap lost someone who was quite special to her before she made her home on Galis."

Kyra bit her lip, her gaze falling to the crystal tabletop. "I see." Silence permeated the chamber for a lingering moment, until the Empress' head shot up and her gaze clashed with her daughter's. "Do you have any holo-images of her, sweetheart?"

Kara's brow furrowed. "Why is this so important to you, *mani*?"

"Please," Kyra said shakily. "Go fetch the holo-image, honey."

Cam waved his hand at a bound servant, instructing her when she approached him that she should go upstairs and fetch a particular piece of his *nee'ka's* jewelry. When he had snatched her away from Galis, it was one of the few possessions she'd been wearing at the time.

When the servant had gone, Gio turned to Kara once more. His jaw was clenched, his expression tight. "Mayhap Dari mentioned to you where 'twas she wished to experience a time of freedom." He spread his hands. "Any information, no matter how trivial you think it, would be of use to me."

Kara blinked, having forgotten that train of thought for a spell. "A time of freedom?" she asked, not following.

"Aye. 'Tis the reason she left me, just as you left Cam."

Kara blushed at the reminder. There had been more to it than freedom on her part, but the reasons were complex and private. But then, so too were Dari's. She decided then and there that she would tell him what little she knew about Dari's troubles without making references to Bazi. Dari had convinced her it was important none knew he accompanied her. "I do not think she fled Arak for freedom, Gio, but because she feared for her safety there."

Gio's gaze narrowed. "She told you I did not care for her well?" he asked icily.

"Nay. Nay! 'Twas not you..."

He frowned uncomprehendingly.

"In truth," Kara whispered, "she did fear for *your* safety more than her own." She knew it was mayhap more than she should have said, but with each passing moment, her fear for Dari and Kari grew more acute. She knew not the why of it, only that she felt thusly.

Zor grunted. "Why in the sands would she fear for Gio's safety? That makes no sense, my hearts."

"Aye," Gio rasped out. "I can see it in your eyes that you are hiding something from us. Please tell me."

Kara bit her lip, but said nothing.

"*Pani*," Cam said softly, "if you know aught, 'tis best do you tell it. Leastways, you would never forgive yourself did Dari meet a bad end."

Kara could feel the eyes of everyone upon her and the effect was nigh unto unnerving. Could she betray a confidence, especially when Dari had kept her and Jana's secret for five *Yessat* years? But then again, could she continue to ignore the nagging premonition that told her it was a matter of life and death that Gio find her younger cousin?

"In truth, Dari told me very little," Kara admitted. "She has ever been the type to hold her own council."

Gio nodded, realizing as much.

"But five years ago when first Jana and I fled..."

"Aye," Zor prodded her, "go on."

Kara sighed. "Dari was supposed to accompany us." She ignored everyone's wide-eyed expressions and plowed on. "Jana and I were to dock at the holo-port in Trader City on Arak and await her there. But before we could land, she sent out a holo-call, instructing us to venture onward to Galis because she could not yet leave Arak."

"Why?" Gio asked, his hearts rate speeding up at the knowledge that he had nigh unto lost her once before without even knowing it. "Why did she wish to remain behind?"

Kara shrugged helplessly. "I do not know. Leastways, she hadn't much time and kept looking over her shoulder as though she feared she'd been followed. But," she said in a whisper of a voice, "she did say something, and 'twas something that ever haunted Jana and I until at last we were reunited with her again."

"What did she say?" Gio murmured.

"She said there was an evil on Arak," Kara said unblinkingly. "An evil that needed to be destroyed before it destroyed her...and you."

Death's body stilled. Every muscle in his large body corded and tensed. "An evil?" he repeated, needing confirmation.

"Aye." Kara shook her head, her expression sad. "Yet she would never confess to me what this evil was, not even when we were reunited with her on Galis. She kept insisting 'twas best if we remained unawares."

Gio was torn between elation that Dari hadn't left him for naught but freedom after all, fear that his betrothed was embroiled in a dangerous situation he wasn't there to aid her of, and a desperate need to find her. Memories of that bedamned male's voice besieged him.

From beside him, Death's mind was reeling, his desperation to reach Kari bordering on fear. Fear that if he didn't capture her anon, something else would. And yet, he said naught of what he knew. He understood now why Dari had held her tongue so many years.

"Dari ventured into Valor City with Kari to seek information she might use to her advantage against this evil." Kara shrugged her shoulders. "I know naught what she learned from the Chief High Mystik there for 'twas the same moon-rising Cam found me."

Gio and Death shot up from their seats, both of them feeling hopeful for the first time. If there was any information at all to be gleaned in Valor City, they would ferret it out for a certainty.

Gio stopped briefly on his way out to place a hand upon Kara's shoulder. "Thank you," he said quietly. And with that, he departed the palace.

Kara took a deep breath as she looked at Cam. She knew they were both hoping Dari and Jana would be found alive and well. And Kari. Kara had lived but five years with the fiery wench, yet she had been like a second *mani* to her.

Just then the bound servant returned, her naked breasts bobbing up and down as she made her way to the raised table. She handed the piece of jewelry to Kara, then quietly left for the kitchens.

"Ah here we go," Kara said to her *mani*. "Now let me find the holo-image of Kari Gy'at Li for you."

Kyra nodded, her eyes widening. She nibbled on her lip, desperate to see it.

Zor studied his wife inquiringly. "Is aught wrong, my hearts?"

"I don't know," Kyra said simply, leaving her answer at that.

Kara flicked through the images that popped out of the small charm that had dangled from the chain about her ankle the moon-rising she'd been captured by Cam. "'Tis not here," she grumbled, flicking rapidly over the holo-images again. "I scarce believe it."

"Damn it," Kyra muttered, her eyes narrowed in thought.

"*Nee'ka?*" Zor said softly. "What is wrong?"

Kyra glanced up at him, distracted. She sighed. "Nothing," she said softly, looking away. "I was just being a damn fool."

* * * * *

"I love you, *pani*." Cam kissed Kara's temple, his hands stroking lazily over the flesh of her buttocks. They had finished making love but moments ago, yet the need for her closeness was upon him as greatly as ever.

"I love you too." Kara raised her head to look at him, her Q'ana Tal glowing blue eyes shimmering. "I've always loved you. You know that in your hearts now, do you not?"

"Aye." He grinned. "I know it."

She placed a quick kiss on his chest then raised her face to his once more. "And I know now that you've always loved me. We will never be apart from the other again."

"'Tis a vow amongst Sacred Mates," he murmured.

"'Tis a vow amongst Sacred Mates," she repeated.

In a lightning-quick movement, Cam rolled her to her back and entered her wet channel with a long thrust. He groaned at the pleasure, greedily wanting to stay within her as he'd dreamed every moon-rising of doing before he'd had the right of it by the Holy Law. He had spent the longest part of his life awaiting the moon-rising when she would at last be his. Now he finally had her. Forever it would be this way.

"Let me watch whilst a *Kefa* pleasures you," he rasped out. "Let me carry you to our bathing hole, *pani*."

Kara wrapped her long legs around his middle. "You were ever the wily one, husband."

He grinned as he bent his neck to kiss her. "Aye. Some things never change."

Epilogue

Naked under the stolen animal pelts she wore, Jana's breasts bobbed up and down as she wound her way through the rocky, iced terrain of the cold silver landscape. It was nigh unto impossible to see where she was going with the night so black upon this planet, yet she had been given no choice but to wait for Yorin to fall in his slumber before attempting to escape him.

And escape him she would.

The things that she had been made to endure—how could any wench humbly submit to them? She ignored the shamefully brazen voice that declared she'd not only endured them, but had in fact enjoyed them, and sprinted at a speed no wench of her species could have moved in without having undergone a metamorphosis to make it possible.

She wanted her *mani* and papa, she thought wildly. She cared not of any recriminations that might stem from having fled all those years back. She would gladly take any of them did it mean she would feel her *mani's* fingers running through her hair once again, or feel her sire's arms clasped about her.

Jana cried out in mental anguish, wondering if it was possible they might reject her when they learned of the species she had become. She was no longer like a Trystonni, she thought in horror. She could do...*things*. Bizarre, frightening things. And the way she drank of

Yorin whilst they mated—good goddess it didn't bear dwelling over.

She put her scared thoughts from her mind, concentrating once again on the mission at hand. She had to escape. It was now or it was never. She had done the unthinkable and thwarted the warriors of Tryston once before. So too could she thwart the Khan-Goris, making them believe she'd died.

Jana was sharp enough to realize that her only hope of successfully fleeing her captor was in finding a holo-port that would transport her to her own galaxy. She refused to consider the fact that in her sennight on Khan-Gor, she had seen not even one holo-port dotting the landscape.

Yorin had firmly told her that there was no sense in running from him for it was impossible to leave Khan-Gor without a ship, yet she refused to give up hope that mayhap he had lied to her. Even if he had been telling her naught but truths, she was a warrior woman now, and a warrior woman would simply find another method of escape.

Jana's nostrils flared, her will growing stronger by the *Nuba*-second. And yet, she admitted, she could scarce contain the little girl words that kept swimming through her mind:

Papa, she thought desperately, sending out the fiercest wave of emotion she had purposely emitted in years, *please come for me...*

* * * * *

"My God," Kari breathed out, her silver-blue eyes wide. "I don't believe it. The Brekkons were correct."

"Aye," Dari murmured, her eyes seeking out Bazi's. "Khan-Gor is real."

Bazi took a deep breath, then nodded. "What will we do now?"

The women and man-child gazed out the wide porthole, their eyes taking in the sight of the large silver-ice planet none in Trek Mi Q'an had even known existed. It was unbelievable. And if the Brekkons had been correct on this score, mayhap their legends of the Barbarians who dwelled here had a basis in truth as well.

"We will land," Kari decided, realizing as she did that they had come too far to back off now.

Dari nodded. "And we will find the key." She sighed, looking back at Bazi. "Mayhap then we can destroy the Evil One," she murmured.

His young eyes were troubled. "Are you certain you wish to do this?" he asked softly. "Mayhap it should be me who does it alone."

"Nay," Dari said firmly. "We made vows unto the other. Leastways," she insisted, "I would sooner throw myself into a nest of *heeka-beasts* than not see this through to its fruition."

"But he will never forgive you," Bazi said quietly, guilt lancing through him. "Your betrothed will never forgive—"

"I know," Dari murmured. She sighed, her gaze flicking back toward the primitive planet coated in ice. "I can never again return to Gio." She closed her eyes. "He will never forgive me for murdering his own sire."

* * * * *

Her thoughts a million miles away, her memories filled with the days so many hundreds of years ago when she'd lived on earth, Kyra swore under her breath when she lost her footing and tripped over—she didn't know what.

"Damn it," she muttered, crouching down to pick up a charm that had fallen from her daughter's anklet. "I am having one hell of a bad—"

Her eyes widened when it dawned on her that the charm no doubt contained holo-images within it as most anklet charms did. She clutched the crystal charm to her breasts, her breathing growing labored as she stood up.

"Maybe this charm holds the holo-image Kara lost," she said shakily.

Kyra didn't know why she was breathing so heavily, or why sweat had broken out all over her body, but she felt desperate to open the charm, to view whatever images lay in waiting within the piece of crystal jewelry. She fiddled with the unlocking mechanism, cursing when it didn't immediately pop open.

"Damn it!" she swore, her nostrils flaring as she continued to fiddle with it. "Why won't this thing…open," she finished softly.

When the charm gave way, when the holo-images displayed before her, her hand flew up to cover her mouth. She backed into a wall, her eyes filling with tears, as the image of a red-headed woman who could have been her twin shimmered then appeared before her.

"Oh my God," Kyra breathed out, chills racing up and down her spine. "Oh my God."

* * * * *

NO FEAR

"Some memories are realities, and are better than anything that can ever happen to one again." – *Willa Cather*

Prologue
The Palace of Mirrors
Dominant Red Moon of Morak, Seventh Dimension
6049 Y.Y. (Yessat Years)

"My nieces could be anywhere." He sighed, his hand running distractedly through his mane of midnight black hair. "Leastways, 'tis all I ask of you. One last request before I release you from your instruction that you might rule o'er your own sectors."

High Lord Jek Q'an Ri acknowledged the King of Morak's words with a barely perceptible nod of the head. "If they have fled into the first dimension, Mighty One, 'tis a vow I shall find them."

Kil grunted as he strolled with Jek toward the west wing of the stronghold. There was only one launching pad within the confines of the palace large enough to host the take-off of a ship so huge as a gastrolight cruiser. "'Tis more like than not that the wenches have remained within this dimension, yet there is also the possibility, slim though it may be, that they would seek refuge in the land their *mani* heralds from."

Jek came to a halt before the warring chamber and motioned for an underling to fetch him his weapons. He turned to look at his cousin, Kil, the warlord who had been his teacher, whilst a young warrior in training snapped *zorgs* on either of Jek's vein-roped forearms. "You will leave with your brothers to scour the seventh dimension, then?"

"Shh!" Kil's glowing blue eyes darted warily about the black crystal corridor whilst he made certain that his cousin's words had not been overheard by his ever-wily *nee'ka*. He frowned. It was Mari's contention that his nieces should not be forcibly returned to Tryston, even though such was precisely what he and his brothers planned to do.

So Kil had said nothing further on the subject of his leave-taking to her, preferring as he did to refrain from yet another tiresome lecture on pigs in power and subverting dominant paradigms. Inevitably, he thought as his eyes narrowed and his lips turned down, conversations such as that one ended up in the King of Morak seeing no action in the *vesha* hides for a moon-rising or two.

He grunted. Definitely not groovy.

"Aye," Kil whispered, feeling every inch the dunce for fearing the wrath of a wife whose height barely surpassed his navel. "Though Mari believes I am traveling to the planet Meridian in the fourth dimension on a mission of peace and goodwill."

Jek shook his head slightly, the beginnings of a grin tugging at the corners of his mouth. He was not a warrior known for smiling over much, so the fact that he was grinning at all was a sign to Kil of how humorous he found his predicament to be. Jek was much more lighthearted than ever Kil was or would be, but he had learned through the Yessat years that it was desirable to remain stoic of appearance at all times—leastways, with other warriors. Only with a Sacred Mate was it permissible to let one's guard down a wee bit.

Kil sighed, exasperated. "What would you have me to say to her? Leastways," he grumbled, "you know how bedamned irritating she is when she gets on one of her femalist kicks."

"Feminist," Jek murmured, his eyes twinkling. "'Tis called a feminist kick."

"Aye?"

"Aye."

Kil grunted. His hand waved absently about. "Femalist, feminist…'tis no difference. Leastways, the wench can irritate me as can no other with her bedamned prattling."

Jek's eyebrows rose fractionally, but he said nothing as they resumed their stroll toward the launching pad. He merely shook his head again, then fell in step next to his cousin.

A topless bound servant passed them in the corridor, her gaze seeking out Jek's as she strode by. Jek ignored her, not out of callousness but because he truly hadn't noticed her presence. Having been raised all his life amongst the most privileged, he was arrogantly accustomed to having bound servants aplenty to see to his every need.

The most favored in his harem he might have noticed had she strolled by with her large breasts bouncing in time with her walk, but even then he might not have. Leastways, it wasn't as if he could feel emotions for a bound servant—not even for a favored.

He would that he could.

It might make his stark life just a wee bit more tolerable.

Since it was not permissible by law for Jek to forsake his duties to the King of Morak in favor of searching for his Sacred Mate, it would have been welcomed had he been able to feel any emotion at all these past long Yessat years for any of the bound servants. But he was to be released from his bonds the soonest, he reminded himself.

Then, finally, could he search the galaxies for the wench that had been born to belong to him.

Yet first there was duty.

Although Jek had been raised amongst the ruling class of Tryston, his power had come at a steep price. Because he would one day be a king by virtue of his birth and not by virtue of his own might, he had found it necessary over the Yessat years to be harsher, stronger—mightier—than every other warrior, that he might prove his worthiness to command.

'Twas ironic for a certainty.

His good friend Cam K'al Ra had followed the same life-course as Jek for the opposite reason. Cam had wanted to prove that he, the son of a lowly *trelli* miner, was worthy of the Emperor's daughter's hand in marriage, whilst Jek had wanted to prove that he, the beloved firstborn son of the Emperor's cousin, was worthy of ruling over his own sectors not because he had been born to rule them, but because he was mighty in his own right.

And so at a very young age Jek had pleaded with his sire to allow him to foster under the King of Morak, a warrior so feared it was common for enemies to surrender unto him without any battling at all. Just the mere whisper of his name was enough to make many insurrectionists forsake their illegal activities in favor of retaining their lives.

Jek had not been disappointed, for the rumors had all been true. Kil was as deadly, if not more so, than legend allowed. The king had mellowed some in the last few years since the birth of his children, at least on the surface for Queen Mari's sake, but for the longest part of Jek's tutelage Kil had been as cold and merciless as his legend.

Jek had learned from the mightiest, the strongest, the most deadly.

No fear.

A weak warrior asked. A strong warrior took.

No fear.

A coward walked away when his enemies outnumbered him. A hero stayed and fought even if it cost him his life.

No fear.

And so it came to pass that Jek Q'an Ri became the very image that Kil Q'an Tal had made him into: ruthless, merciless, cold, and unforgiving. He rarely smiled, wasn't given to jest, and never backed down once he'd set out on a course.

At least amongst other warriors. Whilst visiting with the females of his line he allowed his guard to slip just a bit that he might have the freedom of laughing and jesting in their presence. Mayhap, though, all warriors were given to such dual behavior. It was difficult indeed to remain grim and stoic every hour of every day, so it was probably a necessity of nature that allowed for a warrior to relax in the presence of wenches.

Not that he was complaining. Everything came at a price. The price of respect from underlings was steep, but Jek had paid it.

"You've enough gastrolight stored on board to last you ten lifetimes should you need it." Kil motioned toward the spaceship as they neared the launching pad. "Have a care the pilot hits naught, for the resulting crash would take your lives in the blink of an eye."

Jek nodded. "I take with me Yar'at. 'Tis no finer pilot than he."

"You have named Yar'at your first in command when you become a king and leave for your own sectors then?"

"Aye."

Kil inclined his head. "A worthy choice for a lord."

No more words passed between the warriors until they reached their destination. They absently watched whilst an underling led Jek's harem aboard the gastrolight cruiser, shooing them toward their awaiting bedchamber.

Kil grunted. "You are taking enough bound servants along to last twenty quests. Leastways, 'tis for a certainty that the long trip shan't bore you o'er much," he said dryly.

Jek's eyes twinkled, but he didn't smile. "Aye, Mighty One."

Kil nodded, serious once more. "Be prepared to turn around and hightail it back should I hear tell of my nieces in another dimension or galaxy. Until the laws of succession force me to release you from your duty to me you are still my handpicked first in command." One eyebrow rose arrogantly. "I want you at the ready at all times."

Jek's gaze strayed toward the awaiting gastrolight cruiser. He sighed, actually hoping that the king did call him back. Leastways, the trip was bound to prove a failure, and a dull one at that. No warring. No hunting for a Sacred Mate. No nothing. "Aye, Mighty One." His gaze shot back to his cousin's. "I am ever at the ready."

Chapter 1
Houston, Texas
The United States of America, First Dimension
September 19, 1986 A.D. (Anno Domini)

Brynda Mitchell's eyebrows shot up as her curious gaze strayed toward the old man standing at the opposite side of her desk. His head was thrust back, his eyes closed in bliss as if he'd just reached nirvana, while he thrust open his trench coat and gave her a close-up view of his naked, and extremely wrinkled, seventy-year-old body.

Exhibitionism, she absently thought, letting the scientific term mentally roll around on her tongue. She had just studied the section on sexual disorders in her psychology textbook and could spot all sorts of wicked mental problems from twenty paces. Not that this one was particularly challenging. The trench coat and the nudity more or less gave it away, she conceded.

Brynda shook her head slightly, suppressing the urge to audibly sigh. Having worked in a library since she was old enough to hold down a job, she'd seen it all. Flashers. Junkies. Prostitutes. Once she'd even had to call the cops on an annoying pantomime artist who'd become irate when she couldn't figure out what in the hell his hand gestures had meant. She had calmly informed the pantomime of the fact that he was a failure at his craft, which had enraged him enough to break the cardinal rule of pantomiming—he had spoken to her. Bellowed actually. And none too prettily at that, she recalled.

The public in general tended to think of libraries as sedate places where little to nothing in the way of odd might transpire, but on the contrary, the odd was so commonplace that it seemed rather normal to her. From couples that wanted to spice up their sex life by carrying on in a library aisle to hookers seeking a safe haven from pursuing pimps, Brynda had seen it all. She supposed all the weirdness helped to shake up the monotony of her otherwise staid existence, so she didn't exactly mind any of it. Not even this seventy-year-old man and his naked, if a bit disgusting, body.

"That's nice George," she said distractedly, her gaze flicking back down to the textbook she was reading from. She had an exam in her graduate level psychology course at the university later this evening and wanted to make certain she aced it. "Did you have a book you wanted to check out or do I need to call your daughter to come pick you up again?"

George closed his trench coat with a huff, nirvana forgotten as quickly as it had been found. "No, I don't want you callin' Emmy," he snapped in an amusingly irritated voice only old southern men can perfect. He wagged a skinny finger at her. "I ain't gettin' sent to my room again, Miss Brynda, and that's a fact."

Brynda blinked at him over the rims of her large-framed spectacles. "Then I highly suggest you keep Mr. Wiggly under wraps. And I do mean that literally." Her gaze flicked back down to the book. This particular chapter was actually quite interesting as it not only dealt with various sexual disorders and their remedies, but it had accompanying photographs as well. "There's a new series of books on UFOs that came in today," she said absently. "You might find them interesting."

He hesitated. "Do they got pictures?" George asked begrudgingly, his interest snagged.

She glanced up and smiled. "Artistic renderings. I don't believe anybody's actually photographed an alien yet. Aisle D5, George."

He grunted, curious despite himself. "Oh all right dammit, I'll go have me a look." His bushy eyebrows narrowed, forming one long caterpillar looking creature. "And no tattlin' on me to Emmy while I'm thumbin' through the alien books, y'hear?"

"Loud and clear," she said indulgently as she turned the page in her textbook.

An hour later, when the library was getting ready to close down for the evening, Brynda stood up and headed for the women's washroom to make herself presentable for class tonight. She wished she had time to run home and change into more comfortable clothing, but the visits to the doctor's office directly after work made her free time between the library and the college nonexistent.

When she arrived at the women's washroom, she made a direct beeline for the mirror, wanting to tidy herself up as much as possible. She studied the sensible, dependable image she presented as she straightened her neat little bowtie made out of red ribbon.

Brynda had read in a women's magazine that a spiffy little ribbon bowtie was part and parcel of the proper image a modern businesswoman of the eighties should present. Accompanied by a pinstriped cotton shirt, a pair of matronly black pumps, and a no-nonsense skirt that ended just below the knees, she felt ready to take on the world. Or if not the world at large, she conceded, she at least felt ready to take on the psychology exam at the university tonight.

Sometimes, especially during moments like this when she was tired and not feeling particularly well, she wondered if it was all worth it. Why bother going to class at night when she knew she'd never live to see graduation day? But in the end she always pulled herself together and carried on with life, for she wanted to keep hers as close to normal as possible for as long as possible.

Only thirty-six-years old, Brynda realized she would never marry and bear children. A small part of her grieved the loss of what could have been if only Harry hadn't died, but he was gone, and she had her reasons for not wanting to entangle another man in her life.

Harry had been a good man, if not a particularly fascinating one. He had cared for Brynda wholeheartedly, and while she might have wished for him to be a tad more on the inventive, entertaining side, he had been a dear friend and a thoughtful lover. Unimaginative, even complacent perhaps, but thoughtful regardless.

Not that Brynda herself was particularly fascinating and entertaining. On the contrary, she knew she was a wallflower, knew too that people tended to think of her as a dull little mouse. She was interested in her work at the library, pursued her advanced degree in Psychology at night at the local university, and that, unfortunate as it might sound to others, summed up the whole of her existence.

But Brynda was happy. She might occasionally grow bored with the status quo, might every once in a blue moon wish she led a wilder, more exciting life, but all in all she was quite content with the life she had. Brynda preferred predictability. She sought out stability and normalcy, and she didn't much care for anyone or anything that shook up her ordered, sensible life.

Harry had been good that way. He had been as mousy and sensible as she was, which had made for a smart, if a bit boring match.

Only forty, it had been a shock when Harry had died of a heart attack. It had taken Brynda nearly two years to recover from the loss of him, but eventually the grieving period had ended and now when she thought back on his memory it was more with a small nostalgic smile as she remembered the good times, rather than with tears as she recalled the pain and abject loneliness of losing him.

But it had been difficult. She had always expected it would be her that would go first and not Harry. Now that she understood what it felt like to lose someone you love, she knew that she would never put anybody else through such a horrific event as what she'd gone through herself.

And so the status quo would remain. She would continue on with her life, lead it in the way she knew how to, and she would have no regrets, no wishes that she hadn't dragged somebody else into her life only to leave and break their heart.

Brynda drew in a deep breath as she studied her image in the mirror. She was an average looking woman, she supposed. Neither ugly nor gorgeous. She possessed long blonde hair, clear blue eyes reminiscent of a wolf's, but was otherwise rather ordinary looking. Still, she was fairly certain that if she wanted to she could find another man to date.

But, she reminded herself, she didn't want to. She might be lonely — terribly lonely even — but she would not do to an innocent man what Harry had done to her. She would not allow a man to grow to care for her, only to have her die on him in less than a year's time.

Brynda finished arranging the ribbon bowtie around her neck, shoved the pair of spectacles back onto her face, and reached for her briefcase. She wanted to get an early start before rush hour traffic hit, realizing as she did that traffic on a Friday was terrible. There was only two hours left before the exam tonight and the doctor's office was clear across town.

The doctor, she thought, as she took a deep breath and slowly exhaled. She wondered why she was even wasting her time by driving across town. She knew what he was going to say, knew too what the test results were liable to be—they were going to confirm what her body was already telling her:

The cancer had come back.

What had began as a small tumor in her stomach had spread throughout the rest of her body, slowly eating away at her internal organs until they were rotted. She had gone into remission for a short while—twice in fact—but every time her body began the process of healing itself, the cancer had come back within months, stronger and deadlier than before. She realized that her time on earth was very limited, understood and accepted the fact that she would never live to see her thirty-seventh birthday.

No fear.

Brynda closed her eyes and took a steadying breath. She had lived a full life and had been a good person. She had given her love freely to others and had expected nothing in return. She would die with no regrets.

No fear.

Her eyes opened slowly. She gazed at herself in the mirror.

Except one regret, she quietly admitted.

No matter how much she tried to convince herself otherwise, no matter how many times she tried to deny the desire buried deep within her heart, she knew the truth:

She grieved the fact that she would never live long enough to fall in love.

She grieved too the loss of the child that would never be.

Brynda straightened her shoulders and held her head high as she gathered herself together. She needed courage and strength to get through the next few months, not a sense of grief and regret from having lost things she'd never really had to begin with.

There was no such thing as a miracle. There would be no last minute advances in technology to save her from her impending fate.

There was no such thing as a faerie tale. There would be no magical kisses bestowed by Prince Charming that would awaken her from within the glass coffin.

There was no glass coffin. Just a cold steel cage she'd already bought and paid for, patiently awaiting her arrival at the cemetery.

She was going to die.

No fear.

Brynda left the women's washroom with her dependable briefcase in hand, sensibly determined to carry on with life as best as she could. And if she secretly dreamed of the impossible, if she secretly prayed for a miracle, she would never admit it to anyone. Not even to herself.

Especially not to herself.

Chapter 2

Quietly humming to herself as she flicked through brochures on the jungles of Central America that her travel agent had given to her, Brynda smiled as she found the perfect hotel to stay at during her two-week vacation from the library. The hotel was jungle-themed, each individual apartment made to resemble a small hut. Perfect.

After seeing the doctor last Friday and having him confirm the worst, she had decided to spend her last months of life living it to the fullest. She had no intention of quitting her job for she was ever the dependable, reliable type, but that wasn't to say a little respite from day to day living wasn't in order.

First things first, she wanted to explore a jungle before she died. Well, she conceded, it wasn't so much the jungle in and of itself that had snagged her attention as it was the desire to see and experience a culture and habitat very different from her own.

Native Indians. Predatorial animals. Mayan ruins. Big bugs—

Perfect, she grinned.

Brynda's heartbeat sped up when she came to the part in the brochure that listed the dates of the various guided tour expeditions slated for this year. She immediately noticed that the next scheduled tour into the Belizean and Guatemalan jungles would commence three days from now.

Last minute prices were bound to be sky-high, she considered as she nibbled on her lower lip. She could probably afford it, but the two-week sojourn into the jungle would cost her over half of her savings. She hesitated.

The vacation would be fun, she admitted, but she wasn't really the type to squander money as if it grew on trees. She was a sensible woman. A practical woman...

A dying woman.

Brynda's gaze flicked toward the coffee table where the test results had been laying since she'd haphazardly flung them there last Friday night. She took a deep breath as she straightened her shoulders.

It's time to let go and live a little, Brynda. No Fear.

Determined to take out a new lease on life, she picked up the telephone and rang her travel agent.

* * * * *

Concentrating intently, Brynda squinted her eyes and mumbled to herself as she studied the English to Spanish translation book she'd purchased to take with her on vacation. Sitting at her desk in the library, she went over the phrases she thought she was likely to get the most use out of.

"Excuseme señor," she said in a monotone southern American drawl, "Por donde es el servicio sanitario de las damas?" *Which way is the ladies' room?* She smiled politely as she pretended that a native Spanish speaker had answered her question. "Gracias," she returned. "Muchas muchas gracias."

She frowned. "Maybe just one 'muchas' will do it," she muttered.

"Oh God, Junior – oh my gawd...yes!"

151

Brynda's head shot up. Her gaze flew to Aisle K7 where a couple in their late forties was currently getting it on. Located somewhere between Krentz's latest romance and King's newest horror novel, the Texan couple was apparently more interested in spicing up their sex life than in the Dewey Decimal System. The male's pants were down below his knees as he repeatedly thrust into his female companion from behind. Her sundress was unbuttoned all the way down, showing off everything there was to see about her body.

"Mierda bendita," Brynda mumbled as she absently set down the English to Spanish reference book. *Holy shit!*

"Oh baby yeeeeeah." Junior half grunted and half groaned as he thrust twice more then spent himself inside of her. His cowboy hat fell off mid-thrust. "That was one good fuckin' you gave me, Cindy Ann."

Cindy Ann harrumphed. Apparently she didn't agree. "You stopped before I got started—damn it Junior you're always doin' that!"

Brynda's eyebrows drew together thoughtfully. *Premature ejaculation*, she silently decided, recalling the psychology term for the problem at hand. *Poor Cindy Ann.*

"That ain't true," Junior grumbled as he slapped his cowboy hat down on his head, effectively covering his receding hairline. "Now come on—let's get outta here and head over to my mama's for some beer and barbeque. The ballgame's on tonight."

Cindy Ann rolled her eyes. Her frosted pink lips pinched together in a frown. "Be still my beatin' goddamn heart."

Brynda absently watched the couple adjust their clothing and hightail it out of the library. Cindy Ann mumbled to herself the entire time, her disgruntlement obvious. Brynda didn't know whether she should feel sorry for the woman or envy her. After all, at least Cindy Ann had a sex life to complain about.

Stop it, Brynda. You've made your choices and you've made them wisely.

Besides, she told herself consolingly, she had a two-week trip to the Central American jungle to look forward to. There was approximately fifteen minutes left of work today, then she'd go home and pack and be headed out on the first flight leaving Houston for Belize City tomorrow morning. Perfect!

A cold puff of air hit Brynda squarely in the chest, interrupting her thoughts. She let out a small gasp as the wind hit her, inducing her nipples to harden into tight points.

Her forehead furrowed in confusion as it occurred to her that she was downright cold. Well that wasn't entirely true. Most of her body was warm, but her chest...

Slowly, very slowly, Brynda's gaze flicked downward. *Please, God,* she silently pleaded with the heavens, her heartbeat picking up and her brow perspiring. *Please tell me my medications haven't affected my memory that badly. Please tell me that when I got dressed for work this morning I remembered to put on a—*

Brynda's eyes rounded in dawning horror when she glanced down to her chest and realized that she was completely naked from the waist up. Her nude breasts were there for the world to see, her nipples hard from the chill of the library's air conditioning system.

Oh. My. Gawd.

Her heartbeat picked up dramatically and her cheeks flamed scarlet red when she realized that her indecency hadn't gone unnoticed. *Somebody is here,* she thought hysterically. *Somebody is watching me.*

Mortified, she wondered how many other people had witnessed her public humiliation today as she thrust her hands over her breasts to shield them as best as she could. Her breathing labored, she shot up from her chair, preparing to dash into the washroom.

Only…she couldn't move.

"Oh dear God," she breathed out. "What's happening to me?"

Just then the remainder of Brynda's clothing flew off right before her very eyes. She gasped as she watched first her skirt and then her underwear fly out of her reach and seemingly disintegrate.

Naked. She was completely naked.

Holy shit!

"Optical hallucinations!" she cried out in a panic, the verbal iteration of the psychology term somehow comforting. "Brought about by the repeated use of certain prescription drugs. Chapter five, section three of Heinrick's Thesis on—"

"Uh, Ms. Brynda…"

Brynda closed her eyes briefly to steady herself when the familiar sound of George's voice reached her ears. *You're hallucinating, Brynda*, she frantically reminded herself. *You aren't really naked. George is the only exhibitionist around the library. Address him as if nothing is amiss for crying out loud!*

She plastered on a smile and forced her shoulders to straighten. "Yes, George?"

He studied her as one would an abstract piece of art. "I hate to be the pot callin' the kettle black here and all, but uh…" His wrinkled face scrunched up in confusion. "…why the hell ain't ya got no clothes on?"

Brynda gasped. Mortified, confused, and a thousand other things, she frantically recovered her breasts as best as she could with one hand while her other hand flew down to shield her mons. "What do you mean," she squeaked out. "I'm not naked."

George looked as confused as she was horrified. The seventy-year-old flasher was about to comment further on her state of undress when both of them were startled speechless by the arrival of five huge men who proceeded to surround them on all sides at Brynda's desk.

Her jaw agape, Brynda watched as the largest of the males slowly strode toward her. He was handsome, she conceded somewhere in the back of her mortified mind. Tall and muscular and...

She gulped. And huge, she thought in a panic. At least seven and a half feet tall and so heavy with muscle that he probably weighed in the vicinity of four hundred, maybe five hundred pounds.

And his eyes. Good God in heaven...

"Who are you?" she whispered. She nervously pushed her spectacles further up the bridge of her nose.

The large male cocked his head as if he couldn't understand what she had said. He appeared to think that over for a moment, then slowly raised his massive hands to his neck and unclasped a bizarre necklace he wore from around it. He held it up, then slowly resumed his walk towards her...

Holy shit!

She gasped.

"Holy shit!" George announced, effectively stating Brynda's thoughts aloud. "Let's get outta here! I've got a trench coat you can wear, Ms. Brynda — come on!"

Brynda tried to nod, tried to follow George as the old man scurried away, but found to her rising panic that she still couldn't move. Not that she could escape if she could move, for huge, gargantuan males surrounded her on all sides—all of them dressed in similar leather outfits as their leader. Although the giants had let George pass them by, something inside told her she'd never be so fortunate.

The men were odd looking to say the least. Not only were they the most massively sculpted men she'd ever seen, not only did their eyes glow like something out of a horror movie, but their manner of dress was bizarre. They looked like high-tech Hell's Angels dressed all in leather as they were with unidentifiable contraptions secured to their arms. And their hair...she'd never seen any group of males that braided their hair at the temples. In 1986 men simply didn't do that.

The leader of the group of barbarians stopped a few feet before Brynda and studied her face and her body with such intensity that it frightened her. When his eerie gaze clashed with hers she tried not to appear as though she was scared of him, but failed. She tried to maintain eye contact so as not to look submissive and docile as is the natural instinct for many people when confronted with a larger enemy, but she knew that, again, she had failed.

The intense stare of his eyes was so possessive as to be alarming. He didn't smile, didn't show any outward signs of having emotions at all, yet his eyes—

He softly murmured one single word in a deep, masculine voice that sounded almost computerized, a word she had no idea the meaning of...

"Nee'ka."

Brynda's wolf-blue gaze flicked up to meet his glowing one. Her eyes rounded and her jaw fell open further when, a moment later, the dark-haired giant banged on his chest, let loose a ferocious war cry, and charged the rest of the scant distance toward her.

Oh. My. Gawd.

She gasped, her mind finally panicked enough to do the unthinkable and allow her to faint.

There was only one psychology word that came to mind as her eyes rolled back into her head and her body proceeded to fall backwards like a stiff board:

Sociopath.

And a gigantic one at that.

Holy shiiiit!

Chapter 3

Jek pulled himself up from the raised bed where he had been busily staring at his sleeping *nee'ka* and followed the warrior-guardsman up to Pod One—the sealed off chamber from where his pilot was navigating the gastrolight cruiser. Upon entering the pod, he noted immediately that the mood inside of the command centre was a tense one. Leastways, Jek had ordered that he not be bothered with trivial matters whilst he was attending to his Sacred Mate, so he knew without asking that some sort of trouble was afoot.

His Sacred Mate! He could scarcely credit it. He'd been so stunned upon seeing her and realizing she belonged to him that he'd stared at her for long minutes before he'd gotten his wits about him enough to claim her. His hearts had been pounding, his muscles tense and corded, but claim her he had.

Never had he felt such elation or such a sense of instant rightness. He had been told by other mated warlords that there was no possible way for a warrior to mistake the only woman who could complete him, but because he'd witnessed his cousin Kil do that very thing he hadn't truly believed the sensation of recognition would be so powerful.

It was beyond powerful. It was intense to the point of pain. His thoughts turned to his lady once more, his desire to be close to her overwhelming.

She was beautiful, his *nee'ka*. Gorgeous, perfect, and his. He knew not her name or anything of her, yet she was *his*. The rest would come with the passage of time.

Jek innately surmised from the moment her worried gaze had flicked up to his that his bride feared him. He had been told such a state was normal of all new brides so the knowledge didn't precisely bother him. Still, he was anxious to return to her, to ingratiate himself to her the soonest. He needed to take care of the matter at hand so he could begin the courting.

Jek raised an eyebrow as he turned to the warrior he would soon declare a high lord, the one who was to be his first in command once he was declared a king. "What goes on here, Yar'at?"

The pilot turned in his crystal-carved chair and began to speak. Jek waited patiently for his report, not wanting the soft-spoken giant to feel as though he thought him a lesser warrior because of his troubles with speech. Indeed, Jek knew what sorts of names were whispered about Yar'at behind his back as though his name was but a great jest—idiot, dim-witted, dunce—he'd heard them all...and had severely reprimanded any who thought to make sport of his giant friend.

Yar'at's gaze clashed with Jek's. "W-we..." He took a deep breath and expelled it, then slowly enunciated his words that they might not trip over each other. "We have received a holo-call from the King of Morak, my lord."

Jek nodded. "And?"

"And," Yar'at softly continued, "he wishes us to depart for the third dimension in posthaste."

Jek's eyes narrowed as he considered the king's command. The third dimension was not a safe place for his *nee'ka* to be. Leastways, it was not a safe place for anyone to be, let alone a wife not trained in the warring arts. He would protect his Sacred Mate with his life as would his men, aye, but the necessity thereof would handicap them for a certainty, which caused him to believe their hunting party was ill-suited for such a trek as this one.

"Did you tell my cousin of my Sacred Mate?" he rumbled out, surprised Kil would ask him to go knowing that a *nee'ka* was counted amongst their numbers. Warriors never played a game of chance with the life of a wench who was biologically capable of breeding their kind—not ever.

"Nay," Yar'at admitted. "The c-connection was cut short."

"For a certainty did we try to recontact the king," a warrior-hunter named Kaz seconded. Kaz was another of Jek's favored amongst the warriors. He was younger than Yar'at so not so deadly as the giant, yet it was a given that the young man had proven himself a worthy hunter these past three Yessat years. "Yet did we receive no acknowledgment that our holo-call was received."

Jek sighed as he ran a hand over his jaw. It was possible his wee cousins were in trouble in the third dimension, yet for a certainty he had no desire to take his *nee'ka* into a universe that was riddled with predators, slave traders, thieves, and little else. "Did the king narrow our search down to a specific planet or…?"

Yar'at nodded. "Aye. 'Twas to the three outlying p-planets we are to go."

Of course, Jek thought moodily, it would be to the three planets he least desired to venture into that he had been commanded to hunt within.

His jaw clenched tightly, realizing as he did that he had been given little choice but to see to the task. Without a verbal affirmation from Kil that would release him from the duty, it was treason plain and simple to do aught else but adhere to his cousin's command. If he broke his oath of allegiance and refused to venture onward to the third dimension, he would automatically be sentenced by the Holy Law to death in the gulch pits, high lord or no.

And then what would become of his *nee'ka*? Jek thought grimly. The warriors would never return her to the dimension of her birth if he were sentenced to die in the gulch pits. Leastways, without her having birthed a son, they would keep her in Trek Mi Q'an as naught but a servant if the next eldest of his brothers didn't claim her in time.

Such was the way it was done with the *nee'kas* of the eldest in a line that another male's seed might not infiltrate a royal dynasty. Jek had never seen the wisdom in keeping with this custom. Mayhap many millions of Yessat years ago it had been necessary to do as much, but now after so much biological evolution had transpired it was simply not possible for any male to impregnate a wench the fates did not decree he should mate.

Regardless, to the other warriors his woman was but a potential bound servant for the time—at least until she had born a son.

Nay. Jek's eyes narrowed at the mere thought of it.

From the very moment he had first laid eyes on her, his hearts had gone all aflutter. His stony countenance had never wavered, for he had been taught well never to be the sort of warrior to show a weakness, yet for a certainty he had felt all the giddiness of a young boy by merely locking gazes with her.

His jaw tightened. For a certainty none other but him would ever touch his *nee'ka*. It would never come to pass that his wife was passed about from warrior to warrior, forced to cater to their sexual whims.

And that easily was his decision made. He would not be sentenced to die in the gulch pits. His biological makeup would allow him to do no other but insure his survival that his *nee'ka* might not know the *vesha* hides of any but him.

Jek relented, albeit with grave reservation. "Carry onward by decree of the king."

* * * * *

Wide-eyed and frightened, Brynda wrapped a strange looking animal hide around her naked body and quietly scampered to the other side of the cabin she'd been imprisoned within. *I've got to get out of here! Before that giant comes back!*

When Brynda had awoken some time ago, it had been to the feel of that huge, scary-looking man who'd charged toward her in the library stroking her private parts in the most intimate way imaginable...while staring down at her with an intensity that had been so terrifying she'd been afraid to open her eyes and let him know she was awake. She didn't have to see him to know it was him, nor did she have to visually confirm that he was staring at her—she just *knew*.

And then, much to her mortification, another man had entered the room and seen what the giant had been doing to her. Brynda's eyes had been closed, but she'd known that he could see her. How could he not have? she considered with much embarrassment. She had been lying on her back with her legs spread wide open while the leader of the Hell's Angels had rubbed her clit and labia in slow, methodic circles.

The second man had called the leader away, much to Brynda's relief. But much to her shock and confusion he had done it a language that sounded completely foreign from any known tongue on Earth, and yet…she had understood what he was saying.

As soon as the leader had left, Brynda had bolted up from the bed and searched for clothes to wear for her impending escape attempt. But she had found nothing. The single closet-like structure within the cabin had housed nothing but leather-like outfits for the gargantuan-sized male and these weird little see-through skirts and strapless bikini tops for some floozy to wear.

Not sure of what to do, but knowing that she needed to do something, Brynda had attempted to remove the strange, jeweled chain that had been clasped around her neck. She didn't know why she was so obsessed with the necklace, only that some female intuition deep down inside was telling her that the bizarre piece of jewelry was connected to the entire sordid experience. And so she had pulled at it and twisted at it and gritted her teeth as she'd tried to forcibly remove it, but it hadn't worked. She couldn't find any clasps to loosen it with, and no matter how hard she had tried to break it, the damn thing was impenetrable.

After she gave up her assault on the necklace, Brynda turned her attentions to escaping. With nothing but a blanket of sorts to wrap around her naked body, she was mortified at the thought of escaping like this, but she realized she had no other choice. It was either escape in the nude or remain behind in the nude — either way she was still nude.

And already two men — two strangers — had seen her entire body naked and splayed out, and one of those men had touched her intimately without permission. What if the leader decided to rape her? she thought as she swallowed roughly. What if he decided to share her with the others?

Pale and terrified, Brynda ignored the bizarre voice in her head that kept whispering to her that everything would be all right and that the giant meant her no harm. Her lips pinched together in a frown as she chalked the bizarre voice in her head up to side-effects from her medication and left it at that. No way was that huge guy as harmless as her mind was saying he was!

Determined to escape at any cost, her chin went up a notch as she studied the intricate—and odd—shiny black door before her. If the men caught her and murdered her during the escape attempt then it didn't really matter, she told herself with more staunch than she felt. She was, after all, already dying. Being murdered would simply speed up the inevitable homecoming with the family crypt.

Don't be morbid, Brynda. Just get the hell out of here!

Resolved to do just that, Brynda gritted her teeth and raised her hand to the door. *I'm getting out of here!* she silently vowed. *I'm breaking out of this place! I'm — ah shit…where the hell is the doorknob?*

Her heart beating rapidly, Brynda's eyes rounded as she frantically rubbed her hands up and down the length of the part of the door she was able to reach in a futile effort to find a doorknob. *Please God*, she thought hysterically, *please let me find a way to open this door!*

Frightened, panicked, and somehow sensing that the giant was preparing to return to her, she slammed the palm of her hand up against the door in frustration. *Let me out of here! Let me —*

Her eyes widened when the shiny door whizzed open, the sound of compressed air being freed causing her face to momentarily scrunch up in confusion.

She shook her head. She'd never seen a door like this one except on reruns of Star Trek.

Forget it, Brynda, just get out of here!

Forcibly snapping her mind back to deal with the issue at hand, she stepped through the door, took a quick glance in either direction, then sprinted at top speed down the long corridor. Her breathing labored, her heart pumping dramatically, she clutched the animal skin securely around her body as she ran as fast as her feet could carry to—she didn't know where.

She ignored the eerie pulsing lights she saw every few feet as she ran down the length of the long corridor, ignored the bizarre hieroglyphic writings on the walls as she then veered to the right and sprinted down another. Her head was pounding, a feeling of nausea was overwhelming her, and she understood from experience that she needed to get home and get to her medication before she became so ill that she wouldn't be able to leave her sickbed for days.

Of all the times to get sick, please don't let this be it!

Determined to escape, she ignored her pounding head and concentrated on locating an avenue of escape. She ran for what felt like hours but could only have been minutes, perspiration dotting her forehead and pain lancing through her all the while.

And then at last—*at last*—she spotted…something—something a ways down the corridor that looked like it led to the outside for she could see nighttime and stars through a large window at the mouth of the wide hallway. She smiled for the first time, sprinting toward it at top speed, the animal skin forgotten as it fell toward the ground during her mad dash toward what she assumed to be the exit of the building she was imprisoned in.

"Faster!" she verbally encouraged herself, refusing to succumb to the blinding pain she felt throbbing in her head. "Run fa…"

She stopped abruptly when she reached the end of the corridor and stared wide-eyed out of the large porthole she was looking through.

"…faster," she whispered.

Brynda didn't know what to do, didn't know what to think, as she stared surrealistically at the spacey scene before her. The porthole was not a door leading to the outside, but a mere window showcasing what lay in waiting on the other side of it…

"Outerspace?" Brynda murmured, her eyes round as full moons. Even the sharp, shooting pains lancing through her skull were forgotten in her confusion. "It's not possible," she whispered. She shook her head slightly, too dumbfounded to do anything but stare. "It's not possible."

The blackest night she'd ever seen lay on the other side of the porthole, the occasional twinkling star breaking up the otherwise pitch darkness of the atmosphere. And then surrealistically, horrifically, the structure she was in made a smooth veer to the left and the image of a…*planet?*…appeared before her. It was big, so massive, and toward the middle of it there was—

She gasped.

A giant red spot.

* * * * *

"'Tis called Jupiter by the primitives within this dimension, my lord," Kaz explained to Jek. "Yar'at and I have performed an analysis of the chemical compounds within the large red spot. 'Tis for a certainty the atmosphere within it is naturally charged enough to create the necessary speed for dimension transfer."

Jek raised an eyebrow at Yar'at, satisfied when the giant nodded his head in agreement. "The chemical breakdown is charged enough that 'twill create a wormhole of sorts?"

"Aye," Yar'at softly confirmed.

Jek nodded, then turned away to make his exit. An odd intuition passed over him, telling him it was necessary to return to his *nee'ka* in posthaste. She was frightened and confused and—

He walked faster toward the exit. "Carry on as you were then," he called out over his shoulder. "Enter the red spot."

* * * * *

Her jaw slack, Brynda stared in dawning horror at the planet—and the red spot!—that was getting closer and closer with each passing moment. She had never been particularly interested in science back in college, but the couple of requisite courses she'd taken had been in astronomy. She remembered all too well what her professors had pontificated on at length concerning the atmosphere within the red spot of Jupiter...

Nothing—*nothing*—could survive within it. The gases and chemicals within the massive spot were like a violent, noxious storm that never ceased. No life or synthetic structure of any sort could even enter it, let alone survive it.

And the structure—the ship?—she was in was about to enter it...

Oh. My. Gawd.

Brynda's eyes all but bugged out of her head as she watched the red spot loom closer and closer—so close that she could make out dizzying images of the violent storm torpedoing within it. She gasped, her hand flying up to her throat. *Holy shit!* she thought hysterically. *Holy shiiiiit!*

Frantic, desperate, and not certain whether or not she was dreaming or had indeed been kidnapped by suicidal aliens, she closed her eyes tightly and, not knowing what else to do, screamed loud enough, and bloodcurdling enough, to wake the dead.

* * * * *

Jek came to an abrupt halt before his shrieking *nee'ka* and let out a breath of relief. When he had not found her as he'd left her, asleep and lying abed within their chamber, he had nigh unto panicked. But she was here before him and she was all right, he assured himself, allowing his muscles to unclench for the first time. She had not injured herself out of ignorance for how mechanisms within the gastrolight cruiser worked.

She looked…terribly frightened, Jek thought, a feeling of empathy jolting through him. Alone and scared and panicked. He had not a care for her to experience feelings such as those, for he had awaited her his entire life and wanted only her happiness.

He walked toward her slowly, approaching her as one would a frightened animal. He thought only to comfort her, to tell her it would be all right, when she suddenly looked up, mayhap because she'd become aware of his presence, and stared at him as though he was as horrifying a sight as a hungry *heeka-beast*.

The rejection stung more than he wished it did, causing his hearts to sink and his eyes to dim. He forcibly clamped down on his emotions, telling himself that whether his Sacred Mate found him displeasing to look upon or no, she still belonged to him.

As if she understood what he was feeling, and was confused because she did, her face scrunched up as she continued to look at him. She said nothing for a long moment, simply stared at him, her eyes flicking over his face as she slowly but surely calmed down.

"You're not displeasing to look upon—" She stopped her whispered words abruptly, then shook her head slightly, as if surprised she had admitted as much, surprised too that she'd wanted to restore his pride.

His eyes glowed, though he didn't smile.

"Who are you?" she whispered, her beautiful clear-blue eyes round. "What are you?"

Jek's gaze trailed over her face, over her breasts, then back up to meet her eyes. "Yours," he said softly. "As you are mine."

She closed her eyes briefly as if steadying herself. "I don't understand…"

"You will," he promised her in a voice that was as gentle as it was gruff. "'Tis a vow amongst Sacred Mates that you will."

She looked as though she wanted to comment further when suddenly, as if in pain, she thrust a hand up to her head, closed her eyes, and began to sweat.

Jek narrowed his gaze as he studied her, uncertain as to what malady was ailing her, but very much wanting to put an end to it. "*Nee'ka?*"

Her eyes flew open and clashed with his. "I need my medicine," she said in a strangled voice, her breathing growing labored. "Please…"

Jek's gaze narrowed further in confusion, then widened when her eyes rolled back into her head and she began to collapse before him. His hearts rate soared as he whipped out a heavily muscled arm and snatched her up at the last possible moment.

Dumbfounded as to what had just occurred, he placed her limp body within his embrace and walked briskly toward their bedchamber.

Chapter 4
Meanwhile, on planet Tryston…

High Princess Zara Q'ana Tal glanced warily toward the chained-up male who was her homework. A mere humanoid and not a warrior, she had been taught by her betters all of her life to think of any male not a warrior as inferior to her species and therefore not worthy of her notice.

Leastways, it wasn't arrogance on her part, not even a true feeling of superiority that had her trying to hide her interest in the male…it was simply the way that life worked on Tryston. These lesser males had been captured in battles and taken to the palace that the princesses who lived here might learn how to service their future Sacred Mates on males that the warriors wouldn't mind them touching.

At least not prior to the claiming. After the claiming a Trystonni female was never permitted to touch any male a'tall, save the body of the warrior who owned her. If she didn't go to his *vesha* hides a virgin, and a virgin was considered to be a wench who had never spread her thighs for a warrior, then terrible punishments were handed out. Punishments such as…

Well, they didn't bear dwelling upon.

"For the love of the goddess," her slightly elder sister Zora sighed. "'Tis boring, this."

Zara bit her lip as she quickly glanced away from the captive male she'd been given to practice on. By the holy sands of Tryston she knew not how she would make it through this lesson in her tutelage without giving her deviant feelings away.

Chained to a wall in front of her, the bound and gagged male seemed to watch her through hooded eyes as she stroked his large piece of male flesh in an up-and-down motion. He looked as though he was conscious of what she was doing to him, she thought suspiciously…and very much liking it.

But nay, Zara recalled, comforting herself with the facts. It was impossible for the lesser male to know what she was about. All of these males were held captive by the spells of the priestesses, their chains and gags offering only secondary protection. They could feel sexual pleasure, aye, but they were not able to intelligently process what was happening to them. When she and her sisters had finished their tutelage the males would be released to whence they had been captured, none of them the wiser for what had been done to them.

'Twas the way of it. 'Twas ever the way of it. And such was the knowledge that kept Zara from snatching her hand back in mortification because of her physical reaction to the lesser male.

He was just so odd in form for a lesser male, she told herself. So much bigger and mightier…

That must certainly be why her body was reacting to his like a wanton, she assured her ruffled pride. He was tall like a warrior, solid of muscle and brawn like a warrior, and his cock —

She took a deep breath. For a certainty was he possessed of the large cock of a warrior.

"Aye," Zara muttered to her fraternal twin. "I am nigh unto sleeping from my boredom."

Oh, she thought as she stroked his stiff man-part up and down, she would that it could be true. But unlike Zora and her younger sibling Klea, she was enjoying her homework. She wanted to touch his thick cock and keep on touching it and…

Leastways, she knew not what. Only that she fair craved to do *something* with it.

Zara felt her nipples stiffen as she slowly, methodically, worked her hand up and down the length of the male's shaft. Her breath caught in the back of her throat at the steely silk feel of it, and she found her other hand coming up to inquisitively stroke the man-sac that was tight with arousal.

The lesser male groaned softly.

Zara snatched her hands back as though they had been set afire. Her gaze flew up and clashed with the giant male's.

He seemed to know what she was doing, she thought worriedly. He seemed to understand the effect that his nearness had on her…

Nay, she fiercely admonished herself. *'Tis nigh unto impossible for the male to break the spell of a priestess. You are acting the dunce, Zara!*

Her gaze slowly trailed over the whole of his body. She nibbled on her lower lip. Never had she beheld a man so fine as this one.

His body was carved of sleek bronzed muscle, his legs long and powerful, his arms vein-roped and heavy with muscle. His face was chiseled as if by the goddess Herself—perfect in its masculine planes and angles, and elegant in its rough beauty. His hair was of the night, the blackest she'd ever before seen. It fell to the middle of his back in sleek, sensuous waves, and had been secured in a jade-colored *vesha* thong at the nape of his neck. And his eyes…so vividly green, so sharp and piercing, so…alert.

Her jaw dropped open. His eyes gazed down upon her as if he knew…

Nay, Zara, for the last time you must cease your bedamned mental prattling! It is impossible for him to know what you are about!

Zara drew in a deep breath and blew it out. She was nigh unto crazed, she conceded morosely.

"For a certainty you had better resume stroking your captive's cock," Zora murmured from beside her where she was busily stroking the shaft of a small six-foot male. "You know how surly the priestess becomes when we don't see to our studies properly."

Zara bit her lip. Their sire had seen to it that his daughters were tutored in all things sensual by one of the most acclaimed priestesses in Sand City. Highly skilled in the art of lovemaking, their tutor was none other than the Chief Priestess' second in command. Indeed, Pali's services had cost the Emperor more credits than Zara felt comfortable thinking on. If she disappointed her sire after all the monetary reward he had bestowed upon the priestess…

She sighed. He would be angered for a certainty.

Zara nodded to her twin, then resumed her perusal of the lesser male's body. Her eyes darted up to warily search the captive's, and when he appeared to be unaware of what she was doing to him, she relaxed and allowed herself to enjoy the intimate exploration.

Fascinated by the shaft she held in her palm, she sighed softly. It was like the most finely spun *vesha* silk over uncompromisingly hard crystal, she thought as she stroked his stiff cock up and down. She felt her breathing quicken and her eyes narrow in desire as she stared at the shaft she was playing with. She wanted to do more to it, wanted to…

Closing her eyes, she bent her head to place a sweet kiss on his tight man sac.

The male sucked in his breath.

Zara stilled, momentarily frightened he was aware of her actions. But she knew better, of course, knew it was impossible for him to the break the spell of the priestess, so she forced herself to relax and allowed herself to resume the exploration.

Unable to resist, she parted her mouth slightly and wrapped her lips around the tip of his manhood. She felt him shudder in response, which caused her to feel oddly closer to him rather than frightened. And, perversely, she almost wished it was possible for the lesser male to know it was *her* who was making him feel thusly.

Her eyes still closed, she sucked the head of his swollen cock slowly and thoroughly. She felt his muscles clench and tighten, but ignored it, deciding this was naught but a body's normal response to sensual stimulus.

"Excellent, Zara!"

Zara jumped at the priestess' words of praise. Embarrassed, she released the captive's shaft and looked away from him.

"Nay, do not cease your activity," Pali admonished as she strolled over to where Zara sat before the lesser male. "Indeed, you are getting a feel for suckling cock that your sisters have not yet mastered." She raised an eyebrow meaningfully at Zora, inducing the Emperor's eldest hatchling to blush. "Mayhap you should continue, that Zora and Klea might watch and learn."

Klea merely rolled her eyes at the chastisement, but Zora, ever the diligent and studious twin, glanced away in shame, biting her lip. Indeed, when they had been younger and tutored together in quantum mathematics and the sciences, it had always been Zora who had quietly excelled whilst Zara had more oft than not yawned throughout the whole of the lectures.

Zara's nostrils flared in anger at the not-so-subtle rebuke, for her twin's feelings were gentle in nature and her hearts easily injured. Truly, other than the mane of fire-berry curls they shared in common atop their heads, the glowing blue eyes of the Q'an Tal lineage, and the creamy tanned coloring of their skins, the fraternal twin sisters shared naught in common either in looks or in personality.

Where Zara was flirty and sociable with the warriors, Zora always kept to her rooms, preferring the company of her holo-books to people. Where Zara was ever the life of the feast, Zora was the opposite, keeping to the corner and as far away from the attention of onlookers as possible. Where Zara ever enjoyed traveling about the galaxy with their sire and *mani*, Zora preferred to remain behind in the care of their younger brother Jor whilst their parents were away. If Jor wasn't available to care for Zora, then she would remove herself to the moon of Sypar to stay with her favored uncle and auntie, but never would she stray further than a moon's throw from home.

And so it had always been that Zara was fiercely protective of her elder twin. She knew her as did no other, respected the timidity of her nature, and preferred that others respect it as well. Their uncle Rem and auntie Giselle understood and accepted Zora for who she was, as did their brother Jor, but nobody else was as giving in their understanding, which caused Zara to feel sad in the hearts for the sister who was her twin.

Even their *mani* and sire, as much as they both loved their eldest daughter, often made comments that they wished her to be different, wished her to be more sociable and fun-loving as was Zara, not fully realizing that their eldest hatchling was content in who she was. It was sad indeed that neither the Emperor nor the Empress understood how much their rejection of Zora's true nature hurt her.

And so never would Zara try to change that which her sister was, for she loved her fraternal hatchling deeply and truly. Indeed, the priestess' callous remarks made her fiercely angered on behalf of her timid twin.

Zara's back went ramrod straight. She smiled sweetly and utterly falsely at the priestess. "Indeed, I should love to demonstrate what I have learned." She sighed dramatically. "Though truth be told I will never suckle cock as well as Zora, for 'twas her that showed me how to do it nigh unto two moon-risings ago down in the Pit of Captives."

Zora's eyes widened at the lie. When the priestess' eyes did the same, she grinned at her twin.

"So the deuce of you have been seeing to your studies?" Pali asked, clearly suspicious. In truth they hadn't been doing their homework in the Pit of Captives as they'd been bade, so the suspicion was no great shock to the twins. "Well then," the priestess said disbelievingly, her arms crossing over her *qi'ka*-clad breasts, "do show the lot of us what your twin has taught you, Zara."

Zora looked troubled at the priestess' command, for she knew as did her twin that none of them had seen to their homework. Leastways, they were supposed to visit the Pit of Captives at least once every moon-rising to practice what they'd learned at lecture between Pali's visits.

But until today Zara had felt no great desire to visit the Pit and had instead evaded her homework, just as she'd done when she was younger. And yet now something inside of her admitted she would be visiting the

Pit this moon-rising...and every moon-rising until her captive was removed from the palace.

Zara could feel her twin's distress, knew that Zora believed she'd fail at the task that the priestess had set before her. But then Zora didn't know that Zara nigh craved to suckle the lesser male's cock and that Pali had unwittingly given her the necessary excuse to lavish kisses on it the way her deviant heart desired.

Zara ran her hands over the captive's belly, ignoring the way his muscles there clenched at her touch. She sighed, no longer even bothering to mentally deny the attraction she felt toward the lesser male. "I'd be happy to show you," she said almost morosely. Zora's expression was guilty, assuming her twin's upset was because she knew she'd fail at the task when in fact Zara's distress stemmed from the knowledge that she knew she wouldn't. "Quite happy," she murmured, as she lowered her face to his cock.

She wasted no time, for she was nigh unto desperate to be as close to him as possible. She took his thick manhood between her hands and immediately sucked the head of his cock into her mouth.

The male's muscles clenched.

Zara took him in further, until she felt the tip of his shaft poke against the back of her throat. She worked up and down the length of him slowly and methodically, her eyes closed as her head bobbed back and forth in front of him.

Faster.

Zara stilled, her eyes flicking open and her lips still firmly clamped around the male's cock. She knew not from whence that thought had come but the desire to suck on him faster overpowered her. *His muscles are so tense*, she thought, as she ran her hands up and down his thighs. *So powerful...*

She closed her eyes again and began to suck faster as she rubbed her hands over his hard belly. She felt the muscles there cord and clench as she worked up and down his cock feverishly, loud smacking sounds emitting from her lips on every upstroke. She sucked him faster and harder and —

The male's breathing grew labored. His entire body stiffened.

Zara picked up the pace of her suckling, a soft moan escaping from her throat at the same moment one escaped from his. She felt nigh unto crazed with the desire to bring him completion as her head bobbed back and forth before him, her lips, mouth, and throat working his shaft at an ungoddessly pace.

She sucked him faster and harder and faster and —

The lesser male groaned as his entire body shuddered and convulsed. Her eyes flew open as he spewed a sweet-tasting warm liquid into her mouth, which she wantonly lapped up. She drank everything he had to give, her nipples tightly erect just from knowing it was *her* who had made him feel thusly.

And from knowing it was her whom he wanted to make him feel thusly again.

She knew not how she understood as much, only that she did. Breathing heavily, Zara unwrapped her lips from around the lesser male's cock and warily glanced up at him.

His gaze burned into hers, causing her to realize then and there that, aye, he knew precisely what she had just done to him.

Call out a warning to the priestess, dunce! she chastised herself, her eyes rounded and her heartbeat picking up dramatically. *Call out a warning —*

Her breathing grew more labored as their gazes locked and held. In that moment she knew she would never compromise his secret, would never tell that he had managed to break Pali's spell.

"Excellent!" the priestess praised her, inducing Zara to blink and look away from the captive. "'Tis surprised I am, yet your words were true. The deuce of you truly have been seeing to your studies. Mayhap I shall swoon from the shock of it," she finished, her voice as baffled as it was sarcastic.

Zara glanced hesitantly toward her twin whose jaw was slack and her eyes mayhap more rounded than her own. She blew out a breath. *What has become of me?* she silently cried out.

Zara turned her head slowly and braved a glance up at the lesser male. She nibbled on her lower lip as she stared at him, realizing as she did that the look he was giving her spoke volumes. His head didn't move, his body never wavered from its rigid stance, yet his intensely vivid green eyes spoke volumes.

He knew the strange power of attraction he wielded over her. Knew too that she would visit him in the Pit of Captives the soonest.

Feeling a bit shaken, Zara stood up, her breathing heavy. As she quickly walked away from the captive, she ignored the angry voice in her mind that demanded over and over again that she come to him this moon-rising.

Chapter 5

Brynda awoke feeling better than she had in years. She felt no aches, no pains, no dull throbbing in her head—even her skin felt young and tingly. And, she thought as her eyelids slowly fluttered open, she had a feeling that the reason she was in such good health today had something to do with the gigantic alien with glowing blue eyes who was lounging propped up on an elbow beside her.

She shivered as one of his large hands ran slowly up and down the length of her body, all the while gazing down at her as though she was a goddess. She suspiciously wondered if his sinfully handsome exterior was a ruse and he was really a lizard underneath his skin...just like on that hip new television show *V*.

V, she thought warily. The capital V stood for Visitors. Big alien visitors with sexy humanoid exteriors who were really vicious green lizards with a penchant for eating human flesh. Her eyes narrowed as she studied him suspiciously, expecting at any moment for a forked tongue to dart out from between his lips.

"Mmmm, *nee'ka*," he rumbled out, his voice just as digitized in sound as any Visitor's. She gulped. "Your skin feels so wondrous beneath my finger tips." He pressed his erection against her thigh so she'd know it was there.

"Frottage," she squeaked out, feeling a bit on the hysterical side. She closed her eyes, feeling safer that way. "The inability to stop from rubbing yourself up against other people. Chapter Seven, page—oh dear." Her eyes flew open as he grazed her nipples with the palm of his hand.

"Of what are you speaking, wench?" He grinned and wiggled his eyebrows. "'Tis true I cannot stop myself from frottaging you."

"I—I—uh…" She wet her lips and glanced nervously away as his hand resumed its exploration of her body. She idly considered the possibility that he was trying to find the plumpest part of her flesh to gobble down first, but found that much to her surprise she simply couldn't see him harming her let alone making a meal out of her. In fact, she silently admitted, her thoughts confused, the more he touched her, the more she felt as though she knew him. Weird—very, very weird.

"What are you doing?" she stuttered, her voice squeaky. Her wolf-blue eyes widened. "I, um—I haven't given you permission to touch me," she said in a rush.

What a stupid thing to say, Brynda! Apparently he doesn't care whether he has your permission or not, or he wouldn't have kidnapped you to begin with!

His large hand stilled, the palm covering one of her breasts. "I thought you found my countenance pleasing to look upon," he rumbled out. "Do you speak an untruth to me now or then, *ty'ka*?"

His hand resumed its slow exploration at her breast, softly arousing the nipple until it stabbed up to hit his palm, causing her to forget her train of thought entirely. She sucked in her breath, not certain what to do.

He grinned, feeling more lighthearted than he had in years. "I have asked you a question, my hearts," he said firmly yet gently at the same time. "'Tis best do you answer it."

She gawked at him. Nobody had ever called her by a pet name like that before so she wasn't altogether sure how she should respond. Harry had never used pet names...he had been much too reserved, God rest his soul, for things of that nature.

She hesitated. She was torn between the mad desire to run away as fast as her feet could carry her and the equally odd desire to blush becomingly and bat her eyelashes. Against her will she blushed and batted her lashes, a small smile tugging at the corners of her lips.

Stop smiling at him, you idiot! Quit egging him on!

She frowned disapprovingly when she realized she'd just more or less encouraged his actions.

His gaze found hers. He raked the nipple with the calluses on his palm, eliciting a soft moan from her. "Tell me," he said thickly, his eyes narrowed. "Answer my question, *ty'ka.*" He bent his dark head and drew the nipple into the warmth of his mouth, then suckled it hard.

Holy shit!

"Y-You are pleasing to look upon," she squeaked out, deciding to tell him the truth. Her heartbeat accelerating rapidly, she tried to shove his face away from her breast. It didn't budge. "But—but—oh dear."

Good lord! she mentally wailed as his face left her breast and made a direct beeline for the inside of her thighs, her entire body felt like it had been set on fire. Her nipples were painfully hard, her breathing was labored, and she was willing to bet her eyes were glazed over with lust. What the hell was wrong with her? This man had kidnapped her and she was all but drooling.

She clapped a hand to her forehead and groaned. What the hell is going on!

He grinned as he trailed kisses down her body, a dimple popping out on either cheek. "But what, *nee'ka?*"

he murmured. Settling his face between her thighs, his tongue darted out and flicked repeatedly at her swollen clit.

Her jaw fell open, shocked.

He flicked at it harder, then groaned and slurped the clit into his mouth.

Her hand fell to the bed, numb.

He sucked on the clit hard, *mmmm* sounds purring in the back of his throat.

Oh. My. Gawd.

Fight him, Brynda – fight him! Why the hell aren't you fighting him?

He moaned again, then began lapping at her womanhood in earnest. He suctioned the entire labia into his mouth, toyed with it a bit, then dove once more for her flesh and suckled hard on the clit.

Her eyes crossed as she lay there with her mouth agape, no doubt looking as insane as she felt.

On the other hand I am a dying woman – nothing wrong with living a little!

"What's your name?" she heard herself breathe out as she instinctively spread her legs wider. She had no idea why she wanted to know or why she even cared, but there it was. She suspected he'd performed some weird alien ritual on her while she'd been sleeping, no doubt some hocus-pocus voodoo kind of ceremony that had caused her to feel no fear of him.

I'm insane! I've lost my damn mind! I've been kidnapped, I've been voodooed, I've been touched against my will, and now I'm spreading my legs further apart for –

Her head fell back on a moan as he applied even more pressure to her clit and sucked on it harder. "I'm Brynda," she groaned.

As if he cares what my name is! He's the mad alien who kidnapped you, idiot! Why don't you tell him about being captain of your high school debate team while you're at it!

Jek smiled from around her clit, his glowing blue gaze drifting up to watch her nipples stab up into the air. He couldn't see her face, for her neck was arched back, but the sight of her erect nipples made him desirous of mounting her then and there. He idly wondered how any warrior made it long enough to attend a Consummation Feast before claiming his *nee'ka* fully.

"Jek Q'an Ri," he answered her, mumbling from around her clit.

Knowing he had many, many Yessat years to spend at her side to get to know her, he was less interested in the formalities than she was…and more interested in touching and tasting her. It was a feeling so heady, like an addicting hallucinogen. Leastways, he knew he should talk with her and tell her about himself and the new life that awaited her in his sectors back on Tryston, yet all he could think to do was touch her, taste her, run his hands all over her.

He felt nigh unto crazed. The emotions this wench elicited from him were so mind-numbing as to be painful. It was much like walking about with a great thirst for hundreds of Yessat years and at last finding *matpow* to drink of. He wanted to drink her up all at once, every last bit of her. He wanted to lick her everywhere, then ram his cock inside of her and take her over and over again until he at last felt replete.

"Oh dear — oh goodness."

The breathy sound of her own muttered words startled Brynda. She briefly snapped out of the sensual haze she'd been drowning in and experienced a moment's fear at what was being done to her. But when she glanced down the length of her body and saw the way he was frantically lapping at her pussy, she felt so turned on that the worry was instantly forgotten.

She watched him suck her clit hard, his cheekbones sensually delineated from the slurping motion. "Oh God," she groaned, her head falling back down to the whisper-soft pillows. She rotated her hips, instinctually rearing them up to press her flesh closer against his face.

He growled something imperceptible against her clit about her cunt belonging to him, dug his fingers into the flesh of her hips, and pressed his face as close to her pussy as was possible.

"Oh yes – oh god."

He licked at her and lapped at her, groans erupting from his throat as though he'd never tasted anything better, as though he never wanted to stop. His fingertips burrowed further into the padding of her hips as he sucked on her, the sounds of her clit being repeatedly slurped into his mouth filling the bedchamber.

"Yes – more – yes."

Brynda's back arched and her nipples stiffened as he continued to suck on her clit. Her head began to thrash about as she moaned, her hips violently bucking up to press his face impossibly closer to her aroused flesh.

Jek groaned low in his throat as he sucked on her, again growling against her clit that her pussy was his and no other's.

"I – oh God."

Brynda's eyes closed tightly and her entire body stiffened in preparation of orgasm. She moaned long and loud as her body began to involuntarily shake, her back arching and her nipples stabbing upward as he possessively lapped at her.

"All mine," he growled as he sucked on her clit. "My pussy."

"Oh. My. G – Jek."

Brynda wrapped her legs around as his neck and squeezed his head in closer to her flesh as she burst on a loud moan. Blood instantaneously rushed to heat her face, then downward to elongate her nipples. She moaned and groaned as she rode the long wave of pleasure out, her hips thrashing madly about.

He lapped contentedly at her flesh the entire time, then softly licked around her swollen clit as the peak began to wane. She shivered as he did so, sucking in her breath when one of his hands reached up and rolled a nipple around between his fingers.

When it was over, when she was at last able to form a coherent thought, her cheeks went up in flames, shame filling her at what she'd just allowed to transpire. She glanced away from him when he rose up from between her thighs and lounged back down on an elbow to lie beside her.

"Nee'ka," he murmured. His hand snagged her chin and he turned it gently toward him that she might meet his gaze once again. "What troubles you?"

Brynda tried to turn her face away, but his hand wouldn't budge. She shifted her gaze toward his vein-roped forearm. "I – we shouldn't have done that," she whispered, mortified. "I shouldn't have…"

Reacted that way, she silently finished.

Good lord above, she thought morosely, loathing herself, what in the hell kind of a depraved woman reacted like *that* to the man who'd kidnapped her? She should have fought him. She should have kicked at him and punched at him rather than moaned and groaned and thrashed about like a –

Jek sighed as he gently brushed a wayward lock of blonde hair away from her eyes. "My hearts – *nee'ka* – look at me." And when she didn't comply, but nibbled at her lower lip instead he said again in a non-threatening tone, though more forcefully this time, "look at me."

Slowly, cautiously, her gaze flicked up to meet his. She blew out a breath as she gazed at him, not understanding or particularly liking the fact that she felt so safe and secure with him. The longer she looked at him, the more her eyes studied his, the more connected she felt toward him. It was wrong to react this way—sick and depraved and...

"'Tis sorry I am," he murmured, "that I took not the time to explain the way of things to you." His eyes searched her face. He smiled down at her confused look. "But I should like to remedy that anon, do you desire it."

He bent his head and kissed her softly on the lips. "'Twill be all right," he promised her, his kisses coming down gently and seductively against her mouth. "'Tis naught to fear of me." His head rose and he grunted in arrogant satisfaction when she instinctively snuggled in closer to him. "Leastways, 'tis naught for *you* to fear of me," he admitted.

Brynda's eyes rounded a bit as her gaze clashed with his. She shook her head slightly. "I don't understand—"

"I shall explain."

His large hand trailed over her breast, then settled there to leisurely play with a nipple.

She gulped.

He grinned.

She hesitantly wondered if she'd have been better off as lizard food.

One dark eyebrow rose slightly as he regarded her. "And I shall explain it anon."

Chapter 6

It took Brynda a day or two to let it all sink in...Trek Mi Q'an, bridal necklaces, Sacred Mates, *qi'kas*, warriors, *nee'kas*, *Kefa* slaves, bound servants, Consummation Feasts, missing—royal!—cousins, gulch pits, execution, devolution...

Damn. Somebody really needed to write a guidebook on it all. Perhaps one that came complete with artwork and family lineages, explanations of the various subcultures, and—

Well, whatever, she thought dismissively, waving that idea away for the time being. The point was that she was finally up to speed. She knew why she'd been captured, knew their ship was headed into what Jek referred to as the third dimension, knew too that the huge handsome warrior had wedded her according to the custom of his race. She'd been told everything, denied no information, knew she should have felt excited by this adventure at the very least, but damned if she didn't feel...

Depressed.

Hopelessly, terribly, horrifically depressed.

Over the course of the last few days, Brynda had come to care for this man, this warrior, in a way she'd never thought it was possible to care for any male, let alone one who heralded from a different planet in a different galaxy. She had tried to fight the feelings...oh how she'd tried, but it was as if the feelings had always existed—as if they'd lived dormant inside of her all of her life, merely laying in wait to come out.

If she tried to be standoffish toward Jek, he'd smile down at her with that dimpled grin and make her feel like a giddy teenager. If she tried to physically and emotionally push him away, he'd gaze deeply into her eyes and speak to her of the babies they would have one day and how wondrous their life together would be. He'd tell her of his deep love of the hearts for her and how he cherished her above all others and...

She blew out a breath.

And she believed him.

Had the words come from the mouth of any man but the one who'd uttered them she would have rolled her eyes, shook her head, and never trusted a word of it. Never. If there was one thing Brynda could safely say about herself it was that she wasn't the type of woman given to melodrama, nor was she the type of woman prone toward creating affection in her mind between two people that didn't really exist. Brynda was a logical, calculated thinker...not at all the kind of female who lives with her head in the clouds.

But she did believe Jek and it terrified her. Worse yet, she was beginning to fear that she felt the same way about him.

She sighed. Who was she kidding? She *did* feel the same way about him.

But to what end? she thought sadly, realizing as she did that her days were limited. Whatever Jek had given to her that night she'd passed out — some bizarre sort of sand that was stored aboard ship — had helped put her body into remission for a few days. But she could feel the dull ache coming back and knew from experience that it would grow worse instead of better.

And he loves me.

She closed her eyes briefly and took a steadying breath. This was precisely the situation she had hoped to avoid back on Earth. She didn't want him to love her, didn't want him to care about her, because she didn't want to be responsible for hurting anybody when she died.

You will not die, nee'ka, he had said when she'd disclosed the reality of her illness to him. *This I cannot allow. 'Twould kill me or drive me to my devolution.*

He had looked so serious, she recalled, so matter-of-fact that he'd never let her die, that she had actually grinned at him and his arrogance. It was the first time in the history of her cancer where she could remember laughing in the face of death rather than humbly submitting to it.

And therein lay the problem.

Jek was giving her the one wish she'd carried deep in her heart these past few years, the one simple thing she had secretly longed for but had never voiced aloud...

Hope.

He made her feel hopeful — of living, of loving, of defying the odds, of cheating death. He made her feel hopeful and she hated him for it.

Brynda sighed as she stood at the far end of the gastrolight cruiser, staring out of the porthole and into outer space. She tucked a stray lock of hair behind her ear and ran her hands up and down her arms to ward off the chill she felt creeping into her bones.

She wished she could hate him, she admitted, qualifying her thoughts just a bit. It would make things that much easier. But she didn't hate him. Every day, every hour, every moment, the connection between them grew until it had all but taken on a life of its own.

She took a deep breath.

Don't you realize how it breaks my heart every time you talk about me having your babies, you big brute? Don't you understand that every moment I'm with you, every time I look into those glowing blue eyes, you make me wish for things God never wanted me to have? Damn you!

"Bryn?"

She started at the sound of his deep, digitized voice, not having realized he'd come up behind her. But when he wrapped his arms around her, she found herself relaxing at his touch, allowing him to hold her and to comfort her.

"*Nee'ka*, you gave me a fright. You were not in our bedchamber where I left you," he murmured against her neck before kissing it.

"I'm sorry," she whispered as she stared unblinkingly into outer space. "I couldn't sleep."

He chuckled softly. "Aye. So I gathered." When he felt how tense her body was in his arms, his smile evaporated. Her stance was rigid, her skin cold. "What ails you, my hearts? Have you the need of more sand already?"

When she said nothing, when she merely blew out a breath and continued to stare out of the porthole, he gently turned her around to face him. His gaze found hers and held it.

"I want to show you something. Will you let me?"

She shrugged. "I suppose..."

He smiled. "Come," he said, taking her hand and threading his large fingers through her proportionately much smaller ones. "This way."

Brynda's eyes rounded as she walked with him down a long corridor. The entire corridor was windowed, giving it the look of an underground sea aquarium paying customers could walk through. Only instead of sea creatures to ooh and awe over, there was a vast array of stars and planets slowly drifting by to wow her with.

"This is beautiful," she murmured. "So indescribably beautiful."

He nodded, then pointed toward an orb-shaped planet emitting a dull purple hue. The planet was quite large and was possessed of at least twenty satellite moons in so far as she could tell.

"See you the planet Kampor?" Jek inquired. At her nod he continued. "'Tis very ancient. Mayhap as much as fifteen billion years older than your Earth."

"Wow." Brynda smiled as she walked closer to the crystal wall shielding outer space from the gastrolight cruiser. She had to admit that so far this adventure beat the hell out of trekking through the jungles of Belize. "This is so neat."

He placed a large hand on her shoulder and stared out of the crystal-glass with her. "My people consider the inhabitants of this planet to be crude primitives," he told her, "because the second dimension is far less advanced than the seventh in terms of biological evolution and technology."

She slowly nodded, idly wondering to herself where he was going with this topic of conversation. Jek wasn't the type to state something just for the sake of stating it. In the past few days she had learned much about him, that being part of it.

"And do you realize," he said quietly from behind her, "that the technology of the people of Kampor is approximately one thousand times more advanced than the technology found on Earth."

She froze, at last seeing where he was going with this conversation. If the aliens of Kampor were a thousand times more advanced than Earthlings, and if Trystonnis were far more advanced than that...

Hope. She closed her eyes and warred against it. He was purposely giving her hope.

"Jek," she whispered, her eyes opening, pained. "Please don't—"

"Nay, Bryn," he admonished her. "I will not hold my silence when 'tis obvious you have still not come to trust my promises." He turned her around in his arms and waited patiently for her to meet his gaze. "I will not allow for you to die," he swore, his gaze drinking in her features. "'Tis a vow I shall keep."

She took a deep breath and expelled it, her eyes raking over his heavily muscled body. She stared at his vein-roped forearm, not quite up to making eye contact. "Jek…"

He half sighed and half growled. "Brynda, tell me something true." He waited for her to raise her head and look into his eyes before continuing. "'Tis the truth you were raised amongst primitives in a world where your males have not the biological advancement of ours, and yet…" He sighed. "Can you not feel in your belly that the connection between us was forged by evolution, by destiny, before either of us was ever born? Did you not feel connected to me from the very beginning? Did I not become your best friend as if I'd always been?"

She bit her lip, hesitating. "This is strange to me," she cautiously admitted, wanting him to understand she wasn't trying to be contrary. "My people do not mate like this."

"I know. And they won't, leastways not for millions and millions of years yet."

She sighed. "I want to believe," she whispered, her tone as heavy as her heart. "Don't you understand that I want to believe?"

He placed a tanned hand on either of her shoulders and rubbed them gently. "I understand that the goddess Aparna would not have me wait hundreds of Earth years for a mate, only to find her and have her die on me. 'Tis not the way of Her wisdom, *nee'ka*." One of his hands left her shoulder long enough to slash definitively through the air. "You will be healed, does it take the Chief Priestess Herself to do it. 'Tis my vow unto you."

She smiled slowly, hope rekindling inside of her despite her best efforts to thwart it. "You're determined to make me trust you, aren't you?"

His eyebrows shot up. "Are you deaf of the ear? Or mayhap dimwitted of the mind? Have I not said as much mayhap a hundred times these past few moon-risings?"

She half gasped and half laughed. "I am no such thing! My hearing is excellent and my mental faculties are all that they should be and more!" She smiled. "And yes, you have said as much," she admitted.

He grunted. "If you are neither deaf nor dim, then 'tis insolent you are." His hands trailed down her shoulders, down her back, then lower still until he had palmed her buttocks. He kneaded them gently, his eyes glazing over. "Yet still do I need you," he said thickly, his erection obvious.

She knew he did, and that singular fact both amazed and awed her. She was a nobody back home, the sort of woman men tended to overlook because she was dull and mousy, more plain than beautiful. But Jek...

He was hands-down the sexiest man she'd ever laid eyes on. Tall—very tall!—heavy with muscle, not to mention heavy with emotions that he'd found necessary to suppress for more years than she or even her grandmother's grandmother had been alive.

And, she thought on a gasp as his hands reached down between them and he began to massage her breasts and nipples, he was also the most sensually masterful man she'd ever met in her life...if the oral sex bouts he'd been giving her both day and night were indicators.

Her body responded to his touch immediately, her nipples getting stiff as her eyes did a little glazing over of their own. He began to sensually rotate his hips as if slow dancing, his thick erection grinding against the exposed skin of her belly that a *qi'ka* didn't cover. "I thought," she whispered, her voice giving away her state of arousal, "that it was part of the Holy Law or whatever to wait until the Consummation Feast if at all possible."

He groaned at the reminder, his palms rubbing over her nipples. "'Tis a dimwitted law do you ask me." At her soft chuckle he smiled as he continued to massage her. "Yet I will try to honor you by waiting."

But Brynda didn't want to be honored. She wanted him to take her — and the sooner the better in so far as she was concerned. She prayed to the heavens that he was right and that the pure sands within the ancient dunes of Tryston could heal her, but if he was wrong...

"Cease," he growled.

She blinked, having momentarily forgotten how good he was at guessing her thoughts. "Cease what?" When he gave her a stern look, she sighed and glanced away. "Jek, please—"

"Nay."

She harrumphed. "You don't understand."

He moved the *qi'ka* top aside and deepened the nipple massage. Rolling the tips between thumbs and forefingers, he waited until her breathing had hitched and her eyes had narrowed before continuing. "Aye, I do. I understand that you are either deaf of the ear or dim of the mind."

Her eyes flew open and clashed with his. A smile tugged at the corners of her lips. She snorted. "You are impossible, do you know that?"

He grinned, releasing her breasts in favor of pulling her closer, but not so close that they couldn't make eye contact. "So you keep reminding me." His smile dissolved, replaced with a serious, searching expression. "And yet do you love me," he murmured.

Her eyes rounded. She bit her lip and nibbled at it as she studied his features.

"Admit it," he half asked and half commanded, picking her up and prodding her to wrap her legs around his waist. He backed her up against a crystal wall, then rotated his hips slowly, grinding the steel-hard erection beneath his leathers against her exposed vagina. "Admit it," he said thickly against her ear, grinding his cock against her in sensual, methodic circles.

Brynda wrapped her arms around his neck even as she tightened the hold her legs had on his waist. "I admit it," she whispered, arching her neck so he could kiss her there. "I do love you." She moaned when he began nibbling at her neck, not even embarrassed when she heard three warrior-guardsmen pass behind them to stroll down the corridor.

"I love you so much," he said hoarsely, his hips keeping up their slow, sensual assault. "'Tis torturing me, having to wait to show you how much."

"Then don't wait," she breathed out. "I'm offering myself to you now."

He groaned, burying his face against her neck. She could feel the perspiration that soaked his brow. "I would that I could have you milk my cock of seed, *ty'ka*, yet 'twill be easier for your first time with me do you have a priestess to aid you."

She pulled his head up and latched her hands around the braids at his temples. "I can feel your pain, you know," she whispered. She smiled wryly. "Back home if a guy had thrown me that line I never would have believed him, but I know when you say it's torture for you, you mean that in the literal sense. And yet you put yourself through it...for me." She shook her head. "How can I rage against my feelings for you when you keep doing things like that?"

Jek grunted, arrogantly appeased by her words. "You cannot fight me. 'Tis truth, I am nigh unto perfection."

She snorted at that, her eyes twinkling. "You know what I've just decided?"

"Hmm...mayhap to remove your legs from around my waist before I rut inside of you like an amorous gulch beast?" he teased.

She chuckled as he set her down on her feet. "No, it's something else."

"Aye?" He pulled her close, kneading her buttocks. "What then?"

Brynda smiled, her gaze basking in his. "I've decided to trust you," she whispered.

Jek stilled. His eyes narrowed. "Do you mean that?" he murmured. "Or do you say it in the hopes of appeasing me?"

"I mean it," she said quickly, nodding. She smiled fully. "We're going to go to the third dimension, find your cousins if they are indeed there, and then and only then will we worry about my cancer." She took a deep breath and expelled it. "For the first time, I'm really getting excited by all of this."

"Excited?" He grunted. "Goddess' truth, I know not of another *nee'ka* anywhere who would be excited by a trek through the third dimension. 'Tis nigh unto a hell, that place."

Brynda laughed, holding up her arms so he knew to pick her up. When he did and they were eye to eye, she wrapped her arms around his neck. "I'm not giving up, you know."

"Hm?" He kissed the tip of her nose, then regarded her again. "Not giving up on what?"

"On seducing you," she said unabashedly. She wrapped her legs around his waist, then ground her flesh against his still hard erection. A primitive feeling of feminine power stole over her when he gritted his teeth. "I'm not waiting for that damn feast," she wickedly announced.

His nostrils flared. "You're killing me," he said hoarsely. "I beg of you not to bedevil me—"

"Nope." She wiggled her eyebrows. "We librarians-cum-psychology-students know all about depraved sexual behavior." She rotated her hips, grinning at his growl. "And I plan to use all of my knowledge to bedevil the pants off of you. Literally."

"Insolent wench." Jek plucked her from his waist and threw her over his shoulder, inducing her to yelp. "You may tell me all of the dirty, wicked things you plan to do to me whilst I bathe you in the sands," he grumbled as he strode quickly from the corridor. "But I warn you that 'tis gel-fire you are playing with, vixen."

Brynda purposely wriggled her butt against the side of his face, knowing it would make his jaw clench. "Promises, promises."

Chapter 7
Meanwhile, back in Sand City…

"No way…" Marty gawked at her sister-in-law, shocked. She could feel the anger building up, threatening to erupt. "Are you serious? Why didn't you tell us this before?" she bit out.

Kyra rubbed her temples and sighed. "Because I wasn't sure. Because I wasn't one hundred percent, absolutely certain until Geris sent me a holo-call." She lowered her voice and strolled briskly toward Marty and Giselle. "Ger's pretty upset. Both of her daughters are missing, yet Dak refuses to allow her to accompany him to go and find them." She snorted. "Because as is usually the case around here where females are involved, he thinks she'd be more of a hindrance to finding Jana and Dari than a help."

"Why am I just not surprised?" Marty's hand balled into a fist at her side. "My lying pig of a husband told me he was going on a mission of peace and goodwill to the planet Meridian," she seethed. "I can't believe I ever fell for it!"

"Bloody hell." Giselle shook her head. "And to think I'd believed Rem when he told me he was leaving with his brothers to go holo-dicing for a fortnight." Her lips pinched together in a frown. "He doesn't even like holo-dicing!"

Kyra closed her eyes briefly and took a deep breath. "It gets worse," she murmured.

Marty and Giselle exchanged a curious look before regarding Kyra. They both thought it odd when the Empress began to nibble at her lower lip and pace back and forth. "Worse?" Giselle cautiously inquired. "Precisely how?"

But it was as if the Empress hadn't heard the question for her pacing picked up to the point of appearing frantic. "Kyra?" Marty said softly. "What's going on?"

She turned to face them then, her pacing brought to an abrupt standstill. Her eyes looked wild—and worried. "I think," Kyra said quietly, her hands twisting nervously back and forth in front of her, "I think that the woman who helped the girls escape was..."

When she didn't appear as though she was going to finish her sentence, Marty threw a hand toward her. "Was what?" she asked. "Kyra...what is going on?"

"I think..." Kyra took a deep breath and expelled it. "I think the woman who helped the girls escape is my sister Kara," she whispered.

"Bloody hell." Giselle shook her head slightly, uncertain what to say in the way of comfort. Unfortunately not much could be said. All three women understood the ways of Tryston enough to realize what was likely to come of the situation.

Marty nodded grimly. "And you fear Zor will have her sent to the gulch pits if he catches her?"

"Uh huh." Kyra clutched her stomach, looking as though she might vomit. "He can be so fucking rigid. What if it doesn't matter to him that Kara's my flesh and blood? What if the only thing he cares about," she murmured, her gaze far away, "is getting his vengeance on the woman who helped our daughter to escape Tryston, and Cam?" She shook her head. "I can't let it happen. For all of these years I have grieved..." She glanced up, at last looking at her sisters-in-law. "I can't take the chance of losing her. Not again."

The three women stood there in silence for a long moment, saying nothing as they stared at each other. It was Giselle who eventually broke the quiet. "Are you wanting us to do what I think you're wanting us to do?" she asked carefully.

Kyra didn't pretend not to understand exactly what she meant. "Yes," she said simply.

Giselle took a deep breath and blew it out.

Bloody hell. This was getting interesting.

"Geris," Marty inquired, her eyes narrowed, "is she in on this too?"

"Oh yeah." Kyra laughed without humor. "Ger is as pissed and frightened as I am. Not only was Kara like a baby sister to her growing up, but both of her elder daughters are missing. Do you think she wants to wait at home for hubby to return, hoping against hope he was able to find them but not really knowing?" She slashed a hand through the air, her jaw clenched. "No way!"

Marty snorted her agreement, but said nothing.

"Look," Kyra said, rubbing her temples again. "I hate to drag you two into my personal affairs without so much as a warning, but," she said desperately, "I couldn't think of what else to do! I knew my son Jor would get suspicious and perhaps have me watched like a hawk if I left the palace with Geris, given what's going down as we speak."

"Smart thinking." Giselle nodded. "Nobody will suspect Marty and I of anything if you should all of a sudden be overcome with the desire to visit Sypar and Morak." She sighed. "And yet...Kyra, I'm in—believe me I'll do whatever I can to aid you—but how do you propose we lose our guard?" She waved a meaningful hand toward the bedchamber doors and lowered her voice. "Beyond those doors all of us have guards who stick to our heels like unmated warriors to *Kefas*. How will we ever get off Tryston?" She threw her hands up in the air. "Bloody hell, for that matter, how will Geris ever get off of Ti Q'won?"

"I don't know," Kyra admitted morosely. She slumped down on a *vesha* bench. "I haven't figured that part out yet."

Giselle sighed, perplexed. "Perhaps Jor can be reasoned with?" she asked hopefully.

"Ha!" Kyra shook her head. "He might have been a *mani's* boy as a child, but now that he's grown he is his father's son."

"Which means he can't be trusted." Marty's eyes narrowed as she contemplated various ways to subvert the dominant paradigm they were currently facing. She doubted a consciousness-raising protest would render them any results in a galaxy like Trek Mi Q'an. Well, other than to get them all sent to their rooms like recalcitrant children. "No warrior over the age of thirteen can be trusted. They get a harem and it all goes downhill from there," she said grimly.

Kyra snorted at that. "Ain't it the truth. Why bother shaking up the status quo when you realize at the impressionable age of thirteen that the status quo works out damn well for you?" She sighed. "Jor loves me enough to lay down his life for me, but no, he can't be trusted. Not in this."

"I've got it," Marty breathed out, snagging their attention. She smiled slowly.

Kyra shot up from the *vesha* bench, her expression as hopeful as it was desperate.

"What?" Giselle asked, as curious as Kyra was. "Tell us already."

Marty glanced meaningfully down toward her navel then back up to them. She grinned. "Let's just say I've got connections."

Chapter 8

Brynda's gaze was wary but excited as they exited the gastrolight cruiser at the first planet their party was to hunt through. The planet was called Wassa, an outlying planet in the third dimension's Kabka star system, and according to Jek it was quite small. Indeed, he had made mention that the entire planet would take them but a few days to scour, for it was no bigger in mass than continental Europe.

She immediately noticed upon exiting the cruiser that the atmosphere of Wassa was a frigid one. But then Jek had prepared her for as much, realizing as he did that because the planet was an outlying one and therefore far in distance from the four suns of its solar system, it was apt to be cold.

Brynda immediately likened the daytime atmosphere of Wassa to that of the arctic—but without the snowfall. She could well imagine how frigid it would feel when nighttime fell over the small planet. She shivered, thanking Yar'at with a smile when he wrapped a toasty warm fur around her *qi'ka*-clad body.

Yar'at took her hand and placed it on his bulging forearm, then guided her toward where Jek was currently standing, renting them the use of a submersible conveyance. Most of Wassa's structures were submersed underwater, for great rains that had never receded had fallen from the skies eons past.

"This is amazing," Brynda murmured, her eyes wide. "We will really travel beneath the water, even spend the night there?"

Yar'at nodded. "Aye. 'Tis no land on Wassa I've ever heard tell of, save the p-planet's docking p-port on which we now stand." His muscles clenched and a blush settled over his face at his stuttered out words, but when Brynda didn't seem to take much notice of his affliction, he immediately relaxed. He smiled. "I suppose this would be exciting to an Earth w-wench."

Brynda giggled as her fingers dug giddily into his forearm. "You better believe it!"

Yar'at grinned down at her then resumed their walk toward Jek. "So I feel." His smile faltered a bit as a thought struck him. "Did your Sacred M-Mate warn you that..."

"That the humanoids here resemble fish?" She nodded, then blew out a breath. "I wish I'd had my camera on me when Jek took me," she mumbled.

"C-Camera?"

"It records images."

He inclined his head. "We've what we call holo-cams here that d-do the same job yet better I suspect."

She came to an abrupt halt. "Really?" she asked excitedly as she looked way up to meet his gaze. "Do you happen to have one?"

"Aye." He nodded. "Leastways, you must be circumspect wh-whilst taking holo-images of the natives. The majority of them make their living in illegal slave trading as does the p-people of the next planet we shall scour. They have not a care to have their activities documented."

Brynda swallowed a bit roughly. "Slave trading?" She hesitated, fearing the answer but deciding to ask the question anyway. "What kind of slaves?"

"Wenches," Yar'at admitted. He sighed. "You've naught to fear. I should never have—"

"It's okay." She took a deep breath and nodded. "I know all of you will keep me safe. But..." Her forehead wrinkled. "Why do they not have these *Kefas* Jek told me about? Why do they enslave women instead?"

Yar'at shrugged. "They have not the *trelli* sands from the borderlands here." He sighed. "And truly, would you, a humanoid w-wench, care to spread your legs for a fishman?"

She blushed at his bluntness, but realizing as she did that that's how warriors were, she rebounded quickly. "I suppose not," she muttered. Her lips pinched together in a frown. "But don't they have any, I don't know, fishy women here?"

"Aye." Yar'at shrugged. His difficulty with speech noticeably waned as he gradually became more at ease in her presence. "But they are not so valuable as humanoid wenches to the Wassans."

Brynda harrumphed, feeling oddly indignant on behalf of fishy women everywhere. "That's terrible. Utterly mean."

Yar'at sighed. "'Tis life. In every culture there are people who are valued, and," he murmured, "people who are not."

Brynda bit her lip as they resumed their stroll toward Jek. She wondered if Yar'at had been talking in general...or if he'd been using double entendres to speak of himself.

* * * * *

By the time their group had settled in to eat the evening meal that night, Brynda was as tired as she was excited. It was just so incredibly weird, being on this tiny lime-green planet with its blue water underworld. The waters here were comparable to Earth's but a bit more violent and, of course, the marine life was intelligent.

By the end of the first day Brynda understood that although the Wassans resembled humans who had been interbred with fish, the people were actually amphibians who spent part of their lives in the waters and part of it within the sealed off chambers of the various docking ports. The docking port they were staying the night in tonight was called Tavern Twelve by the locals and was no bigger than a small, country inn.

Having been invited to partake of the evening fare by Tavern Twelve's owner and innkeeper, Brynda tried not to stare at the amphibian males scattered throughout the dimly lit chamber, all seated at various tables, as they watched a naked human woman perform a sexual show for their viewing pleasure on a small stage.

Voyeurism, she recollected from Chapter Eight, idly wondering to herself how she'd done on the last psychology exam. Brent Tallmadge had aced the Chapter Seven test, scoring five points higher than she had, so she was hoping she'd aced—

She rolled her eyes. *As if it matters, Brynda! Try not to be such a studious dweeb!*

She sighed, her attention refocusing on the scene around her.

The males here weren't big compared to warriors, but for Earth standards they were fairly large, standing at approximately six feet in height. They looked more human than amphibian, the only giveaway of their race the blue tinge to their skins and the gills on their sides. But otherwise they looked like human men—muscular, handsome human men at that.

Brynda's attention was snagged a moment later by a human woman who was wheeled into the chamber and placed in front of a group of Wassan men that they might eat their meals. Naked and gagged, the human woman had been strapped to a table, her thighs spread wide, various assorted foods placed strategically all over her body.

She gulped as she watched, embarrassed when it occurred to her that the males here ate their meals using a human woman's body as a serving platter. She heard the male laughter erupting from the group of Wassan men, then heard the woman groan from behind her gag when the males' faces fell to her body and they began to eat their meal.

For at least fifteen minutes Brynda watched, her mouth agape, as the amphibian males lapped up their food from the human slave's body. The male seated between the woman's legs used his hands to spread her thighs further apart. She watched as the male dove for the slave's flesh, her eyes widening when his long tongue darted out and lapped her pussy clean. The slave groaned the entire time, obviously as unwillingly turned on by the Wassan men as she was terrified of them.

The slave began to convulsively orgasm, her moans growing louder and louder as the males continued to feed. Suctioning lips were all over the slave, clamped around her stiff nipples, wrapped around her clit, nibbling at her pussy hole...

The woman's body shook violently as the Wassan male seated between her thighs thrust his long tongue deep inside of her pussy and wiggled it around in a series of fast flicks. The slave came violently, her entire body convulsing, as she moaned and groaned from behind the gag. The woman's nipples shot up noticeably further which caused the males suckling on them to mumble appreciatively around them and suck on the stiff pieces of human flesh all the harder.

The slave came over and over, again and again. Her eyes rolled back into her head and practically stayed there as she was brought to orgasm more times than Brynda could count.

When the largest of the males stood up and impaled the slave with his cock, she watched the woman's breasts bounce with each rhythmic thrust. The slave moaned and groaned from behind the gag, her thighs shaking as the amphibian male fucked her.

Brynda's eyes widened in surprise as the slave began to convulse more violently than ever before, her orgasms growing stronger and stronger. When the male pulled out briefly then plunged his stiff cock deeply inside of the slave again, Brynda realized why the woman was coming so violently.

The tip of a Wassan male's cock worked like a vibrator.

Brynda bit her lip, hesitated, then picked up the holocam...

* * * * *

Later that night in the chamber they'd rented, Jek sat in a lounging chair and splayed Brynda out in his lap, softly stroking her pussy as he gazed down at her. "The *qi'ka* should be outlawed," he grumbled. "'Tis too much clothing for a wench."

Brynda's eyes glazed over as his fingers rimmed the sleek folds of her flesh. "I think what you need is to fuck me," she said boldly, her voice a throaty whisper.

She'd never used words like that before. Yet somehow she wasn't surprised she'd spoken them just now.

Jek's nostrils flared as he slid a finger into her cunt. "You think to bedevil me, *nee'ka*, but 'tis your best interest and no other's that I have in my hearts."

"But why?" she asked for what felt like the hundredth time. She sucked in her breath as he began to slowly finger fuck her.

"Your channel is tight," he said thickly, his eyes narrowing as he repeatedly slid a finger in and out of her. "And my cock is much bigger than a lesser male's."

She gulped, half nervous and half excited. "May I see it?" she whispered. "May I touch it?"

He hesitated, clearly battling within himself. "I fear if you see it 'twill scare you from the *vesha* hides for all times. 'Tis best do you wait until the moon-rising of the consummation when you've a priestess to ease your fears."

Her eyes widened. "Good lord, Jek, you make it sound as big as a small child."

He chuckled, his eyes twinkling. "Not so large as that, but aye, 'tis truth that the sight of my manpart has caused more than one bound servant to swoon."

She rolled her eyes. "What an ego."

"'Tis true," he sniffed. "Leastways, after I join myself to you, you will be thanking the goddess for giving you unto a warlord possessed of a lusty cock so large as mine."

"Prove it," she said in the way of challenge. "Show me."

One dark eyebrow rose. "You think to bedevil me…"

"No," she lied without feeling guilty. She'd arrived at a decision some time ago and that decision was to live life to the fullest. She wanted to be as close to Jek as was possible, wanted to feel the pleasure and closeness of having him inside of her. "Please," she whispered.

His nostrils flared as he guided her hand toward the stiff erection concealed under his leathers and pressed it against him. His teeth gritted as he ground his cock against her hand, the desperateness he felt to be inside of her a palpable thing.

"Take me," she murmured, her hand masturbating him as best as she could manage without being able to have skin-to-skin contact. "Let me feel you inside of me."

She felt as desperate for him as she could surmise he was for her. His breathing was labored, his erection was as stiff as was possible, and she felt herself actually praying that he'd fuck her. For almost an entire week she had done her damnedest every night to seduce him into making love to her, but every night he had gently set her away from him, reminding her it would hurt and that she needed the aid of a priestess.

"Please," she breathed out, sitting up in his lap and thrusting her breasts in front of his face. She moaned when he dove into them, his face smashing into her chest, his mouth latching desperately around a nipple. "Please fuck me."

"*Nee'ka*," he said hoarsely from around her nipple. "Do not do this to me." He closed his eyes and sucked on it hard.

"Please," she begged again, moving her skirt in such a way that she could straddle his lap and grind her wet flesh against his restrained cock. "Jek I *need* you." She felt desperate to be near him, she conceded—desperate and crazed.

Brynda thought she was about to get her way, thought from the grinding of his teeth and the way he reached down to his leathers preparing to free his erection that finally he was about to join his body to hers…

At the last possible moment his eyes flew open. He gently picked her up and set her away from him on her feet.

Her breathing labored, her *qi'ka* askew that it exposed all of her private parts, she balled her hands into fists at her side and screamed. "You're killing me!" she shouted. "You're determined to kill me!"

Jek's nostrils flared. "'Tis you who are determined to drive me to my devolution!" he growled, shooting up from the lounging chair. "I am trying to be the gentleman, I am trying to have a care that I don't split you asunder with my wicked big cock—"

Brynda's eyes rounded. A smile tugged at the corners of her lips.

"—and yet you bedevil me day and night with your lusty charms!"

Her heart soared. Until she'd met Jek, she'd never felt beautiful, had never felt sexy.

His hand slashed definitively though the air. "I can stand no more, wench! Rest assured that if you think to bedevil me again, 'twill get you the rutting you so desperately crave." He pulled down his leathers, and his erection sprang free. She gulped. "If you are desirous of being split asunder, I am the only warrior who will ever touch you thusly!"

"Stop this!" Brynda shushed him, her good humor restored. "And wait right there," she called out over her shoulder as she fled into an adjoining chamber.

Jek was still worked up, still horny and hungry and needful of a rut. "Why?" he growled, his jaw as tight as his muscles.

She reappeared a moment later, the holo-cam in hand. She grinned. "Smile and say 'cheese'."

He harrumphed. And then he complied.

Chapter 9

The next planet the group traveled to was called Dementia, the second furthest planet from the solar system's four suns. They had only to scour this planet, then travel on to the outermost planet called Brekka, and their quest was complete. Brynda didn't know whether to be happy that the end of the journey meant being taken to the healing sands, or sad that the quest would be over because she was having such a good time.

Both Jek and Yar'at warned her repeatedly before their party exited the gastrolight cruiser that Dementia was as wicked of a place as it sounded. Strange hallucinogenic substances could be found in the predatorial plant-life of the entire planet, carnivorous animals roamed about the cold jungles freely, and the humanoids who dwelled here were gorilla-like in appearance.

Jek and Yar'at had expected her to be afraid, but Brynda had been in awe instead, noticeably anxious to explore the outlander planet that sounded as if it resembled her favorite movie as a child, *Planet of the Apes*. Hesitant about bringing her inland, Jek had forewarned her to keep close to either him, Yar'at, or Kaz at all times, for Dementia was a hostile place given to much battling and bloodshed. Worse yet, the gorilla-like males of Dementia kept human female sex slaves just as the Wassans did, and wouldn't turn down the chance of enslaving Brynda, High Lady or no, if they could capture her away from the eyewitness of warrior onlookers.

None of the warriors had any knowledge concerning whether or not the two planets had similar customs beyond that, but all of them doubted it. The Wassans were goddess-worshippers prone toward wanting peace, while the Dementians worshipped a male ape-god and were prone toward war. It had been the experience of both Jek and Yar'at that as a rule goddess-worshipping planets always tended to be less overtly hostile than god-worshipping ones, while polytheistic planets such as the fabled Khan-Gor tended somewhere toward the middle. They didn't know why, only that it was so.

And so it was with much fear, mingled with much excitement, that Brynda exited the gastrolight cruiser with her Sacred Mate on one side of her, Yar'at on the other, and warriors armed to the nines surrounding them. The atmosphere was a bit chillier than that of Wassa, so Jek immediately threw a fur over her shoulders, as both protection from the elements and to keep the heavily-muscled gorilla-men who watched her every move from seeing all of her "charms" as Jek always referred to them.

Wide-eyed, Brynda gulped as their party strode by a slave-trading block, young and frightened looking human girls of no more than eighteen being splayed out naked for the potential buyers to inspect their bodies. The slave girls' wrists and ankles were shackled, chains securing them to a slab of stone, rendering them completely defenseless from the gorilla hands that touched and examined them everywhere.

Brynda's body stiffened, for she was truly afraid for the young girls. The males of this planet were huge and frightening looking. Though not so large as warriors, the males stood at least seven feet tall and were as thick with muscle as any warrior.

Although the body hair of the males was quite short, the shaggy manes atop their heads were long, like medieval warriors from old. Possessed of two deadly incisors, their teeth were otherwise similar to humans, as were their eyes, which glowed a portent green. Their manner of dress was quite similar to a warrior's, though all of the males wore black leather garb instead of various colored leathers to signify rank. Their body colors ranged from medium brown to dark black, just as most gorillas did back home. Their faces were most definitely gorilla in appearance, their noses flat and broad, the skin of their faces a plastic-looking dark brown or black depending upon the color of their bodies.

She supposed that in a ruggedly masculine, dangerously virile sort of way the males here could be considered rather handsome. They personified maleness at its most primitive hour, the danger they were capable of in their well-honed bodies a tangible thing. In many ways their appearances were reminiscent of that of warriors, for even the way they moved about bespoke of a humanoid ancestry.

Or perhaps it was the other way around. Perhaps the warriors of the seventh dimension had evolved from these third dimension males.

Or perhaps it was neither — it could be, she thought to herself, that the warriors and the Dementians shared a common evolutionary ancestor, but neither had been spawned of the other.

The planet itself was rather dark and gloomy, Dementia's nights longer than its days. A barely perceptible red tint hazed the dreary gray skies, making the planet look perpetually overcast, as though it was always preparing to be rained upon, though Jek had told her that it scarcely rained here.

Brynda bit her lip as she watched one of the prettier girl's get her labial lips spread wide apart by one of the gorilla soldiers thinking of purchasing her from the slave trader who'd stolen her away from her planet of origin. The gorilla fighter lowered his face to her flesh, sniffed it, then licked her there in one long swipe that started at her anus and ended at her clit.

The slave girl gasped when his rough tongue hit her clit, her eyes round and terrified. The heavily-muscled male growled something imperceptible against her clit then took the bud into his mouth and sucked on it hard. The girl's head began to thrash about, her desire to not orgasm for the male obvious. But in the end the potential buyer won out and the girl groaned as she came violently for him.

Brynda felt oddly turned on as she watched the slave's young nipples stiffen and stab upwards, then watched the male's fingers pinch and tweak at them as he continued to suck on her clit. She briefly glanced away from the scene, ashamed she'd felt aroused at the girl's expense, but turned back to watch as their party continued down the dirt-trod path that led to what she suspected was somebody's home.

The gorilla fighter brought the human slave girl to peak two more times before his face surfaced from between her thighs and he stood up from his kneeling position. Grabbing her hips, he plunged his thick cock deep inside of her, causing the slave to gasp. Three or four males laughed, strolling over to watch another male of their species fuck a human female.

"The little lass has gorgeous tits," one of the males purred, his gaze clashing with Brynda's.

She gulped. It belatedly occurred to her that he'd probably spoken in Trystonni on purpose so she'd understand what he was saying. It made it easier to intimidate her.

"The unworthy human wench should feel blessed indeed to have a male of our species mount her."

But his friend paid him no heed, for the fighter was lustily stroking in and out of the slave girl's body, his cock pounding over and over again into her pussy. When a rival male reached down and touched the slave's breasts, the gorilla fighter bellowed loudly, then backhanded him with such force that the other male fell to the ground, blood spurting from his mouth.

The girl's eyes widened in growing fright, as did Brynda's. The male mounting the slave murmured something that seemed to console her a bit for she looked a bit less frightened. His large hands settled possessively at her breasts and palmed them as he thrust deep and fast into her flesh.

The girl groaned, the moment of her release obvious, for her nipples stiffened outrageously more as her eyes rolled back into her head.

On a groan the male followed her, throwing his head back and bellowing frighteningly as he spurted his seed deep inside of her body. He sounded like the gorilla he was.

Brynda covered her ears, afraid.

"Do not stare, *nee'ka*," Jek warned her. "The males here will think you are a bold wench desirous of a rutting and try to steal you away."

She gulped, her gaze immediately bolting forward, her hands falling back down to her sides. She thought about the male she'd made eye contact with, the one who had spoken to his allies in Trystonni so she could understand him. "I don't want to stay here," she breathed out. Her heartbeat was picking up at an alarming rate. "I've changed my mind."

Jek pulled her close to reassure her. "'Twill be all right, my hearts. You must know I cannot return you to the gastrolight cruiser now that the males here have beheld you," he murmured. "They would tear it apart to get to you."

She closed her eyes briefly, feeling as though she might be ill. "What about the other women, the bound servants…"

"Shh," he said softly, reminding her to keep her voice lowered. "Their sense of smell is great, yet not so great that they can smell through a contraption so thick as that one. For a certainty they will never know do you not give the secret away."

Brynda nodded like a marionette. She ignored the stares the gorilla fighters were giving her as their party continued onward. "Where are we going?" she whispered, hoping they reached a safer destination sometime soon. Her eyes flicked over the jungles surrounding them on either side. "Not in there I hope."

Jek sighed, then squeezed her hand. "I don't yet know," he murmured. "Leastways, on this moon-rising we shall stay in the hut of General Zaqari. He is leader to the hoard whose lands we are in. Until I break bread with him 'tis impossible for me to know the route we must take, if any."

She held to him tightly, an ominous feeling she couldn't quite pinpoint settling over her. "I'm afraid, Jek," she whispered. "I'm very afraid."

He squeezed her hand again. "No fear, Bryn." He gently lowered his face then raised her hand to his lips and kissed it. "I would die to protect you, *nee'ka*."

Brynda swallowed roughly, her heart palpitating. It dawned on her that that was precisely what she was afraid of.

* * * * *

Jek narrowed his gaze at Lieutenant Zaab even whilst he listened to General Zaqari expound upon some recent political events that had transpired within Dementia. The gorilla fighter known as Zaab was clearly challenging him for the right to Brynda, which caused Jek to feel an anger and a hatred that went beyond anything he'd ever experienced before. He wanted to kill the lieutenant with his bare hands, challenge him to fight in the pits as two prime males with no weapons.

Zaab returned his stare, his gaze unblinking, as two naked slave girls rubbed his shoulders from behind.

"Have you heard a word I've said, Lord Q'an Ri?" The general narrowed his green gaze first at Jek, then at Zaab.

He was an older male, if the general's regal mane of salt and pepper hair was an indication of age, but his sharp green eyes bespoke of keen mental acuity. He turned to the naked slave girl who stood beside him, placed a kiss on the belly that was ripe with his child, then murmured for her to go to their bedchamber and await him there. He turned back to face the men as she wobbled away. "What goes on here?" he demanded.

Sitting next to Jek in the hut around an oblong table made of stone, Brynda bit her lip as she kept her gaze submissively lowered, afraid to look at any of the gorilla fighters overly long. Naked human slave girls scurried around the table, stopping to fill goblets or refill trenchers every few minutes. From what Brynda had overheard, she surmised that the only way a human female could lose her slave status and become mated to one of the gorilla fighters was by proving her worthiness of him by bearing his child.

Indeed, Brynda had listened to the whispers of the slave girls with half an ear as one of them had excitedly announced that she was fairly certain she had been impregnated by the general's brother. A moment later the slave girl had shyly whispered what she believed to be true in Zaqari's brother's ear. The large male had looked arrogantly pleased as he'd bade her to sit upon his lap and partake of the meal with them. Even now the slave girl was feeding him from the trencher they shared as she sat naked in his lap, her legs splayed wide open while he possessively rubbed her cunt for all to see. The girl was smiling and giggly, playfully placing fruit bits on her nipples for him to suck off, then gasping and groaning when he bent his head and relented with a low growl.

Brynda glanced toward Yar'at whom she noted had his hand grasped tightly around a weapon of some sort, as if he expected to use it at any moment. Zaab's first in command was doing the same, both of them ready to step in and protect their respective leaders should a gauntlet of sorts be thrown down. She swallowed nervously, the tense situation at last getting to her.

Jek's nostrils flared, but his glowing blue eyes never strayed from Zaab's green ones. "Mayhap you should ask your lieutenant," he murmured.

"Zaab?" The general threw a hand toward him, absently glancing at the naked slave girl who was seating herself on his lap to feed him. "Either issue challenge for the wench and fight to the death for her as is our way, or let it go." He folded his heavily muscled arms over his massive chest, then, thinking better of it, wrapped one of his arms around the slave to hold her securely while she simultaneously fed him and massaged his chest. "The choice is yours but make it quickly."

Holy shit!

Brynda gasped, drawing all eyes toward her. She felt a moment's fear at being the center of attention, but ignored it. "Please don't," she breathed out. "If I've done something wrong, or in any way led you on, I apologize for my ignorance of your ways, but please—"

"Stay out of this, Brynda," Jek softly ordered her, his eyes relocking with Zaab's. "'Tis between the lieutenant and me, this."

Her nostrils flared. "This is ridiculous," she hissed under her breath to him, not aware of the fact that Dementians were possessed of acute hearing. "I'm not letting you kill that man just because I didn't understand I was flirting with him by making eye contact."

Zaab's eyes widened. His gaze darted over to Brynda. "You think to save me, lass?" he asked incredulously, his tone shocked. "Think you I cannot hold my own against the warlord?"

Brynda bit her lip, afraid she'd inadvertently done something else offensive. "W-Well..." she stuttered.

Zaab folded his massive arms over his chest. He was a wickedly handsome man, gorilla in appearance or no, she'd give him that much. "Speak only the truth of it to me."

She reached up to nervously push her spectacles up the bridge of her nose, only then remembering she'd quit wearing them days ago. "Well, um, the thing of it is, you see..." She gulped. "No," she squeaked. "I don't think you can win."

The atmosphere inside of the hut was so quiet she could have heard a pin drop. Brynda bit her lip as she glanced at Jek, idly noting the look of arrogance that smothered his features. And there was something else there. Something dangerous and primal. She deeply suspected he wouldn't be waiting for a Consummation Feast to breach her after the events of this night.

Well at least something had come of it all, she thought with down-turned lips.

The dead silence within the hut was broken a moment later when Lieutenant Zaab threw his head back and laughed. His men joined in, all of them believing Zaab would emerge the victor from any challenge that took place.

Jek exploded at the insult, growling as he sprang up from his chair and jumped towards Zaab. The naked slave girls jumped out of the way, looking as though they were quite accustomed to brawling and thought little of it.

Jek hoisted the lieutenant up from his chair and held him over his head, his massive muscles bulging, then hurled him across the hut's dirt floor. Zaab sprang to his feet the moment he landed, snarled at Jek, incisors showing, then charged toward him with a guttural growl. Their bodies clashed as they lunged toward each other, two massive males in their prime battling hand-to-hand.

Oh. My. Gawd.

Brynda gawked at the sight, deciding she must have done something very, very wrong to have caused this. "Oh goodness."

"'Twill be all right," the general assured her, patting her hand. "They are but sparring, my dear, no challenge has been issued."

She took a deep breath as she looked at him, blushing when she noted that two slave girls were kneeling before him, taking turns sucking on his cock. "Nobody will die then?" she asked wearily as she glanced down at one of the slave's heads bobbing up and down before the general, moaning as she sucked on him.

Brynda sighed as she rubbed her temples. The weirdness of the past week was finally catching up to her.

"Nay." General Zaqari shook his head. "A bit of blood and bruising, mayhap, but no more."

She expelled the breath she'd been holding in. "Is this common here?" she asked dryly. She didn't know if she meant the sex or the fighting.

"Aye."

Her eyebrows shot up. She didn't know if he meant the sex or the fighting. "I'd never fit in here," she muttered.

A few minutes later when the fight escalated, Brynda shifted her eyes about the hut to make certain nobody was paying her much attention. When she was fairly sure that nobody was, she shrugged her shoulders, bit her lip, and reached for the holo-cam...

The fighting continued, slave girls fleeing to the hut's kitchen to get out of the line of fire.

"Why does the lass defend you thusly, warlord?" Zaab asked as he punched Jek squarely in the jaw. "I cannot smell your scent upon her, so 'tis obvious you have never mounted her."

Jek's nostrils flared as he landed a punch to Zaab's eye, busting open the flesh there. "Because she loves me, dunce. Mayhap if your kind tried love instead of slavery you'd understand," he sarcastically replied. He kicked him in the stomach. "Leastways, you shall smell my scent upon her by the morrow, fighter. 'Tis for a certainty, that."

Zaab grunted, then tackled him, both males falling to the hut's floor.

Brynda's mouth hung open the entire time, having never seen such a primitive display of brute male strength before. "This is positively barbaric," she said in a disapprovingly matronish tone even as she held up the holo-cam and snapped a few good images.

Zaab's brow furrowed right before he punched Jek. "Why does your woman take holo-recordings?" he asked, perplexed.

Jek shrugged before he punched him back. "She heralds from the first dimension," he said in the way of explanation.

Zaab nodded as if that explained all. "Go to the heart of the jungle, warlord, and within it find the hut of the Mantus hoard leader." He grunted as his next punch found Jek's jaw line, cutting it. "If any have heard tell of the royal lasses, the old man would know."

"'Tis grateful I am," Jek grunted back as he kicked him in the face, "for the information."

"I warn you now, warlord," Zaab said as he regained his footing, swiping the blood from his jaw. He ceased the sparring and reached for his hand to shake it. "The Mantus hoard is not known for playing fair. Mount your woman before you go that your scent is upon her, permeating her skin and her cunt. Give them no reason to issue challenge for her."

"Tis done," Jek growled, his eyes darting toward Brynda. The intensely possessive look he gave her made her gulp, made the holo-cam fall to her side forgotten.

"'Tis done," he murmured as Lieutenant Zaab picked up two slave girls and strolled from the chamber to fuck them both.

Chapter 10

Jek knew Brynda was frightened as he slammed the wooden door that partitioned off the bedchamber they'd been given to use from the rest of the hut. Leastways, when she turned around to face him, she began to slowly back away from him, as if afraid he would hurt her.

He strode slowly toward her, his boot heels thumping on the tightly packed dirt floor, his gaze never leaving hers. He summoned off her *qi'ka*, mentally throwing it to the floor, causing her to gasp.

His jaw clenched. "I would sooner die than hurt you, *nee'ka*," he said hoarsely, his eyes raking over her body. "This you know."

She wet her lips and glanced nervously away. "Then quit staring at me like that," she breathed out. "You're behaving like a madman."

He realized he mayhap was, realized too he should probably not touch her this moon-rising when he felt like a crazed gulch beast in heat, yet knew too that there was no chance of her leaving this bedchamber unbreached by him. Zaab's near challenge, harmless or no, had brought out a predator in him far more deadly than even he had known lurked within him.

"I need to join with you, *ty'ka*," Jek said thickly. His nostrils flared as he came to stand before her, his hands possessively tangling themselves in her hair. "I need for these males to smell my scent upon you."

Brynda's eyes widened. "You want to mark me," she breathed out.

Jek's hands unwound from her hair and trailed down her naked body. He ran his large hands over her breasts, his callused palms grazing the nipples. "Aye," he growled.

She wet her lips. And then she smiled. "Oh Jek...that is the sexiest thing a man has ever said to me!" She held up her arms for him, laughing as he instinctively picked her up.

He sighed, looking bewildered.

She wrapped her arms around his neck and placed a series of quick kisses all over his face. "You are so sexy," she mumbled between kisses. "And I want you to mark me so incredibly badly."

"You are mayhap the most bizarre *nee'ka* in existence," he groaned as he carried her to the chamber's wood and *rama*-hide bed and splayed her out on it. He grinned as he summoned off his leathers and settled himself atop her. "Thank the goddess," he murmured.

She ran her hands over his vein-roped forearms, feeling his skin beneath her fingertips as she trailed up, then wrapped her arms around his neck once again. Her grin faded as a serious expression commanded her features. She searched his eyes, her feelings there for him to see, to feel. "Thank you," she whispered.

His eyes glowed even as they narrowed in desire. He brushed a lock of blonde hair out of her line of vision as he studied her eyes. "Do you know how lonely I was all of these years, waiting on you to be born?" he murmured.

When she considered that he'd lived hundreds of years according to her time standards and that he had been subjected to stark loneliness for the majority of them, it damn near made her cry. She took a deep breath instead, not the type to tear up. "No," she admitted, albeit a bit shakily. "Not like that." She expelled the breath she'd drawn in. "I can't begin to imagine—."

"Aye, you can." He stared deeply into her eyes. "I had the comfort of knowing all these years that one day I would find you," he admitted, his body covering hers fully as he settled himself between her thighs. "And yet oft did I despair, letting the black moods settle in out of misplaced sorrow for myself. But you..." He bent his head and placed a kiss on the tip of her nose. "You knew naught of my existence, believed you would die alone and without knowing love of the hearts, yet never did you weaken, never did the light inside of you cease to shine."

"Stop it," she whispered, tears welling despite her best efforts to thwart them. She took a deep breath. "I might have been stoically resolved on the outside, but on the inside I..." She sucked in her breath. "I prayed every night for you to find me," she whispered.

"And so I did," he murmured. He rotated his hips a bit, poising his erection at the entrance to her vagina. "I love you, Bryn."

She smiled. "I love you too." Then she hit him. "Now quit getting me all teary and mushy, you big brute. It's ruining my lusty mood," she teased.

He grinned. "If you love me, then mayhap you will forgive me."

Her brow wrinkled. "For—*whaaaat!*" she screamed.

He groaned as he plunged his cock deeply inside of her, seating himself fully. He gritted his teeth, a sheen of perspiration lining his forehead. "For that," he said hoarsely.

Holy shit!

Brynda blinked a few times in rapid succession, her fingers digging into his steely buttocks as she adjusted to the length and width of him. "No problem," she squeaked.

Jek drew himself up on his elbows, palmed her breasts, and gently kneaded them as he began to slowly stroke in and out of her. His eyes closed on a groan as he thrust in and out, his hips grinding in slow, methodic circles. "Do you hear the sound your pussy makes for me," he murmured against her ear. "'Tis wet for need of me."

"Yes," she gasped. Wrapping her legs around his hips, Brynda arched up, already wanting more. "Please," she urged him. "I'm fine now. We've waited too long as it is."

His nostrils flared as he continued to slowly plunge in and out of her. "Don't tempt me, Bryn," he said hoarsely. "I'm still feeling nigh unto crazed from Zaab's near challenge."

Her eyes widened when she realized he wasn't lying. She could feel the controlled rage still simmering below the surface. Every muscle in his body was clenched tightly, his jaw was set, his breathing heavy.

"I want to rut inside of you like a beast marking his territory," he murmured.

Her eyes narrowed lustily as she arched her hips up and ground her cunt against him. When she heard him growl, it turned her on all the more. "You better mark me," she brazenly challenged him, hoping to make him snap, wanting him to unleash on her, "before we have to go deeper into the jung—"

She moaned as he slammed into her, his hips rapidly pistoning back and forth. He growled as he pounded deeply into her flesh, his thrusts possessive and branding.

"*Oh God*," she groaned, her head falling back and her eyes closing. "*Oh yes*."

"Mine," he said dangerously, his teeth gritting. "All mine."

He mated her hard, rocking in and out of her with mind-numbing speed, his muscled buttocks clenching and contracting again and again as he slammed his cock deep inside of her. She moaned and groaned, her fingernails digging into his arms as she threw her hips back at him, meeting him thrust for thrust, her breasts jiggling beneath him from the hard mating.

"*Harder*," she demanded. "*More.*"

He growled against her ear as he buried himself inside of her, his cock violently rocking in and out of her cunt. He rotated his hips to the left, then quickly to the right, see-sawing back and forth, then slammed forward again and again, causing her body to shake and her moans to grow louder and louder.

Brynda gasped as her eyes flew open, the sound of their flesh smacking together reverberating throughout the hollow walls of the hut's bedchamber. She squeezed her legs around his waist as tightly as she could, holding on with everything she had as he rode her hard.

"Tell me no other male shall ever fuck you," he ground out as he rotated his hips and slammed into her pussy. "*Tell me*," he growled.

"No other man," she breathed out as she threw her hips back at him, rearing them up to get as much friction against her clit as possible. Her breasts jiggled with every thrust. "*Never*," she groaned, her eyes closing as she felt an orgasm fast approaching.

The feel of his perspiration-soaked body mounting hers, the feel of his cock slamming possessively into her flesh, the sounds of their mating when their sexes pounded together, the dangerous excitement of being with a man you knew would kill another just for touching you...

Brynda's body instinctually prepared for orgasm, her hips thrashing up madly to meet his deep thrusts. Her head fell back on a low moan, her neck bared to him as he fucked her harder and harder, slamming his cock possessively inside of her, over and over, again and again.

"*Oh God.*"

She broke on a groan, blood rushing to her face to heat it. Her back arched as her nipples stabbed upwards, and her eyes closed as she rode out the wave of exquisite pleasure.

He moaned as he pounded into her, groaned when he felt her tremors and her pussy began milking his cock for seed. "*Nee'ka,*" he growled, his eyes closing tightly as his teeth gritted. He held her body possessively as he slammed into her once, twice, three times more and—

"*Brynda.*"

He came on a groan that sounded half delirious, his eyes opening on a primal growl as he rode her hard, draining his tight balls of seed. He didn't stop, took her over and over again, then bellowed as the bridal necklace began to pulse.

Brynda's eyes widened when the shockwave of sensation hit her, not having realized this was to happen when they mated. She held onto him tightly and rode it out, the mind-numbing release causing her groans to sound hysterical and tortured.

When it was over, when they lay in each other's arms relaxing from the intense release, Jek grinned at the dumbfounded expression written all over her face.

He raised an eyebrow. "'Twas wicked good, aye?"

She could only gawk at him.

He chuckled. "Think you they have a psychology term for our mating?"

Her teeth clicked shut. She shook her head as if in a daze. "No. But I sure as hell wouldn't complain if I got that disorder."

Chapter 11
Meanwhile, back in Sand City…

Naked, Kyra sank into the warm, lulling water of the bathing pool within her bedchamber. She smiled at Giselle who was already in the bathing pool, her three-year-old son Kalïq sitting between her legs while she combed out his hair. "He's got the sweetest little curls."

She grinned. "Bloody hellish to work a crystal-comb through, though."

"Are you taking him with us?"

She shook her head. "No. I'm leaving him here with the rest of the kids now that he's weaned."

Kyra's eyes flicked over the baby, then to the other side of the bathing pool where Zy'an and Zari were giggling and splashing at each other. She sighed. "Gis—"

"You didn't drag us into anything," she interrupted without looking up from her work. She nodded definitively. "Marty and I had a choice and we've made it." She glanced up. "Besides, it's not as if we've no manner of protection at all. Those Wani warriors…" She grinned. "Wow."

Kyra grinned back. "Wow is right." She nibbled at her lip and glanced away. "Still, I feel a bit guilty."

"Zari," Giselle called out, "come get Kalïq from *mani*." She set the crystal-comb down on the side of the bathing pool and sighed as she looked up at Kyra. "Well don't. Dari and Jana are my nieces too—Marty's as well. And if we can help your sister whilst we find them, then even better."

"I hope we find her," Kyra murmured, her gaze far away. "I don't know why I'm supposed to go find her, only that I am." She climbed up on a soft gel-rock and laid down on her belly, careful of her engorged breasts by propping up on her elbows.

Giselle kissed the baby on top of his head before handing him over to his big sister and cousin. Zari and Zy'an waded with him to the other side of the bathing pool and put him in the Trystonni version of a floatie toy. They giggled as he grinned and splashed the water up and down, his feet energetically flailing beneath him.

Just then Marty strolled in, an arrogant smirk on her face. She quickly discarded her *qi'ka* and waded into the water, stopping next to the soft rock Kyra was lounging on. She frowned down at her breasts, muttering something about gigantic floating melons.

"Well?" Kyra asked.

Marty grinned. "Well, my dears, I just spoke with Jor and we're all set."

Kyra bit on her lip. "Shit, I feel so guilty lying to my son."

"Which is why you didn't and I did."

She snorted at that. "And? What did he say?"

"All three of us are permitted to visit Morak, provided our guards escort us." An eyebrow shot up. "Our 'guards' that day will be, of course, Tulip, Gardinia, and Flora."

Kyra blew out a breath. "Good job," she murmured. "I just hope Jor doesn't get in trouble with the big oaf if we get caught."

"He won't." Marty waved that way. "We'll think of something. Kil always accuses me of being manipulative and wily, so in this case I'll just have to make sure I am."

"And Geris?" Giselle inquired. "Have you spoken with her yet today? Has she figured out a way to get away from Dar and meet us at the rendezvous point?"

"Yep. I told you, we're all set." Marty grinned. "This is so fucking groovy."

Giselle's lips curled upward. "Kinda like *Thelma & Louise* except, you know, there's like four of us." At Marty's baffled look, she waved a hand dismissively. "Never mind. Forgot it was after your time."

"Subverting the dominant paradigm," Marty said nostalgically as she climbed up on the gel-rock next to Kyra. "Too bad we don't have a doobie to take with us."

Kyra chuckled. "Maybe not, but Death sent over some moonshine *matpow* a while back." She wiggled her eyebrows. "I've been saving it for the right occasion."

"Far out." Marty grinned as she laid back. "Bring it on, sister."

* * * * *

Zara clamped her hands over her ears, the mental call of the lesser male driving her daft. For a fortnight he had been calling her thusly, and every moon-rising became harder than the next to resist the lure of visiting the Pit of Captives.

She wanted him.

Fiercely. Possessively. Mayhap insanely.

But there was something not quite right about him, something too foreign about the idea of mating him. Something that warned her it would change her fate forever did she mount him.

Zara rolled over onto her back upon the raised bed and began frantically massaging her pussy, the need for completion greater than the need for breath.

She groaned. For a certainty something was not right.

Chapter 12

"Khan-Gor?" Jek bellowed. "Do you take me for a fool, old man?"

The leader of the Mantus hoard growled low in his throat as he surged up to his feet, his muscles clenching. He and Jek locked eyes.

"I have been called many things in my life, warlord, but liar was never amongst them."

"That planet is naught but a fable," Jek hissed, his words precise.

"He speaks the truth, Lord Q'an Ri," Lieutenant Zaab said from behind him. He shrugged when Jek turned to look at him. "Or mayhap at least in so far as he knows it."

Jek sighed. He had come to trust the judgment of Zaab this past fortnight they'd been trekking through the treacherous highland jungle together. The lieutenant had taken it upon himself to serve as both guide and bodyguard to their traveling party. When first Zaab had made the offer Jek had been insulted, assuming the lieutenant was trying to defame his warring skills in the witness of his *nee'ka*. But the gorilla fighter had assured him that wasn't the case and he meant only to aid him.

In the end Jek had agreed, deciding it was probably best to have a male familiar with the jungle counted amongst their numbers. Leastways, he had been correct on that score for the rugged highlander terrain was filled with predators the likes of which none of the warriors had ever heard tell of. Zaab had proven invaluable. Not to mention trustworthy.

He pinched the bridge of his nose for an indecisive moment then turned back to General Kwall. "These Brekkons you captured," he said on a sigh. "They claimed to have seen two royal wenches?"

"Nay."

Jek's brow furrowed. "Then…"

"They claimed to have seen one royal wench, accompanied by a female below her in rank." The general sat back down, a naked slave girl resuming her massage of his shoulders when he did. "An onyx-skinned lass with the eyes of your lineage…"

Jek stilled.

"…accompanied by a lass with hair of fire." He waved a dismissive hand. "The eyes of the fiery-headed wench did not signify a royal lineage."

"Did the Brekkons mention a royal lass who is golden both of hair and body?" Zaab inquired of the general as he strolled over to stand before him, asking the question he knew would be put to the old man anyway.

General Kwall scratched his chin as he thought that over for a moment. "Nay. Only a male."

Jek sighed. It was best if Gio was not told as much for he knew the warlord carried about the hope that the male had been long removed from Dari's presence. "And these Brekkons were able to convince my cousin of the existence of Khan-Gor?" He sighed and shook his head. "Dari is either panicked of being caught or the Brekkons speak an untruth of her," he muttered under his breath to Zaab.

"General," Lieutenant Zaab intoned, "my friend here assures me that the princess is not a lass easily fooled. What proof did the Brekkons offer unto her? Were you told?"

"Nay." The old gorilla fighter sighed as he accepted a chalice of hallucinogenic brew from a slave girl. He nuzzled her large breasts, waiting for her to giggle before turning back to face them. "If 'tis that important for you to know, then ask them yourselves."

Jek nodded. "You've my thanks. I'll hunt them in Brekka and get them to talk."

The general chuckled. "Not necessary, that." At Jek's raised eyebrow, he waved a hand toward the hut's door. "My prisoners still hang in the cage, warlord. You may interrogate them at your convenience."

Jek didn't wait to hear more. He turned on his boot heel and strode briskly from the hut, Yar'at and Zaab bringing up the rear.

"Now then," General Kwall said as he pulled the naked slave closer to him. "Mmm," he growled, "what young, stiff nipples you have, lass."

She giggled.

He used his rough tongue to lick them thoroughly. "Now," he said arrogantly, "put my thick gorilla cock inside of your tight little human cunt."

* * * * *

Brynda swallowed nervously as their party made its way through the eerie Dementian jungle. She yelped when a carnivorous bug landed upon Jek's arm and stabbed him, her hand flying up to cover her mouth when her husband hit it with such force that it exploded, bursting like a blood-filled balloon. "That was just so gross," she mumbled from beneath her hand.

He sighed and took her hand, rethreading their fingers together. "One more fortnight and we'll be on our way home."

Her wide eyes tracked the slow movement of a predatorial vine. It curled itself around a low-hanging branch, then relaxed, as if preparing to sleep. Or to watch. "Two weeks can't come soon enough," she muttered.

* * * * *

Groggy with sleep, Brynda's brow furrowed in confusion as she woke up in the middle of the night to the feeling of being gagged.

Her eyes flew open. Her heart began palpitating rapidly.

There's nobody here, she thought, dumbfounded. *Am I dreaming or —*

A vine wrapped itself around her leg, shocking her. Another vine lassoed her arms, tying her wrists together above her head.

A hysterical scream bubbled up in her throat, desperate to erupt but unable to do so. The gag, she realized in dawning horror, was part of the vine itself. Her body shook and her head thrashed from side to side as she tried to scream, tried to wake up the husband who was asleep beside her.

Please wake up, Jek! she mentally screamed. *Please!*

She turned her head and her eyes widened in shock when, a moment later, a tiny spike within the vine shot into her thigh, injected her with some sort of substance, then retreated back inside of the plant just as quickly as it had emerged.

I'm being drugged. Oh God I'm...

Brynda smiled dreamily, the need to giggle overcoming her, as the hallucinogenic properties of the plant's drug took effect. She closed her eyes and slept blissfully, not even aware when the vines dragged her out of the animal hide tent and into the heart of the jungle.

Chapter 13

Meanwhile, in the far reaches of Zyrus Galaxy...

Kari Gy'at Li, nee Kara Summers, narrowed her gaze at the gigantic ice-coated planet that seemed as if it was taking forever to reach. She sighed as she switched the gastrolight cruiser onto auto-pilot, then settled back in her seat. "It looks a lot closer than it is," she announced in a monotone. "It'll be days still before we reach its perimeter if the holo-reading is correct," she said tiredly.

Princess Dari Q'ana Tal nodded to her companion. She turned her head to the front, her glowing blue gaze absently flicking over the planet Khan-Gor. "Rest whilst you can," she murmured. "I've the feeling it shan't last."

Kari turned her head, her eyes studying Dari's profile. She was silent for a long moment, just simply stared at her, but then she murmured, "tell me about him."

Dari stiffened, knowing precisely who she meant. "There's naught to tell of Gio," she said quietly.

Kari snorted. "Don't give me that." At the princess' sigh she said, "Come on, Dari. You tell me your story and I'll tell you mine."

Dari turned her head long enough to grin at her. "Ah. Like two warriors of old reminiscing on battles won and lost."

"Something like that," she said on a smile. Kari was quiet for a moment, then gently prodded her again. "We don't know what's going to happen down there. One of us could die or all of us could die," she said softly. "Let's at least face the unknown as friends."

Dari's wary gaze darted toward her. "I keep you in the dark not out of disrespect, Kari, but—"

"I know." Kari smiled. "And thank you for trying. But I'm too entangled to back out now."

The women sat in silence for a long moment, the only sound the dull whirl of the gastrolight cruiser's auto-pilot navigation system. Kari had almost drifted off to sleep when Dari whispered, "where should I begin?"

Kari opened her eyes slowly and smiled. "At the beginning."

Chapter 14

Brynda awoke slowly, her mind in a daze, as if everything around her was taking place on a surreal plain. It was the middle of the night. It was frigidly cold. And yet she felt warm and bubbly and...

Aroused.

The vines. The vines were—

Her eyes widened when it occurred to her that her clit was being licked.

She closed her eyes on a groan, not needing to look down her body to know that somehow it was the plants doing this to her. Her mind was hazy, so incredibly dazed...

"Beware of the vines, lass," Lieutenant Zaab had warned her. "They feed upon the juice of wenches."

She swallowed nervously. "They drink their blood?"

"Nay." He chuckled, his gaze raking over her naked body. "'Tis the intoxicating juice of the cunt they crave."

She blushed, but grinned. "That doesn't sound so bad..."

"Nay, lass." Zaab shook his head, his expression serious. "Between the amount of juice they take and the hallucinogens they feed to you..." He sighed. "Let us just say 'tis the method with which my people break human slaves to our bidding."

His eyes trailed down to where Jek was possessively rubbing her pussy, her husband having commanded her to spread her thighs wide so the gorilla males could easily smell his scent upon her. "The vines can drive you daft."

Brynda glanced down her body, visually confirming the gorilla fighter's words as the truth. Two vines were wrapped around her, pinning her spread eagle to the jungle's floor, one of the vine's flowers clamped around her clit, suctioning it into a peak of delirious arousal.

She groaned from behind the plant-gag, unable to move, unable to do anything besides lay there and submit with her thighs spread wide open and her arms thrust up over her head.

Her eyes rolled back into her head and her back arched as the suctioning mouth of the flower drew harder from her. She came on a low moan, her nipples stabbing up into the frigid nighttime air, then groaned when two flower-mouths clamped onto them and suckled vigorously.

She whimpered from behind the gag, another orgasm fast approaching. The flower bud working on her clit drew harder still, sucking and sucking and sucking and—

She burst on another groan, her body shaking as she came violently, the beautiful red bud soaking up her cunt juice while the two pink buds that were clamped around her stiff nipples suckled them harder still.

"It only gets worse," Zaab *murmured, his erection obvious as he watched Brynda's body convulsively orgasm around Jek's cock. Jek had placed her on his lap, her back to his chest, and bade her to ride him in front of the gorilla fighters that they might be given proof of his claims of ownership according to their own customs. Her tits jiggled as she groaned and rode him.*

"The more cunt juice you give the vines, lass, the more they will crave of you."

He growled as two slave girls began to suck him off. They took turns pleasuring him, one sucking his staff while the other one suckled his tight balls.

"Day and night, unrelenting in their passion…"

He spurted on a loud, reverberating growl.

241

"...drinking of your witch's brew until you've been driven insane..."

Brynda's body shook violently as she came harder than she had the last time. By this point her system had been pumped full of too much hallucinogen to experience panic, but oddly enough, knowing that she should have felt panic but didn't somehow served to panic her.

The flowers of the vines continued their assault, suckling harder and harder still, making her burst and groan and moan, over and over, again and again.

It kept up for three more hours. Three mind-numbing, unrelenting, violently orgasmic hours.

By the time Jek found her, by the time he'd killed the vines and unwrapped their limp fibers from around her body, Brynda's eyes were wild, her body shaking, her mind splintered from the combined effect of hallucinogen and climaxes.

"'Tis best do I mount you," Jek gently assured her as he lowered himself between her splayed thighs. Without ceremony, he plunged his stiff cock into her cunt, his teeth gritting. "My cock will make you feel better, *nee'ka*."

Brynda whimpered as he fucked her long and hard, her mind half-crazed, not altogether certain what was happening. All she knew for sure was that she needed his cock buried inside of, knew too that her husband was in a great deal of pain for he refused to orgasm lest he set her bridal necklace off.

"Why?" she whispered weakly, the world around her fuzzy and skewed. She could focus on nothing, see no one, so she concentrated on her Sacred Mate's voice and the cock he was ramming inside of her.

"Zaab says the vines pumped you full of aphrodisiac," he ground out, his eyes closed as he fucked her harder, his cock slamming into her cunt again and again. "'Tis how they break the slaves, making them ravenous for cock."

He rotated his hips and plunged deeper, her soft moans telling him he was giving her the proper amount of gentle release without allowing her too much. "You must allow yourself as much woman-joy as you need, *ty'ka*," he said hoarsely. "Know that I will not send you to your madness by allowing you too much."

His words made no sense to her. Nothing made sense to her. She only knew that she felt good, that she needed to keep feeling his thick cock plunging into her, that she needed the friction.

He fucked her for what felt like hours and probably was, giving her warm and fuzzy releases that served to calm her. She moaned and she groaned as the cock she so desperately craved fucked her, ramming into her cunt over and over, again and again.

Surrealistic — like a dreamstate.

When it was finally over, when she was weak and exhausted but momentarily feeling rational and sane, Jek lifted her up into his heavily muscled arms. He carried her from the jungle, determined not to stop until they reached the gastrolight cruiser.

* * * * *

The hallucinogens had long since worn off, but it had taken two days of constant sex before she'd felt completely calm and normal again. The deep impalements Jek gave her had worked for no more than an hour at a time when she'd feel desperate and crazed again, needing to be relieved.

But now it was over.

Brynda stared out of the porthole as the cruiser lurched upward, waving goodbye to Lieutenant Zaab and

General Zaqari. Odd as it sounded considering what had happened to her in the jungle, she was going to miss Dementia. And the Dementians.

"I've a feeling we'll see them again," Jek murmured in the way of comfort as he too waved goodbye.

She smiled. "I hope so," she said softly, watching as the gorilla hunters disappeared into the jungle. She glanced up at Jek. "If it wasn't for Zaab's near challenge I'd still be waiting to make love to you."

He chuckled as he planted a kiss atop her hair. "Mayhap," he said. "But I doubt it."

Chapter 15

Jek frowned, his brow furrowed. "For a certainty I cannot understand why you are sulking." He grunted as he threw a hand toward her, watching from the gel-rock he lounged upon as she combed out her hair in their bedchamber bathing pool. "Leastways, 'tis o'er. You are healed. You have cheated death." His look was perplexed. "Why the sadness?"

Brynda sighed as she set down the comb. "You don't get it? You really don't get it?"

"Nay," he said slowly, over-enunciating his words as if speaking to a dimwit, "I do not."

She waded toward him in the lulling water. When she reached the gel-rock she propped her elbows onto it and plopped her chin down onto her hands. "Me neither," she admitted.

Jek snorted. "Ah, at least 'tis good sense you are making, *nee'ka*." He bent his neck and kissed the tip of her nose.

She smiled. "I guess it was just so…so…"

"So what, Bryn?"

"So…anticlimactic." She sighed. "I've been fighting this disease for years and years. I was so sick, in fact, that I would have died within a few months had you not shown up and whisked me away."

"Ah." He nodded. "I see what you mean."

She groaned. "I know I'm being ridiculous! I mean, the point is I'm alive and well and scheduled to live for oodles and oodles of years, but..."

"...but," Jek finished for her, "you mayhap wanted a bit more of a dramatic healing than Ari waving a hand at you and announcing 'twas done."

"Exactly!" Brynda's lips pinched together in a frown. "Damn, I'm a moron."

He chuckled, bending his neck to kiss the tip of her nose again. "But 'tis my moron you are, Lady Q'ana Ri."

She playfully slapped his chest, grinning up at him. "Gee thanks."

He held her hand against his chest, then growled when he felt her other hand wrap around his erection. "'Tis gel-fire you play with, vixen."

She chuckled as their lips met, smiling as they performed a little tongue duel. She ground her hand against his swollen cock, loving it when he hissed in response. "Please," she teased, "split me asunder anon, big boy."

Jek grinned as he raised his head. He wiggled his eyebrows. "'Tis wicked big, aye?"

She rolled her eyes. "What an ego." She grinned. "But yeah, it is."

His smile faded as his expression grew serious. "You know something, Bryn?"

"Hm?" She smiled.

"I think you were healed," he admitted, "before ever you had an audience with Ari."

Her brow wrinkled. "I don't understand..."

"Aye you do," he murmured.

She thought about that for a moment. "Because I let myself believe?"

Jek nodded. "The mind is quite a powerful ally. Leastways, you have seen what I can do with mine."

She inclined her head, conceding the point. "I think you may be right," she said on a smile.

"'Twas either that or…" Jek grinned, the teasing light back in his eyes as he grabbed his manhood by the base. "Or 'twas this wicked big cock."

Brynda laughed, realizing as she did that he was trying to keep her mood light. The past no longer mattered. Old battles no longer mattered. Only the present and the future were of importance now. "By the way, what happened to all those hatchlings you promised me?"

Jek plucked her out of the water, causing her to yelp, then set her astride him that her legs straddled his hips. "I've the feeling you will get with my *pani* this very moonrising, my hearts." He wiggled his eyebrows. "Best grab the recorder, Bryn. I've a feeling 'tis a holo-cam moment."

She chuckled as she enveloped his cock inside of her, then grinned when the slow undulation of her hips made him growl.

And later, when the belly flutters began, she would learn that he had been correct.

It *had* been a holo-cam moment.

Epilogue

Chained to a narrow raised bed, Vandor commanded himself to move not a muscle whilst the fiery-headed High Princess walked slowly towards him, her expression defeated. He had felt her distress on each occasion that she had disobeyed his mental summons, and verily, it had taken its toll.

She looked tired. Tired and weak and defeated.

"What do you want of me?" she brokenly whispered.

Weak — far too weak. He should have forced his will upon her days ago, weeks ago.

She stood before him naked, not having bothered to don the customary dress of her people, for verily she must have known he would only remove it anyway.

When one of his chained hands rose up and his thumb began to massage her erect nipple, she shuddered breathily, no longer trying to shield herself from him for she had to have realized by now it would do her no good.

His jade-green gaze found her glowing blue one. One side of his mouth kicked up, displaying his fangs. "Everything," he purred.

* * * * *

Yar'at tried to keep his attention on what was being said unto him by the High King Jor Q'an Tal. He had trekked into Sand City to the Palace of the Dunes this moon-rising to report his third dimension mission under High Lord Jek Q'an Ri unto Tryston's ruler. And yet, try as he might to focus on the High King, it was to the beautiful fiery-headed wench standing quietly behind him that he found his gaze continually straying toward.

He could tell from Jor's stance that the High King was fiercely protective of his elder sister, for he kept her securely a foot behind him, shielding her from the need to speak with others.

Yar'at had heard whispers of Zora Q'ana Tal's beauty and he could see for himself that they were true. But he had also heard cruel jests spoken of her name because she was so different from other wenches. It was said she wasn't given to flirting with the warriors and from what he'd heard amongst rumormongers she rarely even spoke to any of them save the males of her lineage.

And yet he found her shy gaze constantly straying upward to meet his...

Yar'at forcibly clamped down on the emotions he felt, telling himself he was delusional if ever he thought the eldest daughter of the Emperor Himself would have a care for his affection. It was ridiculous in the extreme to even hope, let alone to test her.

And so with heavy hearts he prepared to leave the Palace of the Dunes after his verbal report was complete. When the High King finished handing out his instructions, Yar'at's gaze strayed one last time to clash with Zora's. He inclined his head respectfully to her, garnering him a wide-eyed expression and a sincere smile that did more to his hearts than he wished it did.

Yar'at turned on his boot heel and walked briskly from the dining hall lest he do something foolish that would cause others to make more jest of him — such as test the eldest hatchling of the Emperor for the ability to mate with him.

He would that it could be true.

But he was slow of the tongue, he reminded himself.

And if ever the High Princess had heard the rumormongers speak of him, she would also believe him to be slow of the mind.

* * * * *

"The beginning," Dari sighed, her head arched back on the seat's *vesha*-pad. She absently watched as the legendary planet Khan-Gor loomed closer and closer in the encroaching horizon. "'Tis hard to decide just where and when it all started."

A *vesha* hide wrapped around her, Kari laid her head on the padding of the pilot seat and smiled. "How old were you when you were sent to live with Gio on Arak?" she murmured.

Dari glanced over to her. "Fourteen."

Kari nodded. She was silent for a moment and then, "and how old were you when you fell in love with him?"

Dari's eyes widened. She smiled softly as she looked away, staring out into the night.

"Fourteen and a day," she whispered. "Fourteen and a day."

* * * * *

Next in the Trek Mi Q'an Series:

DEMENTIA

In the anthology *Taken*

ISBN # 1-84360-390-X

Dee Ellison is catapulted from earth and ends up in a mysterious alien world reminiscent of Planet of the Apes. The males of the planet, she soon discovers, keep human females as sex slaves. More terrifying yet, the Alpha Male of the Hoard is hot on Dee's trail...

About the author:

Critically acclaimed and highly prolific, Jaid Black is the best-selling author of numerous erotic romance tales. Her first title, *The Empress' New Clothes*, was recognized as a readers' favorite in women's erotica by Romantic Times magazine. A full-time writer, Jaid lives in a cozy little village in the northeastern United States with her two children. In her spare time, she enjoys traveling, horseback riding, and furthering her collection of African and Egyptian art.

She welcomes mail from readers. You can visit her on the web at www.jaidblack.com or write to her c/o Ellora's Cave Publishing at P.O. Box 787, Hudson, Ohio 44236-0787.

Why an electronic book?

We live in the Information Age—an exciting time in the history of human civilization in which technology rules supreme and continues to progress in leaps and bounds every minute of every hour of every day. For a multitude of reasons, more and more avid literary fans are opting to purchase e-books instead of paperbacks. The question to those not yet initiated to the world of electronic reading is simply: why?

1. Price. An electronic title at Ellora's Cave Publishing runs anywhere from 40-75% less than the cover price of the <u>exact same title</u> in paperback format. Why? Cold mathematics. It is less expensive to publish an e-book than it is to publish a paperback, so the savings are passed along to the consumer.

2. Space. Running out of room to house your paperback books? That is one worry you will never have with electronic novels. For a low one-time cost, you can purchase a handheld computer designed specifically for e-reading purposes. Many e-readers are larger than the average handheld, giving you plenty of screen room. Better yet, hundreds of titles can be stored within your new library—a single microchip. (Please note that Ellora's Cave does not endorse any specific brands. You can check our website at www.ellorascave.com under "how to read an e-book" for customer recommendations we make available to new consumers.)

3. Mobility. Because your new library now consists of only a microchip, your entire cache of books can be taken with you wherever you go.

4. Personal preferences are accounted for. Are the words you are currently reading too small? Too large? Too...**ANNOYING**? Paperback books cannot be modified according to personal preferences, but e-books can.

5. Innovation. The way you read a book is not the only advancement the Information Age has gifted the literary community with. There is also the factor of what you can read. Ellora's Cave Publishing will be introducing a new line of interactive titles that are available in e-book format only.

6. Instant gratification. Is it the middle of the night and all the bookstores are closed? Are you tired of waiting days—sometimes weeks—for online and offline bookstores to ship the novels you bought? Ellora's Cave Publishing sells instantaneous downloads 24 hours a day, 7 days a week, 365 days a year. Our e-book delivery system is 100% automated, meaning your order is filled as soon as you pay for it.

Those are a few of the top reasons why electronic novels are displacing paperbacks for many an avid reader. As always, Ellora's Cave Publishing welcomes your questions and comments. We invite you to email us at service@ellorascave.com or write to us directly at: P.O. Box 787, Hudson, Ohio 44236-0787.

Printed in the United States
110377LV00001B/28-33/A